Works by David Wood

The Dane Maddock Adventures
Dourado
Cibola
Quest
Icefall
Buccaneer
Atlantis

Dane and Bones Origins
Freedom (with Sean Sweeney)
Hell Ship (with Sean Ellis)
Liberty (with Edward G. Talbot- forthcoming)
Dead Ice (with Steven Savile- forthcoming)
Splashdown (with Rick Chesler- forthcoming)

Stand-Alone Works
Into the Woods (with David S. Wood)
Callsign: Queen (with Jeremy Robinson)
Dark Rite (with Alan Baxter)
The Zombie-Driven Life

The Dunn Kelly Mysteries
You Suck
Bite Me (Forthcoming)

Writing as David Debord
The Silver Serpent
Keeper of the Mists
The Gates of Iron (forthcoming)
The Impostor Prince (with Ryan A. Span- forthcoming)

ATLANTIS

A Dane Maddock Adventure

David Wood

Gryphonwood

Atlantis: A Dane Maddock Adventure by David Wood

Copyright 2013 by David Wood

Cover art by Trisha Thompson Adams
Edited by Michele Wilson and Michael Dunne

ISBN: 978-1-940095-12-7

Published December, 2013 by Gryphonwood Press
www.gryphonwoodpress.com

Dedicated to my dear friend Tamara "Myra" Bodrick, the real-life Tam Broderick. Thanks for letting me steal your identity and pithy sayings.

From the Author

Thank you for coming along with Dane and Bones on another adventure! As always, I've played free and loose with a few factual details here and there for the sake of the story, especially Rachel, Nevada, which bears little, if any, resemblance to the actual town. Apologies to anyone who finds my embellishments a distraction.

I want to say a special thank-you to Michael Dunne and Michele Wilson for their contributions to this book.

If this is your first Dane and Bones story, and you'd like to read more, please visit me at www.davidwoodweb.com to learn about all of their adventures.

David

PROLOGUE

"We have emptied the city, Eminence." Albator shifted his weight and stole a glance at the temple door. "It is only the two of us and a few acolytes who wait to block the door as you instructed."

"You have done well, my son. Now it is time for you to go." Paisden pointed a long finger at the exit. "You don't want to be here when they arrive."

Instinct battled obligation in Albator's gray eyes. Clearly, he wanted to get away, but as Paisden's highest-ranking acolyte, his place was here in temple. His lips formed soundless words and his feet continued their dance of indecision.

"Perhaps it won't come to war," he finally managed. "Why would the lords do this to us? We are of their line."

"We are their greatest mistake, or so they believe." Paisden's outward calm reflected the serenity that came with accepting one's fate. "They feel they never should have let us leave the mother city. We did not hold to the old ways. We interfered."

"We helped!" Albator swept a shock of stringy hair off of his high forehead. His voice took on a strident tone. "The people knew nothing. We taught them so much. We bettered their lives."

"The lords do not see it that way. To their minds, the knowledge was not ours to give. And then there were those of us who did not rein in our baser instincts."

Albator's red cheeks confirmed something Paisden had long suspected.

"Who is she?" Paisden now regretted the long

hours he spent in the temple. Perhaps if he'd ventured outside more often, he'd have known more about Albator's life.

Albator's eyes fell. "Her name is Malaya, and she is kind and beautiful. If the lords could only see how much we care for one another, perhaps they could understand that a union such as ours…"

"Will always be an abomination to them. On this, and many other things, they are intractable." Paisden hated to bring the young man up short, but the sooner this conversation came to an end, the sooner Albator could make his way to safety. "Now, go to your woman. It is not too late for the two of you to build a life together. I hereby discharge you from your obligations to the temple."

"I don't want that." Albator held up his hands and took a step backward.

"What you want no longer matters." Paisden delivered the words like a slap to the face. "By this time tomorrow there will be no temple."

"We should fight them." Albator looked around as if searching for a weapon. "There are more of us than there are of them."

"Impossible. You know we have nothing with which to fight. For years, under the guise of needing resources in other parts of the empire, the lords have gradually stripped us of our weapons and energy sources. By the time we realized what was happening, we had but one machine and nothing with which to power it."

Paisden winced. The memory of his own naiveté stung. He remembered the pleas for help from their sister cities—pleas to which he was helpless to respond. Disasters, none of them natural, befell the cities, until only Paisden and his followers remained. He sent envoys to the lords, but none returned.

And then, yesterday, a single messenger, so weak from hunger and exhaustion that he could scarcely walk, staggered into the temple and uttered three words.

"They are coming."

Paisden sprang into action, ordering everyone to flee inland, taking only what they could carry on their backs, for he knew the weapon the lords would use against them, and he was powerless to stop it. When the messenger recovered sufficient strength, he told Paisden that the lords were, perhaps, a day behind him. And thus, did Paisden finally know the number of his days.

"There is nothing more you can do. Our people will need leadership, and you are their strongest remaining link to the temple. You and the other acolytes must close the door and then go, before it is too late."

"I'm not a stronger link than you." The flash of puzzlement in Albator's eyes dissolved in understanding. "You mean to remain here."

"I do. I am sworn to this temple. If fate wishes me to live, it will be so."

"You can't." A tear trickled down Albator's cheek. "Is there anything I can say to change your mind?"

"No." Paisden embraced the young man who was the closest thing to a son he would ever have. He kissed Albator once on each cheek, tasted the salty tears and perspiration, and then, gently, pushed him toward the door.

Albator stole a single glance over his shoulder as he stepped out into the sunlight. Moments later, he and the others began piling up stones at the temple door. Soon, it would be dark and Paisden would be alone.

Paisden took one last look around the place he had called home since his youth. Though wrought by human hands, the temple was perfect. Every stone fitted together seamlessly, every line was perfectly straight, just as Paisden's people had taught them. He took one last look at the sun, breathed deeply of the tangy salt air, and then went about his business.

He spared not a glance at the statue that dominated the room, but trailed his hand across the cool, smooth surface of the altar rail as he headed deeper into the temple. In the adyton, he clambered up into the steep shaft that led to his hidden quarters. Despite his years, he still had little trouble making the climb. With his demise looming, he savored every breath, every sensation. The rock shaft seemed alive beneath his hands, each trickle of sweat a living thing dancing along his flesh.

At long last, he crawled into his cell. It was a tiny, dark room, but he found comfort in the close quarters. He wanted to sleep, but he had set himself a task worthy of his final years, and he would see it completed. He lit a taper, plugged the tiny doorway with a stone block, and gathered the tools he would need.

He forsook the hammer, chisel, and stone tablets. There was too little time. Instead, he filled several wooden frames with dry clay, added water, stirred, and then smoothed them. His tablets ready, he found a sharp wooden stylus, settled onto his pallet, and began to write the story of his people.

CHAPTER 1

Sofia Perez mopped her brow and looked out across the sunbaked flats of the Marisma de Hinojos. Heat rose in waves from the parched earth, shimmering in the summer sun. Sunburned workers chipped away at the baked mud, excavating the canals that ringed the site. The scrape of digging tools on hard earth, and snatches of conversation, drifted across the arid landscape. It was hard to believe the transformation this drought-ridden salt marsh outside of Cadiz, Spain had undergone since early spring. Considering the level of funding their primary donor provided, progress was not just expected, but demanded.

"It's hot as Satan's butt crack out here." Patrick fanned himself with his straw pith helmet. His fair skin was not holding up well under the Spanish sun. In fact, his entire body glowed almost as red as his hair beneath a thick layer of sunscreen. "I don't know how you handle it."

"I'm from Miami. This is nothing." That wasn't entirely true. She kept going to her backpack for the can of spray-on sunblock to protect her olive skin. She hated sunburns—the itching, the way her clothing rubbed raw in all the wrong places. It was something she avoided at all costs. She noticed the way the corners of Patrick's mouth twitched and raised an eyebrow. "So, are you going to stand there trying not to smile, or are you going to tell me what's up?"

"You're needed in my section." He stopped fanning. "We think we've found the entrance to the temple."

Now it was her turn to keep her emotions in check.

"*No vendas la piel del oso antes de cazarlo,*" she said under her breath.

"What's that?"

"Something my abuela used to say. It means, *Don't sell the bearskin before you hunt it.*" She permitted herself a sad smile at the memory. Her grandmother had been so proud when she'd graduated from college, but wasn't impressed by her choice of Archaeology as a vocation. She'd been hoping for an attorney in the family.

"It's more colorful than, *Don't count your chickens before they hatch*, I'll grant you that. Now, are you coming?"

They navigated the busy work site, waving to workers who called out greetings to them. Spirits were high. This had been a controversial undertaking from the start, and everyone feared it might end up a black mark on their résumés. Sofia had more hope than confidence, but the money was too good to pass up. Since then, her results continued to vindicate her. The circles originally spotted in satellite imagery and scoffed at by almost everyone had proven, upon excavation, to be ringed canals. And at the center…

"The Temple of Poseidon." Patrick's beatific smile made him look ten years younger. "I can't believe we've really found it. It's almost like a dream."

Sofia tried to ignore the flutter in her chest at his words. "You're a scientist, Patrick. Be professional."

"Even if it's not what we think, it's still a spectacular find. The architecture is classic, the golden ratio is everywhere. We uncovered a shaft that runs down into the temple at precisely the same angle as one of the shafts in the Queen's Chamber of the Great Pyramid, except it's much bigger. A few inches wider and I'd have climbed down there myself. It's a great find, Sofia. We're going to be in the history books."

"We can't draw any conclusions until we get inside and see what, exactly we're dealing with. It would be pretty embarrassing if we told the world we've found the legendary temple at the heart of Atlantis and it turns out to be a grain storage building."

"I'll bet you a romantic, candlelight dinner that it's not a grain storage building."

Sofia laughed. "Even if I win that bet, I still lose. I'm only saying we need to be sure before we tell anyone outside the dig about this. It's just common sense."

Patrick's eyes fell and he turned away.

Sofia stopped in her tracks, grabbed him by the shoulder, and yanked him around to face her. "Tell me you didn't." The look in his eyes was all the answer she needed.

"I only sent one text. I was supposed to report in if we found anything promising. You've got to admit, *this*," he pointed to the peak of the temple roof where it rose out of the earth, "is interesting."

She couldn't argue with him. The temple, for, despite her professed reservations, it was clear that's what it was, was remarkably well preserved. The carving on the pediment, the triangular upper portion of the temple facade, showed an angry Poseidon slamming his trident into the sea, sending ferocious waves in either direction. The supporting columns were massive pillars fluted with parallel, concave grooves. At their peaks, the capitals, the head pieces that flared out to support the horizontal beam beneath the pediment, were carved to resemble the scaled talons of a sea creature, giving the impression that the roof was in the clutches of a primordial beast. The sight of it sent chills down her spine.

"Who did you tell?"

"Mister Bishop. I mean, I told his assistant. That's the only number I had. They're staying somewhere nearby, so we can expect a visit." His voice took on a pleading tone. "Come on, Sofia. They're practically footing the entire bill for this dig. They've given us everything we could want. You think we could have written grants to find Atlantis in southern Spain and gotten anything but ridicule for our trouble?"

"I know." She hated to admit it, but he was right. "It's just weird that the Kingdom Church is paying us to find Atlantis. Noah's Ark, I could see, but this? It's weird."

"I don't care as long as the checks keep coming in. Now, how about you quit worrying and let's get down there so they can open this door? You said not to open anything without you, and we took you at your word."

"Good. I'm glad to know you can use common sense when you have to."

Patrick mimed thrusting a dagger into his heart and then stepped aside so she could be first down to the dig site. A forty foot ladder descended into the pit where the excavation was ongoing. She climbed down, almost losing her footing once as she daydreamed about what they might find inside.

Several people stood around the entrance to the temple. They had cleared the entire front of the temple and back through the pronaos, the covered area that led back to the naos, the temple's enclosed central structure, and now waited for her to give the word. She could almost feel their excitement as she mounted the steps and approached the doorway. This was the moment!

"The door is weird." Patrick removed his helmet and scratched his head. "It's not really a door at all. It's more like a patch."

She didn't need to ask him to explain. The exposed portion of the naos was solid marble. The entryway, by contrast, was sealed with loose stones and mortar.

"Looks like they wanted to keep something out." She ran her fingers over the rough stones. "Maybe they knew the flood was coming?"

"Or they wanted to keep something in." Patrick made a frightened face, eliciting a giggle from a plump, female grad student.

Sofia brushed her hands on her shorts and stepped back. "Clear it out carefully. Try to keep it in one piece, if you can."

The crew didn't need to be told twice. Clearly, this was what they'd been eager to do since uncovering the entryway. They worked with an efficiency that made her proud. Sooner than she would have thought possible, they worked the plug free.

"Ladies first." Patrick made a mocking bow and motioned for her to enter the temple.

Sofia paused on the ambulatory, crinkled her nose at the stale air wafting through the doorway, and tried to calm her pounding heart. Was she about to make one of the greatest archaeological finds of all time? Heart racing, she fumbled with her flashlight, turned it on, and directed the shaky beam inside.

The cella, the interior chamber, hadn't gone unscathed in the disaster that befell the city. The floor was covered in a foot-deep layer of silt and all around were signs of leakage, but it could be worse. Much worse. This place had been closed up tight and must have been quickly covered by dirt and sand, at least, quick by geological standards, to have kept it in such pristine condition. Mother Earth had wrapped it in her protective blanket, protecting it against the ravages of time.

She played her light around the room, and what she saw took her breath away. Twin colonnades, the columns shaped like the twisting tentacles of a sea serpent, ran the length of the room, framing a magnificent sight.

"What do you see?" Patrick had hung back, like he knew he was supposed to, but his anxious tone indicated he wouldn't wait much longer.

"Poseidon!" A twenty-foot tall statue of the Greek god stood atop a dais in the middle of the temple. Like the image on the pediment outside, this was an angry god, driving furious waves before him. Unlike so many modern interpretations, he was not a wise, grandfatherly figure, gray of hair and beard, but young and virile, with brown hair and long, sinewy muscles. Wait! Brown hair?

"You can still see some of the paint!" Through the use of ultraviolet light, researchers had determined that the Greeks had painted over their sculptures, sometimes in bright primary colors, other times in more subdued, natural tones. Thus, the classic marble statues seen in contemporary museums did not accurately reflect their appearance in ancient times. This sculpture appeared to have been done in the latter style. Besides the traces of brown in the hair, she could see hints of creamy skin, as well as flecks of silver on his trident. The waves beneath his feet were speckled with aqua and the crests streaked with white. Had leaks in the roof eroded the paint, or had the pigments faded over time? One of the many questions they would doubtless try to answer as they studied this fabulous place.

Her crew could wait no longer, and crowded in behind her, adding their own flashlight beams to the scant light hers provided.

"Whoa." Patrick, focused on the Poseidon statue, stumbled on the soft, uneven dirt. "It's just..." Words failed him, so he shook his head, continuing to gaze at the sculpture of the god of the sea.

"What's the Stonehenge thing?" The grad student, who had been so amused by Patrick, indicated a circle of stone that ringed the statue. Though they were marble, and their lines sharp, the thick bases and circular arrangement did suggest Stonehenge in miniature.

"I guess it's an altar." Overwhelmed by the temple, Sofia found thinking a challenge.

"And there's an obelisk where the heel stone should be." Patrick rounded the statue, kicking up a cloud of dust as he went. "Hey, wait a minute." He froze. "Sofia?"

"What is it?" She joined him on the far side of the statue and followed his line of sight. The back wall that divided the cella from the adyton, the area to which only priests were admitted, sloped away from them, and each layer of stone grew progressively smaller, giving the illusion of...

"A pyramid," Patrick whispered.

"Why not? We've got an obelisk here. Perhaps Atlantis was, in some way, a cultural forerunner to both the Greeks and the Egyptians." She wanted to kick herself for uttering such an unexamined theory. Such speculation was unscientific and unprofessional. She turned the beam of her flashlight into the adyton and almost dropped it.

The light gleamed on a contraption of silver metal supported on four stone pillars. It was a pyramid-shaped frame made of a metal that looked like titanium. Suspended beneath it was a metal bowl shaped like a satellite dish. The pyramid was capped by a grasping silver hand. Only the hieroglyphs running around the cap just below the hand looked like something from the ancient world. Otherwise, its appearance was thoroughly modern…

…and thoroughly alien.

(HAPTER 2

"**What the hell** is that thing?" Patrick's words, whispered in a reverential tone, gave voice to Sofia's own thoughts.

"Everybody stay out until I call for you." She wanted to make a complete photographic record before anyone else entered the chamber. But more than that, she wanted to experience it by herself, to get the feel of the space and let her intuition speak to her. It was something she'd always done—her way of communing with the past.

She circled the odd contraption wondering just what in the world it was. She'd never seen its like in an ancient world site, but here it was, inside a temple that had spent the last few millennia buried under twenty feet of silt. She took a few minutes to photograph the chamber before turning to a tiny doorway in the back wall. She ducked through and found herself in a small room that was, surprisingly, faintly lit by sunlight. She identified its source as a shaft high in the opposite wall above a stone shelf that might have been a priest's bed. Moving closer, she looked up and saw a square of sky at the far end. This was the shaft her crew had uncovered. Patrick was right. It looked like a larger version of a pyramid's air shaft.

"Sofia." Patrick called, soft but urgent, from the cella. "Mister Bishop's here and he's brought armed men with him."

"What?" She whirled around. "That doesn't make sense. Why would they need to be armed?"

"I don't know. A few of them are Guardia Civil, and others look like Americans."

Just then, gunfire erupted somewhere outside, reverberating through the stone chamber like thunderclaps. A final scream pierced the air, cut off in an instant by a single shot.

"You've got to get out of here!" Patrick hurried up to her. "The shaft. I'll give you a boost."

Before she could argue, Patrick scooped her up and lifted her toward the opening. She struggled to find handholds in the smooth stone, but Patrick kept pushing. He was stronger than she'd imagined. A few more shots rang out just as Patrick got his hands under her feet and shoved her the rest of the way in.

"What about you?" She felt like a coward, fleeing this way.

"I'll be fine. He likes me." His words rang hollow. "You just climb as fast as you can. I'll stall him."

Fighting back tears, she scrabbled up the shaft, her feet finding purchase on the sides and forcing her upward. Why had Mister Bishop done this? Behind her, she heard Patrick's voice.

"Mister Bishop, what happened out there?" His voice quaked with every word.

"Nothing you need concern yourself with." Bishop's deep voice echoed in the shaft. "Where is Doctor Perez?"

His words chilled Sofia to the bone. She had no doubt he planned on killing her and Patrick once he'd extracted whatever information he sought. She didn't know why he wanted to find Atlantis, but now that she'd discovered it, she, and her people, were expendable.

"She's out on the dig site. Inspecting one of the outer canals on the south side, I think."

"There are two sets of footprints." His voice was cold.

"One of the assistants took some pictures and then I sent her back out."

If she hadn't been deathly afraid for her life, Sofia would have admired Patrick's ability to invent on the fly. The fear was gone from his voice. She wished he could have escaped along with her but, should the worst happen, she was determined not to let his sacrifice be in vain. She continued her climb, now almost halfway to the top.

An unfamiliar voice, rough like sandpaper, spoke up. "What's that opening behind you?"

"We think it's an air shaft like the ones in the Great Pyramids." Patrick reply came out fast and unnatural. Sofia could hear it, and she was sure Bishop and his cronies could too. "We got lucky. It was capped up at the top. Otherwise, it and this whole chamber would have filled with silt. We'd have had a heck of a time uncovering this thing, not that we know what it is." He was clearly trying to divert their attention to the strange contraption.

"Oh, we know exactly what it is." Bishop cleared his throat. "To be more precise, we know what it does."

Don't say anything else, Patrick. The more you know, the worse it is for you. Just run away.

Perhaps if Sofia were a telepath, Patrick would have heard her plea and clammed up. Instead, he rambled on. "Really? What does it do? It looks like…"

A gunshot rang out and Sofia muffled a cry of grief and fear. She looked up at the square of light at the end of the shaft. It was no more than ten meters away, but at the rate she was going it might as well be a thousand. If Mister Bishop, or one of his men, looked into the shaft, she was dead. She tried to quicken her pace, reaching out as far as she could, and her hand closed on cold metal.

"Pack up the machine." Bishop was all business. His voice carried no hint that he had just witnessed the slaughter of innocent people. "Carefully, now, and be certain to crate it up before you take it out."

"Yes, Bishop," the man with the rough voice replied.

"I wonder." Mister Bishop now sounded thoughtful. "Could a person fit inside that shaft?"

Sofia's pulse roared in her ears, and panic dulled her senses. She realized she was gripping a metal handle of some sort. She scooted closer and saw two brass handles embedded in a block of stone. It was a plug like the one archaeologists found in the Great Pyramid! She grabbed hold of them and yanked with all her might.

It didn't budge.

"I'll check it out, Bishop."

With renewed strength born of abject terror, she heaved at the plug, and it came free in a cloud of dust and stale air. There was a chamber there! It was pitch black, but instincts honed from years of experience told her there was a large, open space inside. She slithered through the opening and took the plug along with her. Moments later, she heard the rattle of gunfire. Bullets pinged up the shaft, inches from where she squatted.

"Did you see someone?" Mister Bishop asked.

"Just being thorough. It's not like there's anyone left out there for me to hit." The man's guttural laugh echoed through the chamber.

"Doctor Perez is still unaccounted for. Find and dispatch her with all due haste. I'll meet you back on the ship."

"Yes, Bishop. We'll have the machine out of here in ten."

Sofia bit her lip, thinking hard. If they were looking for her, it would be too dangerous to try and climb out right now. She'd have to wait them out. She hefted the plug and pushed it back in the hole, handles facing inward, and then took out her small LED flashlight and flicked it on. Through a curtain of dust that tickled her nose and made her eyes burn, she followed its beam.

The space was no more than three meters square, its walls smooth and unadorned. She directed her light down onto the floor and her heart skipped a beat as it fell on a skeleton. It lay on its side in a pool of dust that might have once been clothing or a blanket. Near its hand lay a thin wooden rod with a pointed end—a stylus, and a jumble of rectangular tablets not much bigger than index cards. She knelt down for a closer look and saw they were all covered in tiny hieroglyphs. Many she recognized as identical to their Egyptian counterparts, but most were either slight variations on the Egyptian writing, or were unfamiliar.

"A codex." Depending on what was written here, this could be the single most important find of the dig. After first checking to make sure the opening to the chamber was sealed, she photographed each one, moving them about as if handling a newborn baby. They were made of clay, and she feared they would crumble at her touch, but they held together. When she'd made a photographic record, she took another set of pictures with her phone, vowing to text them to… she didn't know… someone she could trust, the moment she got out of this temple and into cell phone range. If she and the tablets should fall into Bishop's hands, she didn't want the secret to die with her.

The absurdity of her thoughts struck her in a flash. Here she was, hiding from men who had apparently just murdered her crew, and now were after her, and her paramount concern was preserving a codex. She would have laughed, had the situation not been so dire. This was her life's work, and she wasn't going to let a crazy man stop her. With great caution, she stacked the tablets and wrapped and bound them in a bandanna. It was the best she could do for now.

She checked her watch. Nearly twenty minutes had passed since she first entered the adyton. Were the men gone? As carefully and quietly as she could, she shifted the plug aside and strained to listen.

"We can't find Doctor Perez, Bishop. If we'd kept Patrick alive we might have extracted her whereabouts from him."

"The Guardia Civil will put her on our list." The speaker's voice was deep with a Spanish accent.

"Thank you," Mister Bishop said. "Are we certain she is not among the dead?"

"I can't be sure. My men like to aim for the head. It's good for target practice but bad for identification purposes."

Bishop let out a long, slow breath. "In that case, she is most likely dead. If not, it won't matter for long. We will cleanse the site, as planned."

She froze. What did he mean by that? She knew what it meant for her—she had better find a way out of here sooner rather than later. She listened for more sounds, but Bishop and the others seemed to have gone. She performed some quick mental calculations, and decided she should wait ten minutes to make certain the men were well clear of the temple before she climbed out. She watched the minutes pass by with agonizing slowness until, finally, it was time.

She tucked the codex into her shirt, listened again for a few seconds, and heard nothing. Heart pounding and dizzy from fear, she took a deep breath and clambered out into the shaft. The ascent seemed to take hours. Every second she expected to hear the gunshot that would end her life. Her breath came in ragged gasps and cold sweat soaked her clothes, but labored on until she reached the top.

She peeked her head out and scanned up and down the trench her workers had dug in order to reach this part of the temple. The trench was empty and all was quiet, save the rush of distant waves. Of course, she had no idea who might be waiting up above. It didn't matter. Her gut told her she needed to get as far away from here as possible, and fast. She hurried to a nearby ladder, ascended in silence, and paused at the top to peer over the edge.

A small whimper escaped her lips as her eyes fell on the bodies of two crew members. Bullets to the head rendered them unrecognizable, but she grieved for them all the same. She wondered again at the reason for this senseless slaughter. Furthermore, how had Bishop gotten the local authorities on his side? Money, she supposed. There would be time enough to figure that out once she'd gotten clear of the dig.

She heard the faint roar of an engine in the distance and looked to the south to see a van driving across the flats, escorted by two pickup trucks, their beds packed with men. She couldn't quite make them out, but the light glinted off of what she presumed to be firearms. Bishop was leaving, which meant it was a good time for her to go, too.

Not wasting time, she scrambled out onto level ground and sprinted in the opposite direction. It was not until she'd run for an hour, the stabbing pain in her lungs and leaden feeling in her legs reminding her how long it had been since her last 10K road race, that she felt safe enough to stop in the shelter of the tall grass in one of the few remaining marshlands.

She took out her phone and first used it to pinpoint her location. She would need it when she made her next call. But would he want to hear from her? It didn't matter. She didn't have many connections in Spain, and certainly no one else who would be okay taking in a fugitive from the Guardia Civil, perhaps Spain's most corrupt branch of law enforcement. And then there was the matter of the codex, her taking of which violated all kinds of laws. Of course, he couldn't possibly take the moral high ground on that score. Besides, he owed her after the way he'd left her in Peru. She punched up the number and held her breath. He picked up on the first ring.

"Sofia, is that you?"

So he hadn't deleted her number from his phone. That made her smile.

"Hey, Arnau. Long time, no speak."

"Oh my God, it is you! Are you all right?" The genuine concern in his voice moved her, but then a different thought chased the good feeling away.

"Why wouldn't I be?" Had word of the killings already leaked out?

"You don't know?" He sounded befuddled. *"Where have you been? There was a tidal wave or something down on the salt flats. Your whole dig is gone."*

(HAPT€R 3

"Yeah! I freaking love this thing." Bones tapped on the transparent ceiling of the small submarine. "It's sturdier than I expected. I know! Let me try the torpedoes."

"No way." Dane Maddock stifled a grin as he took the craft into a steep dive. "Tam just gave us this new toy. We're not getting it taken away after our first test run."

Down below, the barnacle encrusted hulk of a sunken ship grew ever closer as they approached. Dane slowed the craft and drifted toward the gaping tear in its hull. The two former Navy SEALs turned treasure hunters, along with their crew, had recently agreed to work for a clandestine branch of the CIA that sought to root out the Dominion, a powerful group of religious extremists that had given Dane and his partner, Bones Bonebrake, more trouble than they cared to count. This submarine, which Bones christened *Remora* after the suckerfish that attached itself to a larger host for transportation, protection, and food, was just one of the benefits.

"I don't think we can make it through that gap," Bones said from his seat behind Dane. "How about I make that hole bigger?"

"Fine, but no torpedoes. What do we have in our arsenal?"

"How about this?"

Dane watched as a mechanical arm extended from the sub and, with a flash of white light, began slicing through the hull. A cloud of silt and debris engulfed the sub. When it cleared, Bones had carved out a semicircular section of hull large enough to pass through.

"Laser cutter, baby!" Bones sounded like a kid on Christmas morning. "Hey, you know that riverboat casino my Uncle Charlie's all worked up about? With this, we could send that thing to the bottom of the river in no time."

"You know something? I was kind of hoping you wouldn't be able to fit inside here. Being at close quarters with you gets old fast." It seemed something of a miracle that the hulking Cherokee had managed to squeeze his broad-shouldered, six foot-plus frame, into the tiny sub.

"Always hating. I can't help it if you need a gallon of hair gel to get to six feet tall."

Dane shook his head. It wasn't only the contrast between the blue-eyed, blond haired Maddock and the dark-skinned, long-haired Cherokee that made them an odd pair. Bones was brash and aggressive, while Dane was prone to think twice before taking action. They hadn't cared for one another in the early stages of SEAL training but, over time, found that their strengths complemented each other. Now, though they still managed to annoy one another, they were closer than brothers.

Dane poked *Remora's* nose into the ship's open cargo hold. The hull had collapsed in places, leaving insufficient room for the craft to make it all the way in. He shone the light around, revealing indistinguishable piles of silt and rubble. Nothing to see here. "Why don't you try out the retrieval arms and then we'll head back?'

Two more mechanical arms extended from the bottom of the sub. Dane followed their progress on a video display. Bones used them to lift and move items of various sizes. Finally, one of the arms came up with a thin chain hooked on its grip. Bones raised the arm so they could examine the object through the transparent bubble that topped the pilot's area.

"A necklace. That'll clean up nice," Bones said. "Hard to believe it didn't break. I am good."

"What are you going to do with it? Give it to Avery?" Avery Halsey was Dane's sister whom his father had kept a secret from him. They'd met a few months before and now she was dating Bones.

"Yeah, Maddock, I need to talk to you about that." Bones stowed the necklace in the sub's tiny hold and retracted the arms while Dane reversed the craft and turned back toward shore. "She says she's found a job and is moving down here so she can be closer to us."

"From Nova Scotia to the Keys? That's quite a change, but that's cool. Wonder why she didn't tell me." Dane paused. "Hold on. Are you two moving in together? If so, you're moving out of my guest room."

"Hell no! I broke up with her. That's what I wanted to tell you." Bones hurried on. "I just hope it doesn't make it weird between us."

"Why would that be weird?" Dane rolled his eyes. He wasn't entirely surprised that the relationship hadn't lasted. A few months was actually a long time for Bones, who sometimes referred to himself as "Pollinator in Chief," considering it his duty to expose as many women to his charms as humanly possible.

"You know what *was* weird?" Bones ignored the sarcasm. "Each of us dating the other's sister. That was messed up."

Bones' sister Angel, a model and professional mixed martial arts fighter, was Dane's girlfriend. Unlike Bones and Avery, they were still together. She had joined them on a couple of their adventures, but was currently in North Carolina training for a championship fight. The very thought of her made him smile. After years of forcing himself to think of her as a friend, she'd finally broken through the wall he'd constructed between them.

"What is this, a pajama party? Cut the relationship talk and take over." Dane chuckled at Bones' triumphant shout as he took control of the craft and they surged forward, climbing up toward the light.

"Let's see if we can find a military ship and try out the cloaking on this baby."

Dane's good-natured groan died in his throat as the power in their sub flickered. When it returned, all the displays went crazy for a split second before returning to normal.

"Looks like we've found our first bug," Dane said. "What did you do? Turn on the cloaking?"

"No, I was kidding about that." Bones sounded puzzled. "I was taking us in, holding steady, when everything went on the fritz for a second, if that long."

"Everything looks normal now. Let's take it back to shore and give Tam our report."

"Aye aye. Let's hope this thing doesn't crap out on us before we get there."

"I hope they're enjoying themselves." Willis Sanders cast an angry look at the dancing blue waters of the Gulf of Mexico. "Me and Matt are getting that sub tomorrow. I don't care what Maddock says."

"I'm the boss, not Maddock," Tam reminded him for what felt like the hundredth time. "I said you two can take it out tomorrow and that's final. Now shut up before I change my mind."

She'd recently brought Maddock and his crew onto

her team, and Willis, in particular, found adjusting to the new power structure difficult.

"Girl, you're grouchy. Is the Key West humidity getting to you?" He grinned down at her. He was a handsome man, tall, and well-sculpted, with skin just dark enough to lend him a hint of mystery, but even if he wasn't her subordinate, he got under her skin way too often for her to take an interest in him.

"What have I told you about calling me girl? I used to think you were too arrogant to stop, but now I think you're just a slow learner." She would never admit it, but there was some truth in his words. She felt as if she was in a steam room most of the time, and the humidity played hell with her hair. More and more, she found herself in a foul mood, and she was putting far too many dollar bills into her cussing jar. She mopped the sweat from her damp brow and attempted to maintain her stern expression.

Willis hung his head and attempted to look chastened, but failed badly. His mischievous grin seemed permanently fixed in place.

For a moment, Tam considered shoving him off the pier, but he'd probably find that funny, too.

"It's your fault for hiring a bunch of SEALs." Matt Barnaby, a sturdily built man with brown hair and a fresh beard that he couldn't stop scratching, gazed out at the water. "The Army actually teaches discipline." He was a former Army ranger, which led to plenty of good natured ribbing amongst the crew members.

"Crazy talk." Willis shook his head.

"One word: Bones."

"All right, you got me there." Willis threw his head back and laughed. "I'll bet he's down there testing out the torpedoes right now."

"All right, ladies, break time's over. Let's finish our

run." Tam raised an admonishing finger. "And I don't want to hear any more complaints about cardio. I don't care how well you boys swim..." The words died on her lips. Along the shoreline, the water receded across a wide swathe, and the gentle roar of the waves dissolved into an ominous, sucking sound.

"You were saying?" Willis folded his arms across his chest and cocked his head.

"It's a drawback!" she shouted. "Tsunami!"

CHAPTER 4

Tam dashed down the pier, the sunbaked planks trembling beneath her feet as she pounded along its length. All around, people looked at her in confusion.

"Tsunami!" she shouted. "Everybody get to high ground as fast as you can!"

Everyone looked at her like she was crazy, and well they should. The idea that a tsunami could hit with zero warning, and from the inland side of the island, was absurd. That, and there was no "high ground" to be found here.

She slowed her pace and turned on her most commanding voice. "Move it! Get to the upper floors of a building! Now!"

The authority and urgency in her voice seemed to convince a few people, who began trotting along in her wake, but others just stared.

"Come on, y'all. Look at the water!" Willis pointed to the receding waterline. "I'm a Navy SEAL and that's a warning sign of a tsunami. Now move your asses!"

Whether it was the bizarre sight of the water drawing back, or the force of Willis' words, the people on the dock were finally convinced. That was both good and bad, as some turned and ran, while others froze in fear, and some even began to scream.

"Sure." Tam put her hands on her hips and frowned. "The woman yelling *tsunami* is hysterical, but if a *man* says it, they jump. Forgive me, Lord Jesus, but stupid people do vex me."

Matt and Willis brought up the rear urging the stragglers along, while Tam ran ahead, continuing to call out her warning to those who might not have heard.

She knew they didn't have much time. The wave period for a tsunami averaged twelve minutes, but there was nothing average about this situation. She stole a glance over her shoulder to check on Matt and Willis. They were falling farther behind as they tried to get everyone moving off the pier. She knew enough about them to know they wouldn't want to leave anyone behind. A tsunami in Key West! Why had she let Maddock talk her into setting up shop here?

By the time she hit the end of the pier, the warning had spread and people all along the shore were streaming away from the beach, but it wouldn't do any good if they couldn't get above the waterline. She scanned the area, looking for anywhere safe. Most of the buildings in this area were small waterfront bars, restaurants, and shops, but beyond them, she spotted a four-story hotel building.

"Everybody to the hotel! Get to the second floor or higher!" She ground her teeth in frustration. These people were slower than boyfriends to a bridal shower. She grabbed a dazed-looking, heavyset woman who seemed to be clogging the flow of traffic, took her by the chin, and looked her square in the eye. "You see that hotel right there?" The confused woman nodded. "Good! You're in charge of getting everybody to the top floor. Can you do that?"

The woman nodded again, shook like a dog fresh from its bath, and turned around the face the oncoming throng. "We're going to the hotel!" she bellowed in a voice suited for a football coach. "Follow me!" With that, she lumbered away, the rest following in her wake.

Tam could almost hear her grandmother chiding her for lack of tact, but she'd gotten the job done, hadn't she? Matt and Willis trotted up as the last of the stragglers cleared the deck of the pier.

"Where to now, boss?" Matt didn't look the least bit concerned about the impending disaster.

Down the shore, a crowd milled about, some staring at those fleeing the beach, but not making a move to escape the wall of water that would soon sweep them all away if they didn't get away. Willis and Matt followed her line of sight and they took off running. All three were in good shape but Willis outpaced his shorter colleagues, reaching the crowd well ahead of them and ushering them away from the beach. It didn't take long for panic to take over as people realized what the receding water meant, and they fled in every direction.

"If that's all the stragglers, we need to get ourselves to some place safe." Tam pressed her hand to the stitch in her side, hoping she wouldn't have to run any farther.

Matt turned toward the water and his expression grew stony. "I think we're too late."

Sure enough, a wave rolled toward them. It was difficult to tell at this distance, but Tam estimated it to be least four meters high, which meant the swell behind it would be powerful. They'd never outrun it.

"Time for some body surfing." All signs of fear were absent from Willis' face, but a hint of resignation lay beneath his words. "I always did like riding the waves."

Tam looked around for anywhere close by they could go to escape the water. "We ain't done yet. Come on!"

A nearby sign read "Glass Bottom Boat Rides" and two of the crafts sat on damp sand where the drawback had left them high and dry. Willis untied one from the dock while Matt kicked in the office door and retrieved a key ring. He tossed them to Willis and joined them in the boat.

"You think we'll make it?" Tam tried to sound braver than she felt. The wall of water was now a hundred yards away and closing fast.

"The boat's pointed the right way." Matt couldn't keep his eyes off the wave. "We've got a chance."

"Y'all put on your life jackets." Willis said found the proper key and put in the ignition. No sense cranking up the engine until they were actually afloat. If they managed to ride the wave, that was.

Tam strapped on her life jacket and braced herself as the wave broke fifty yards from where they waited and an avalanche of foamy white water came roaring toward them. When it struck, the boat shot straight up, its bow pointed to the sky. For one, heart-stopping instant, she was sure they were going to flip over backward, but then, as if in slow motion, the craft fell forward and hit the water with a loud crack. She felt the impact from head to toe, and icy water soaked her, but the boat didn't capsize. She spat out a mouthful of salty water and blew more from her burning sinuses. This was crazy, but they were alive. For the moment.

The boat rocked and spun as Willis fired up the engine and struggled to gain control, but the water carried them inland at a breathtaking pace. They rode a swell and teetered perilously as they crested it and came down, sending up another curtain of cold salt spray. "Can't you drive any better than this?"

"It's just like a ride at Disney World!" Willis laughed. He was enjoying himself. Gradually, he turned the craft, but not out into open water, as Tam expected. Instead, he pointed it back toward shore.

"What the hell are you doing?" The roof of a

submerged beachfront bar stuck up like an iceberg in their path, and they bore down on it with alarming speed.

"We can't fight the water." All traces of humor had vanished from Willis' face. "Engine can't handle it."

"Well, you better make a right turn quick."

With agonizing slowness, the boat turned, but not fast enough. The stern struck the roof of the bar, sending them spinning. Tam tried to see where they were headed, but couldn't focus. She felt, more than heard, another crash. The next thing she knew, she found herself lying face down on the glass bottom, staring through drops of blood and churning water at a paved road beneath the swirling water. She touched her forehead and her hand came away red and sticky. That was going to be attractive.

Matt hauled her to her feet and leaned in to inspect her wound, but she shoved him away. Grasping the side rail for balance, she blinked to clear the cobwebs from her mind and looked around. The boat still turned, but slower now, and the surge carried them along a thoroughfare through the middle of town. Buildings, half submerged, spun past, making her dizzy. She tried looking down, but the transparent bottom was little better.

"Hang on!" Willis shouted and, moments later, they careened off the top of a lamppost and crashed into a brick building. The impact jolted them, but the craft took no serious damage. "Man, this thing is tough."

The current slowed as it swept them inland, and Willis gained control of the boat. Tam looked around, surveying the damage. She didn't know what the rest of the key looked like, but this section was devastated. Only buildings two-stories or higher were visible. The tops of palm trees rose like shrubbery just above the surface of the water. Debris clogged the surface, and she spotted the occasional body carried along by the current. She was no stranger to death, but the sight made her wince. How could such a tragedy occur with no warning whatsoever?

"It doesn't make sense." Matt seemed to read her mind. "This is the twenty-first century. We detect these things ahead of time and issue warnings, but not this time. If you hadn't noticed the drawback, no telling how many people would have been caught off guard."

"That ain't the strangest part." They turned to look at Willis. "Didn't y'all see? That wave, it wasn't natural."

"What do you mean?" Tam felt her insides turn cold.

"It was, I don't know, concentrated. I could see where it ended on both sides. It was like somebody aimed a surge of water right at this spot."

"Are you sure?"

"Definitely."

"What could cause a phenomenon like that?" Tam mused. "Setting off a nuclear bomb underwater?"

"No." Matt shook his head. "That would send out waves in an ever-widening circle, which isn't what Willis saw."

"I'm dead serious. It seemed like the devil scooped up some water and pushed it right at us."

"I hope Bones and Maddock are okay." Matt turned and looked back in the direction from which they'd come.

A shrill scream rang out. Tam turned and saw a woman clutching a child in one arm and hanging on to a treetop with the other. The current battered her as she struggled to maintain her grip. Instinct kicked in.

"Somebody needs help," she barked. "Step on it."

CHAPTER 5

"Muchas gracias! Dios le bendiga!" The sodden woman lay in the bottom of the boat, her body limp, but her eyes were alive with gratitude. She clutched her son, probably no more than five years old, to her chest. The boy stared up with glassy eyes, but he had no visible injuries.

"It's fine. We just need to get you somewhere safe." Tam didn't know if the woman understood her, so she made sure to keep her voice calm and her expression friendly. Not her strong suit under duress, but such was life.

"I see somebody over there." Matt pointed to woman clinging to a boogie board. "You get these two to safety while I get her." He didn't wait for a reply, but kicked off his shoes and dove in.

"You boys expect me to believe you were ever in the military when not a one of you knows how to take orders?" Tam glanced at Willis. "You see anywhere we can take these two?"

"How about that church over there?" Willis indicated a high-steeple white church backed by a two-story brick building. A few faces peered out of second floor windows, gaping at the devastation. Willis guided the boat to the church and pulled up next to one of the open windows. A blocky, middle-aged man stared at them with unfriendly eyes.

The man didn't give Tam a chance to speak. "We're full up. No room here."

"These people need help." She couldn't believe what she was hearing.

"Get it somewhere else. I told you, we've got no

more room." He set his jaw and fixed her with a flinty gaze. Those eyes held no compassion.

"I don't know how full the rest of your church is, but I can tell from here that the room you're standing in is empty, save for you." Tam pointed to the space behind him. Soft music and the aroma of fresh coffee and cinnamon rolls wafted out into the air. The people inside were having a social while the world outside lay in chaos. "You can take them in."

"Come on man," Willis said. "This is a church, and you're supposed to help strangers in need. Do I need to start quoting scripture to you?"

"I don't need a Sunday school lesson from an uppity…" The man bit off his retort and swallowed hard. He didn't need to complete the sentence for everyone to know what he'd been about to say. "Just move along. There's a Methodist church around the corner. They'll take *anybody*." He screwed up his face to show what he thought of the Methodists.

"I want to talk to the pastor." Tam had to stop herself from slapping the fool look off the man's face.

"I am the pastor." More than anything else he'd said, this news stunned Tam. "And I will go to any length to defend my flock. He opened his jacket to reveal a holstered revolver.

Tam's fingers twitched and she felt the lack of her Makarov, which she'd left back at headquarters. She vowed she'd never go jogging unarmed again.

"Let's go before I take that toy away from him and give him an enema." Hot fury burned in Willis' words.

Tam nodded. "This is no house of God. We'll shake the dust off our feet and move along."

The pastor's face turned beet red at the insult, but he didn't reach for his weapon. Apparently, he believed Willis could, and would, follow through on his threat.

"Do you keep office hours, Pastor?" Willis asked.

"Why?"

"Because, when this is over, I just might drop by and teach you some manners. Keep your appointment book open." Willis gunned the engine, drowning out the man's sputtered retort.

Tam kept her eye on the pastor as they drifted away. If he wanted to shoot them, there was nothing they could do but duck, and she wanted to be ready. Thankfully, the man settled for staring daggers at them until they were out of sight.

They collected Matt and the woman he'd rescued, a Hooters girl who declared him her hero and offered to give him her number. While Matt searched in vain for pen and paper, they continued on until they came upon a group of survivors gathered on the roof of a local bar.

"Oh man, not Sloppy Joe's." Matt raised his hands in dismay. "Best joint in town underwater."

The survivors atop the building welcomed the newcomers, particularly the Hooters girl, who was already eying one of the men on the roof. Their charges now safe, Tam decided they should continue to look for others who might need help, at least until they ran low on fuel.

They continued their search, finding victims, but few survivors. They passed two more churches, both packed with refugees. They were considering trying to make their way to safety when they caught sight of two men clinging to a child's inflatable raft and struggling to keep their heads above water. Here, floating debris choked the streets. They had scarcely closed the gap between them and the struggling swimmers when a diver surfaced near the two men.

"Thank God!" one of them cried. "Can you help my partner? He can't hold on much longer."

Something glinted in the sunlight and the man fell back, clutching his throat as a curtain of scarlet poured from the gaping wound below his chin. He treaded water for a moment, the disbelief in his eyes evident even at a distance, and then he sank. Still clutching the boogie board, his partner managed only a startled cry before the diver's knife flashed again and the second man disappeared beneath the water.

"What the hell are you doing?" Tam shouted. The diver jerked his head in her direction, and then disappeared beneath the water. Tam gaped at the empty space where, moments before, two cold-blooded murders had been committed before her eyes. The world had gone mad. "Get after him!" she shouted to Willis.

"He could be anywhere," Matt said.

"Just go that way." She pointed to the spot where she'd last seen the diver. After a few minutes of searching, though, they had to give it up as a bad job. The man was nowhere to be found. "Dammit." She pounded her fist into her palm.

"Sorry," Matt said. "There are just too many places he could have gone."

"It's not just that. He made me cuss, and I had a three day streak going." She sighed. "Well, another dollar in the jar."

"You might want to add a few more dollars." Willis pointed down the submerged street to a boat speeding toward them. A man stood in the bow. At first, Tam thought he was pointing in their direction. Then a bullet smacked the water a foot from their boat, and she heard the report of a rifle.

They were being attacked.

"Something strange is happening up on the surface."

Dane checked the readouts on the display in front of him.

"How so?" Still distracted by the bells and whistles of this new craft, Bones sounded disinterested.

"I'll skip the details and just say I think Key West has just been hit by a tsunami."

That got Bones' attention. "No freaking way! Corey would have let us know about any warnings." Corey, their crew's resident techie, was minding the shop back at their temporary headquarters.

"I'll bet you a bottle of Dos Equis." Dane wouldn't mind losing that bet, but he knew better. His heart sank at the thought of his home being struck by such a disaster. And then he thought of Matt, Willis, and Tam. "Say, do you know what Tam and the guys had planned for today?"

"Besides bitching about us getting first crack at the sub? They were going to... Holy crap! They were going for a run somewhere around the pier. She's been ragging Willis about his conditioning."

"I'm taking over. See if you can raise Corey on the radio."

Bones made several attempts to reach their friend, but failed. "He's got to be okay. He's minding the radio, so he wouldn't be down on a bottom floor."

"He probably lost power," Dane said as the sub sliced through the water, headed for the dock. As they approached, he gradually brought the sub to the surface.

"Up periscope." Bones tapped a button and an image of Key West appeared on their monitors.

Dane groaned. The island, or at least this part of it, lay under a good eight feet of water. The topmost portions of buildings rose above the churning surface, and all around, people sat perched on roofs or leaned out of second-story windows to witness the disaster.

"What do we do?" Bones asked.

"Let's see if we can get closer. Maybe we'll run into the others." Dane felt the conspicuous absence of conviction in his voice, and he tried to force down the rising doubt. "They've been in worse situations than this. I figure they're partying on a rooftop somewhere."

He grew concerned as they made their way into the city and began to navigate the flooded streets. He wasn't sure how far he dared take *Remora*. The sub was small and maneuverable, but the streets were choked with debris and submerged vehicles. If they found themselves stranded, at least they'd have a chance to try out some of the special features.

"Hey, check this out. An external mic!" Bones exclaimed. A moment later, a cacophony of noises filled the cabin: rushing water, people shouting... and gunshots. "What the hell? Surely nobody's looting when the water's this deep."

"I don't know," Dane said. "Let's find out."

CHAPTER 6

"Listen up!" Willis shouted over the whine of the engine and the crackle of gunfire. "When we round the corner up ahead, there's an office building with a broken window. I remember passing it. I'm going to swing in close and you two are going to jump in there. I'll draw them off."

"You can't outrun them." Matt stole a glance back at the boat that followed in their wake. "They'll catch you in no time."

"I don't need to outrun them. I just need to draw them off of you and then I'll swim for it."

"Without diving gear? You're crazy. I won't allow it." Tam grabbed for the wheel. "Let me."

Willis gave her a level look and held on to the wheel. "I know you're the boss, but this time, neither one of you needs to argue with me. I'm the only one of the three of us who can pull this off."

"I hate it when he's right, but of the three of us, he's by far the best swimmer." Matt turned to Willis and gripped his friend's shoulder. "If you don't make it back in one piece, I'm going to kick your ass."

"You just fire up the barbecue and have me some ribs and a cold one waiting. Now, you two better be quick about it. Don't let them see you."

They approached the corner at a rapid clip. At least, rapid for the glass-bottom boat. As they turned and swung toward the gaping window, Tam and Matt moved to the edge of the boat and tensed to spring.

"You first, and be quick about it," Matt said. "One... two... three!"

Tam flung herself through the window, tucked her

shoulder, and rolled out of the way as Matt followed on her heels. He landed at an awkward angle and hit the floor with a thud.

"That sucked." He rolled over and drew in a deep breath.

"Get up. We need to help Willis." Tam didn't wait for him, but dashed through the empty room and out into a hallway. To her right, she spotted the door that led to the stairs. With Matt hot on her heels, she dashed to the top floor, the fourth, and hurried along the hallway until she found the room closest to the corner of the building. Inside, she spotted what she'd hoped to find: a heavy wooden desk. "Help me turn this over."

Matt bared his teeth in a predatory grin. Clearly, he understood what she had in mind. Together, they flipped the massive desk over onto its smooth top.

"You ready?"

"Just like football practice." Matt put his shoulder to the desk and they pushed, gaining momentum until the desk slammed into the floor-to ceiling window. The sturdy glass cracked but did not shatter.

"Again," Tam huffed. They repeated the maneuver two more times. The first time sent a spiderweb of cracks splaying across the glass. The second time, the glass shattered, leaving a gaping hole four feet high. "That's what I'm talking about."

Matt peered around the edge of the window frame. "Here they come. "Let's do it."

The boat rounded the corner, traveling as fast as the tight quarters would permit. Its momentum forced the craft to swing wide, bringing it right up to the side of the building where Tam and Matt waited. She caught a glimpse of the armed man in the bow. His eyes were locked on Willis. Slowly, he raised his rifle.

"Now!" Tam said. They threw their weight against the desk. It slid forward, teetered on the edge, and then plummeted down onto the unsuspecting men. It struck the boat near the stern with a resounding crash, taking a chunk out of the boat's side and eliciting cries of alarm as the boat tipped hard to port, taking in water over the damaged section. It didn't, however, sink, and a hail of bullets answered their improvised bomb. Broken glass scoured their exposed flesh as they dove away and scrambled out into the hall.

"What do we do if they send men in after us?" Matt said as they dashed for the stairwell.

"I don't know. Hide and pray, I guess." It galled Tam to admit it, but she could think of no better plan.

"Is that Willis?" Dane looked at the boat that filled his screen as it churned through the debris-filled water, coming right at them. Sure enough, their friend stood at the wheel, jaw clenched. As he piloted the boat, he stole the occasional glance back over his shoulder. He appeared to be running from something. And he was alone. "Where are the others?"

"Maybe they're in that other boat down the way?" Bones said.

In the distance, a second boat appeared. And then an odd thing happened. A desk came tumbling down from an upper story of a nearby building, and smashed into the corner of the boat. After a moment of shock, the passengers raised weapons and sent a barrage of bullets up at the building from which the desk had been dropped.

"I think we've got our answer," Dane said. Up ahead, the gunfire ceased and the second boat roared off in pursuit of Willis. Two men took potshots at him as they pursued the glass-bottom boat. At their rate of speed, they'd catch up with Willis quickly.

Just then, Willis spotted their sub and slowed down.

Dane flipped on the two-way audio. "Need a lift?"

"I'm trying to draw them off of Tam and Matt!"

"You won't last long. Here's what we're going to do." Dane hastily outlined his plan, then took the sub down as far as he dared.

"Think it will work?" Bones asked.

"We'll know soon enough."

"**You two, into** the building and find whoever dropped that desk!" Karl shouted. The men obeyed immediately, and Karl gunned the engine as soon as they were clear of craft. Though the debris in the water slowed their progress, he felt confident he'd catch the glass-bottom boat quickly. Three of them, armed, against one man made for fine odds. One fewer witness, and an undesirable for good measure. He smiled as the gap closed between him and his quarry. It was a fine day on the sea. Beside him, Abel and Henry fired off a few shots.

"Looks like he's slowing down, sir." Abel pointed at the boat ahead of them.

Sure enough, the glass bottom boat drifted to a stop. The pilot, a tall, black man, had apparently lost control, and the craft slowly rotated until it faced them broadside. The pilot spared them one panicked glance, then dropped down into the bottom of the boat.

"Broken down or out of fuel, I gather. It doesn't matter. He is ours." As they approached the foundering craft, Karl slowed their own boat and ordered his men to exercise caution. He assumed the man they pursued was unarmed, but there was no need to make a mistake.

"Where is he?" Abel leaned over the starboard rail and narrowed his eyes.

"Hiding, no doubt. You and Henry will board his boat and root him out. I'll cover you."

With a loud thump, their boat shuddered and a high-pitched grinding sound filled the air. "What the hell?" A whirring blade sliced through their hull. They gaped as it tore a ragged line across the bottom of the boat. What could do such a thing?

Panicked, Henry fired off two shots at the protruding blade, adding two holes to their already damaged craft.

"Stop it, you idiot!" Karl began working the controls, trying to break free of the blade before they sank. When they began to take on water, Abel and Henry grabbed buckets and bailed. Above the sound of the cutting blade, the engine roared and, with a jerk, they started moving in reverse. The blade disappeared, but the damage was done. They'd be lucky to get away before they sank. They needed to get to the church, and get there unseen at that.

As Karl turned the boat about, an alien-looking metal claw appeared over the port bow, clamped down on Abel's head, and plucked him out of the boat. Abel screamed in terror and fired his AK-47 with wild abandon. Henry went down, clutching his stomach as a seeping flow of crimson spread across his midriff.

Karl let loose a stream of curses and gunned the engine, hoping extra speed would help keep the craft afloat until he could get away. He spared no more than a single glance at the building where he'd left his other two men, but didn't slow down. There was no time. If he stopped for them, the boat might sink, or, worse, whoever… whatever had attacked them might catch up. Right now, the only thing he wanted was to get as far away from this disaster as possible.

"This had better work," Matt grunted, the strain evident in his voice. "I don't think I can hold myself in place up here much longer."

"Shut up. I hear them coming." Tam had little confidence in her plan, but, as improvised attack plans went, it wasn't the worst. She stood just outside the door that led into the darkened stairwell and listened as the footsteps drew closer. Thinking they had nothing to fear, the men who pursued them weren't making any effort to keep quiet. Tam didn't care if they were arrogant or just plain stupid, either was a point in her favor.

The sounds grew louder until she was sure they were almost upon them. This was it. Whispering a quick prayer, she dropped to one knee as she heard a loud thud and a shout of surprise as Matt dropped down onto the man in the lead. By pressing his hands and feet against the stairwell walls, he'd managed to climb up to ceiling level and wait until he could take their pursuers by surprise.

Before either man could react, Tam squeezed the lever on the fire extinguisher she'd taken off the wall nearby. She heard another surprised shout as gas filled the stairwell. She emptied the canister and then flung it into the cloud, then rolled aside as bullets flew through the open doorway.

"Come after me," she whispered to herself. "I dare you." She clenched her fists, ready to spring. She'd have to get the drop on the gunman, and that was an iffy proposition since she and Matt had just sprung an ambush on them, but it was her only hope. Every nerve alive, every muscle tensed, she readied herself to spring.

Another burst of gunfire rang out.

And then silence.

She waited, not daring to breathe. Her heart pounded out a steady beat.

"I'm okay."

She sagged with relief at the sound of Matt's voice. "What took you so long?"

"You try wrestling a gun away from a guy and knocking him out before his buddy shoots you. Of course, I knocked him out after I shot the other guy. Now, help me haul this dude out of here."

"Not bad," Tam said as they dragged the unconscious man out of the stairwell and into the nearest room. "I don't think your crew mates give you enough credit."

"Please. I'm a Ranger. I eat SEALs with barbecue sauce."

"If you say so." Tam smirked. "I'm going to grab the other guy's rifle and make sure he's dead."

"Oh, he's done, but check if you like." The semi-conscious man was already beginning to stir, and Matt took a step back and trained the procured rifle on him. By the time Tam returned, their captive was awake, if not fully alert. He gazed up at them with hate-filled eyes, but he didn't move.

"Who are you?" she asked.

No reply.

"How hard did you hit him?" she asked Matt, who shrugged. "Okay, dummy. You don't know your own name, so how about telling me why you're out there shooting at people instead of saving them?"

"You can't talk to me like that."

"I believe I just did. What's the problem? Mister murderer don't like taking orders from a woman?"

"It's not murder. It's a cleansing." As soon as the words left his mouth, the man blanched. Faster than Tam would have thought possible, he sprang to his feet and ran, not at her and Matt, but for the closest window.

"Stop!" she called, but the man flung himself against the glass, which shattered on impact. He flew out into open air and disappeared from sight. She ran to the window and looked down, where their prisoner of seconds before now floated in the water, his head caved in on one side. He had struck the top of a lamppost just before hitting the water.

"So much for questioning him," Matt said. "What do you think he meant by a cleansing?"

"I don't know for sure." Tam felt cold inside. "But I think we'd better figure it out."

"I think I squeezed his head too hard. He looks pretty out of it to me." The man Bones had snatched out of the boat using one of the sub's remote appendages lay atop an awning just above water level, held fast by the remote arm. He'd lost his weapon, and now stared up in disbelief at the sub's high-density cutting blade, which hovered inches above his chest.

"We'll see how he handles questioning." Dane once again engaged the external audio and spoke into his mic. "Nod your head if you can hear me." The man nodded. "Good. What's your name?" The man frowned and pressed his lips together. "Let's try this again," Dane said. He spun the cutting blade and lowered it an inch for emphasis. "Give me your name or this is about to get painful for you." He wasn't about to slice this fellow apart, but hopefully, his bluff was convincing.

The man's face twisted in anger then sagged. "Abel." He looked like he was going to be sick.

"See how easy that was? Now, tell my why you were shooting at my friends."

Abel took a deep breath and narrowed his eyes. For a moment, he looked as if he might refuse to answer. "The Cleansing."

"What the hell is that supposed to mean?" Bones asked.

Abel's eyes bugged out and he gaped, but it wasn't the sound of Bones' voice that elicited the reaction. A diver rose from the water, inches from him. With a single, swift movement, he sliced Abel's throat, and sank back into the water.

Dane released Abel's body and tried to snatch the diver using the mechanical hand, but the man moved too fast. Dane took *Remora* down while Bones engaged the sonar and began pinging the area all around them, but the diver was gone.

"We're not going to find him," Dane said. "Too much silt and debris in the water for visual or sonar, and he's not a large target. Besides, he could swim through any of these submerged buildings and get away."

"What just happened?"

"Not a clue," Dane said. It was the truth. Try as he might, he could not construct a scenario in which the murder they'd just witnessed made any kind of sense. "Let's pick Willis up and then find Matt and Tam. Maybe they can help us figure it out."

CHAPTER 7

Sofia rolled the mechanical pencil back and forth between her teeth, her index finger tracing an invisible line under the row of symbols. She cursed, dropped the stack of papers onto her lap, and fell back onto the pillow. She needed sleep, but she couldn't turn her brain off. Since her arrival in Huertas, a barrio of Madrid, she and Arnau had made progress deciphering the codex. As she had suspected, the codex bore a strong similarity to Egyptian hieroglyphs, but too many of the symbols still eluded them.

She moved to the window and gazed down at the street below. Streetlights shone on a young couple enjoying the night life, and a few stray singles who cast envious glances at the two lovers. Under different circumstances, she'd be down there among them, drinking in the local culture and perhaps enjoying tapas and cerveza at Magister or Viva Madrid. Right now, though, she couldn't bring herself to put the codex aside.

"Five more minutes, and then lights out," she told herself. She sank down on the lumpy bed in Arnau's guest room and returned to her stack of papers. Wanting to protect the ancient codex, she and Arnau were working from blown-up images of the artifact. She had abandoned her plan to send copies to colleagues skilled in ancient languages because she could think of no one whom she could completely trust. Some would turn her in to the authorities for stealing the codex. Others would seek to discredit her find, while still others would try to translate it on their own and steal the credit for themselves.

And then there was Arnau. She was not entirely comfortable working with him. His dealings with her, as far as she knew, had always been honest, but the fact he'd been caught trading in stolen antiquities strained his credibility. Then again, considering her present circumstances, who was she to judge?

She decided to begin by re-reading what she'd translated so far. It was not a literal translation. The symbols conveyed meaning, but could not be directly transcribed into complete sentences, so she and Arnau had fleshed things out, using a combination of educated guesses, wild speculation, and trial and error. In the places where they were least confident about the translation, they'd inserted their best guess in brackets.

The words of Paisden, priest of [Atlantis?] We are betrayed by our [Fatherland? Motherland?] Our crystals have been taken and our [machines?] [fail?] My [servant?] leads our people to [safety?] but I remain [steadfast? Dedicated?] The deluge shall soon [unknown] I believe we are the last [remnant]...

The rest remained untranslated, save for a few words, including an intriguing reference to temples. She gained no new insights, and put the papers down even before her allotted five minutes was up. Weariness weighed heavy on her and her eyelids drooped. Tomorrow, she'd look at the codex through fresh eyes.

"Let's see if the Marlins have made any more stupid trades." She took out her phone, opened the web browser, and punched in the Miami Herald's website. She gasped when she saw the headline.

Killer Tsunami Strikes Key West

She read on, concern turning to disbelief as she read the report. A freak wave had struck Key West without warning, causing death and devastation to a small section of the island. The tsunami was odd, not only because it seemed to come out of nowhere, but because its size and behavior were so far out of the norm. It had come from the direction of the mainland and was reported to be a concentrated wall of water rather than a typical, broad wave. Strangest of all, scientists could determine no cause for it. Seismic detectors all around the Gulf of Mexico and in the Atlantic detected no activity whatsoever. The sole clue was a brief burst of energy, emitted by an unknown source, minutes before the wave struck.

Sofia leaned back and considered this terrible news. It wasn't just the tragedy that impacted her, but the similarity to the wave that had swamped her dig site. In both cases, a wall of water appeared out of nowhere, with no obvious cause, and behaved in a way no known tsunami ever had. The articles she'd read hadn't mentioned a surge of energy preceding the event in Spain, but that didn't mean it didn't happen.

Something in the back of her mind nudged at her thoughts. What was it? The codex mentioned machines, and a deluge to come. The machine in the temple! What if… No, the very idea was absurd. Of course, belief in Atlantis seemed absurd until she'd unearthed the city.

"Oh my God. I have to tell somebody." But who? Could she really go to the American embassy with this story? They'd think her a lunatic. But she couldn't just let this drop. She was certain she was onto something.

A loud knock startled her. Someone was at the apartment door. She heard Arnau moving through the front room. He opened the door and whispered something unintelligible.

"Why the need to be so quiet?" a deep voice said. "We are alone, no?"

"I don't want the neighbors to hear us."

"Always overcautious," said a second voice.

"Perhaps it is for the best. There is no harm in taking a few precautions. Now, where is it?"

"Just a minute. It's in my safe."

Sofia's heart lurched. Damn Arnau! He thought to sell the codex. She gripped the doorknob, ready to storm in and confront him, but then she paused. Some of the people who bought stolen artifacts were little more than wealthy eccentrics or gluttons who wanted to own a piece of history. Others, however, were dangerous. What sort were the men outside? Indecision rooted her to the spot.

"Here. Give me the money and go." Arnau's voice trembled. "I want this out of my house."

"Let us see what we have here. Ah, very nice. You say this came from Atlantis?" The man's tone expressed his obvious skepticism.

"That's what I was told. I've studied it enough to be satisfied that it's a genuine artifact. "

"You've studied it." The voice sounded flat.

"Yes, but only to authenticate it. Nothing thorough." Arnau spoke quickly. "I don't know what it says."

"From whom did you acquire this piece?"

"You know I can't reveal my sources."

A dull pop made Sofia jump. On the other side of the door, she heard a thump and Arnau's cry of pain.

"It is not a fatal wound, but the next one will be unless you tell me the truth. I ask again, from whom did you acquire the codex?"

Sofia's stomach heaved. She had a feeling the fatal wound was inevitable, regardless of what Arnau told the men.

"I only know his first name," Arnau groaned. "It's Abed. He lives in Cairo."

Another muffled pop and another cry of pain. That

must be what a silenced weapon sounds liked.

"I've given you a measure of grace, Arnau. You'll lose your leg, but you might live if you receive medical attention soon." The speaker lowered his voice to a husky whisper. "You got this from Sofia Perez, didn't you?" Arnau's silence was all the answer the man needed. "Very well."

Sofia didn't need to hear any more. She was halfway out the window, her few belongings stuffed inside her shirt, when the next gunshot sounded. She clambered down the fire escape, dropped the last ten feet and rolled her ankle when she landed hard on the pavement. Fear gave her strength and she hobbled down the street at a half-run. The hour was late, but the hotel district wasn't far, and there were always taxis about.

By the time she flagged down a cab, she was soaked with sweat and her white tank top wasn't quite opaque any more. If the driver thought it odd to pick up a young woman in her nightclothes, he gave no indication, though he didn't bother to hide the way he undressed her with his eyes. He sat up straight, though, when she told him her destination.

"United States Embassy. I'll double your fare if you get me there fast."

Tires screeched and horns blared as the cabbie stepped on the gas and pulled the cab out into traffic. Sofia watched the lights and the people flash past and wondered if anyone would believe her story.

CHAPTER 8

"I expected something fancier from a government agency." Bones scowled at the faded carpet and plain, white walls as they moved along a narrow hallway at the back of the Truman Little White House. The famed building had suffered a great deal of water damage, but this section must have been waterproofed. The carpet was dry and the sheetrock walls unblemished.

"After all those years in the military, you still think the government splurges on people like us?" Dane shook his head and chuckled. "Come on."

"We're, like, agents now. James Bond gets all those fancy toys. Why not us?" Bones scratched his chin. "Must be a British thing. You think I could fake a British accent?"

"I've heard your accent. Hate to tell you, but it's not the best." He ignored Bones' expression of feigned insult. "Besides, this building was underwater only a few days ago, or have you already forgotten?"

"Sloppy Joe's and Captain Tony's got washed out. Trust me; I'll remember this for a long time."

"They'll be back." Already they'd seen many of the island's residents pulling together in the wake of the tragedy that had taken so many lives and caused such devastation. It was both sad and heartening to witness.

"Misters Maddock and Bonebrake?" A husky man dressed like a banker, barred their way. Dane didn't need to see the holster inside his coat to know he was a professional, probably military. His rigid posture and clipped manner of speaking spoke volumes.

"That's us," Dane said.

"Very good. Follow me, please." He led them to a

bookcase.

"Thanks, but I've switched to e-books." Bones ran a finger down the spine of a very old copy of Tom Sawyer. The shelves held complete works of Alexandre Dumas and Mark Twain. "Besides, I don't read anything published before nineteen hundred. Not enough sizzle, if you take my meaning."

The man grinned and withdrew a battered copy of The Count of Monte Cristo, revealing a small keypad. He entered a code and re-shelved the book as the bookcase swung forward, exposing a blank wall of gleaming metal and a small black screen. "Left thumbs on the scanner, please."

Bones held his thumb up. "Mine's been up my butt half the day. Is that going to be a problem?"

The corners of the man's mouth twitched. "Not for me. I never touch that scanner."

Dane and Bones pressed their thumbs to the scanner and, with a hiss, a previously invisible door slid to the side, opening onto an elevator. Inside stood Tam Broderick. She checked her watch and gave them an impatient look.

"Late for the first team meeting. Not the way to impress me."

Bones yawned and stretched. "Whatever gave you the idea that I care about impressing anybody? Besides, we're five minutes early."

"Five minutes early is ten minutes late to me. Now get in here and let's get to work."

"All I see is a down button," Dane said as he stepped inside and the elevator began its descent. "Should I have brought my dive gear?"

"Sweetie, this place has been here longer than you've been alive, and we know how to waterproof when we want to."

"I can't believe there's been a secret installation here all this time," Bones said. "Seems like a conspicuous place to hide spook central."

"Sure has. The government built it during World War II and kept it going all through the Cold War. It got shut down for a few years, but reopened again right after the start of the War on Terror. They were about to close it again when I requested we be headquartered here. Now it's all ours."

The elevator stopped and the door slid back, revealing a welcome area with plush, blue carpet, leather sofas, and an attractive receptionist with shoulder length, black hair and blue eyes, seated behind a mahogany desk. Five doors were evenly spaced along the wall behind her, with no signage to indicate where they led. Fine works of art lined the walls to their left and right.

"Everyone's in the conference room, Ma'am."

"Everyone except for these two." Tam rolled her eyes in Dane and Bones' direction. "Joey, meet Dane Maddock and Uriah Bonebrake." Tam smiled sweetly as Bones' smile flickered. He hated his given name.

"Call me Bones," he said, taking Joey's hand in a familiar way. "How about you and I get to know each other while Tam and Maddock go to their meeting?"

"Bones?" Joey frowned, and then realization dawned in her eyes. She stole a quick glance at Tam and then smiled at Bones with what Dane could have sworn was a touch of sympathy. "It's very nice to meet you and I look forward to working with you."

"You ain't getting out of the meeting that easy, Bonebrake. Let's go." Tam led them through the door on the far right and down another hallway.

"Did you tell Joey not to talk to me or something?" Bones asked.

"No, I just warned her that, ever since your injury, you try to overcompensate by hitting on every woman you meet, and she should be patient with you but not encourage you."

"What injury?"

"You got shot in the pelvis and now you can't do your manly duty. That's why we call you 'Bones.' It's one of those ironic nicknames."

Dane smothered a laugh in a rasping cough while Bones' cheeks turned crimson.

"That *was* you, wasn't it?" Tam asked with a straight face. "Or did I confuse you with somebody else? I'm sorry."

"Not bad," Bones admitted. "You do realize the next move is mine?"

"I'm counting on it, sweetie. Just don't forget I'm the boss."

The door at the end of the hallway opened into a well-lit conference room painted in bright colors and furnished with tropical plants. A giant, high definition screen on the far wall showed rolling surf and palm trees swaying in a gentle breeze. Just above the edge of hearing, the sound of waves crashing onto shore whispered from invisible speakers.

A long, oval table sat in the middle of the room. All the seats were occupied but three. Some of the faces were unfamiliar, but Matt, Willis, and Corey, the rest of Dane's crew, were there, smirking at Dane and Bones like the two were school kids who'd just come from the principal's office. A blonde sat with her back to them, but Dane didn't need to see her face to recognize her.

"Avery?"

At the sound of her name, his sister turned around. He'd expected her to look contrite, if not downright guilty, but instead, she set her jaw and raised her eyebrows.

"Yes?"

"What are you doing here?"

"I work here. You have a problem with that?" The look in her eyes told him it would be a bad idea to answer in the affirmative.

"Man, I love it when she gets all Maddock Junior on him." Willis laughed and slapped his thigh. "That's exactly what you look like when you act stubborn," he said to Dane.

"Come on, now. Maddock isn't stubborn." Bones put a protective arm around Dane's shoulders. "When he knows he's right, he sticks to his guns. And he's right *all the time*."

Everyone joined in the laughter, even the unfamiliar faces. Dane shrugged Bones' arm away and turned to his friend. "You knew about this, didn't you?"

"I told you she was moving down here because she got a new job."

"You left out one important detail."

"Not that long ago, you didn't even know I existed," Avery said. "This way, we get to spend even more time catching up on all those lost years."

He couldn't argue. It had only been a few months since he learned that his father, Hunter Maddock, had a daughter a few years younger than Dane. Avery was the sole blood relative he had left in the world, and the idea of her being a part of their new team, worried, even frightened him a little. Except for Angel, all the people he cared about were now part of this team, and that meant their lives were in peril. He knew they were adults and the responsibility was not his, but he couldn't like it.

"It doesn't matter," Tam said. "I needed to add to

our research staff. I like her and, more important, I trust her. She's one of the few people in the world I can be one hundred percent sure isn't connected to the Dominion. Are we clear?"

Dane nodded. As he took his seat, the others greeted him. He shook hands with Greg Johns, a tall, lean man with close-cropped, dark hair. They'd worked together once before, and Greg was a solid agent. The other two agents were Joel Berg, a sandy-haired man of about forty, and Kasey Kim, an attractive woman of Korean descent, who looked to be in her late twenties.

"You forgot to save me a seat." Bones smiled at Kasey, who made a wry face and shook her head. "It's cool. I'll grow on you."

"Like a fungus," Corey chimed in.

"You two can paint each other's toenails after the meeting. Let's get to work." Tam picked up a remote, clicked a button, and the image on the HD screen changed to a satellite image of Key West. Red circles dotted the map. "The circles are places where someone witnessed a murder during the tsunami, or a body was found with a gunshot or knife wound."

"I don't see a pattern, but that's a lot of people," Dane said.

"Twenty three. And those are just the ones we know about. The waters receded quickly. No telling how many might have been washed out to sea."

"But the island was under water for, what, an hour?" Bones cupped his chin and stared thoughtfully at the map.

"Exactly. Think about that. What are the odds that the killers saw the tsunami hit, spontaneously cooked up a scheme to ride around in a boat murdering people, and pulled it off in such a short period of time?" Tam looked up and down the table.

"Or that a guy would run home, strap on his diving gear, and start cutting throats," Matt added.

"You're saying they knew the Tsunami was coming and they were ready." Dane shook his head. "But how?"

"We'll get to that in a minute. You said you didn't see a pattern in the circles, and that's true, but Corey's found something." The screen now filled with head shots. "These are the victims. See a pattern there?" No one answered. "Corey?"

"They're all minorities."

"Most of them are, but there are a couple of white dudes up there too." Bones gestured at the screen.

"I did some checking and they're gay." Corey ran a hand through his short, red hair. "Willis told me about the killing they witnessed. He said one man referred to the other as his partner. That was my first clue."

"That church we went to turned away the Latina woman and her little boy." Willis scowled. "Bet you they'd have taken her in if she was white."

"It could be a coincidence," Tam said, "but I've got a feeling we're on the right track. There's more. We've been checking on our dead men—the one who came after me and Matt, and the one Bones snatched with his new toy. Both were members of the same church. The one who turned us away." She paused, letting that sink in. "As far as we can tell, no other members lost their lives. Seems like every one of them just happened to be in the church at the time the tsunami hit. Every one."

"On a weekday during business hours." Dane didn't bother to hide his disbelief.

"You catch on quick."

"What is this church like? Conservative?" It was the first time Joel had spoken, and Dane noted the man's rich voice and the way he enunciated each word.

"Not conservative—crazy. Separatist, racist, misogynist, every bad stereotype you can think of."

"That guy we caught, the one who was killed, said something about a cleansing," Bones said. "That definitely sounds like something this church would approve of. What's a church like that doing in Key West? This place is chill."

"Good question. The building has been around for a long time, but this pastor and congregation are new. He moved here from Utah less than a year ago, bought the church and grounds, though we don't know for sure where the money came from, and managed to run off all the old members with his hate mongering."

The back of Dane's neck began to itch. He was beginning to understand why this was an issue for their team. Tam suspected the Kingdom Church in Utah was the driving force behind the Dominion in the United States, though she hadn't yet managed to prove it. "You think this is a front for the Dominion."

"I think it's a possibility, even a probability."

"I've been running background checks on the church members," Corey said. "So far, I haven't found one who's from around here. It's like this whole group was planted here."

"Let's assume that's the case." Dane chewed his lip, turning the details over in his mind. "We've got a group associated with the Dominion hiding out on the upper floor of their church, waiting for a tsunami to hit. While their own people are safe from the disaster, they send out killers to take out any undesirables who might have lived through the flood."

"We're still left with the question of how they knew the tsunami was coming when no one had any warning," Avery cut in.

"We think we know how it happened." Tam grimaced and looked away for a moment.

"Spit it out. We've seen all kinds of craziness in our lives. Can't be any worse." Dane propped his feet on the table, folded his arms, and waited.

Tam took a deep breath and let it out in a rush. "We think the Dominion has found Atlantis."

CHAPTER 9

"You have got to be kidding." Kasey stared at Tam in disbelief.

"It's not as crazy as it sounds," Bones said. "Stick with us and you'll see all kinds of things you never thought were possible."

"So what's the story?" Dane knew Tam would not share this with the team unless she was reasonably certain that the information was correct.

"As to that, I have someone I'd like you all to meet." She opened the side door and escorted a young woman inside. "This is Doctor Sofia Perez. She has a story I think you all need to hear."

Sofia Perez was an attractive Latina woman in her early thirties. Her soft brown hair hung just below shoulder length, and her brown eyes were big and round. Her skin was bronzed by the sun and she had about her an air of youthful vigor. She settled into the last empty seat, while Tam remained standing, and looked around, giving everyone a tight-lipped smile.

"Doctor Perez," Tam began, "why don't you begin by telling everyone about your most recent project?"

"Please, call me Sofia." She shifted in her seat, took a deep breath, and began. "I'm an archaeologist and one of my areas of interest is Atlantis. It's something I've mostly kept private for obvious reasons."

Dane nodded. Professional archaeologists frowned upon colleagues who treated seriously what they considered far-fetched legends. Publicly declaring belief in something like Atlantis could derail a career, and someone like Sofia would be especially vulnerable, being both young and female.

"I spent a number of years researching Atlantis and made what I believed was a major breakthrough—a site in southern Spain that, I believed, fit Plato's description. But I lacked the resources and connections to excavate. About a year ago, a man, known to me as Mister Bishop, contacted me. He had somehow found out about my work and wanted to fund my research. I was suspicious at first, but when the first check didn't bounce, I stopped worrying about it."

Joel cleared his throat. "I have to confess my ignorance of the Atlantis story. Forgive me, but I always considered it nothing more than a myth, and an absurd one at that."

"Believe me, I understand." Sofia smiled at him.

"Why don't you give us a quick summary of the Atlantis story?" Tam asked. "Other than Bones, I suspect even those of us familiar with the story are fuzzy on the details."

"All right." Sofia rose from her chair and smiled. Clearly, she loved her subject.

"The story is told in Plato's dialogues: the "Timaeus" and the "Critias." He claimed to have learned the story from the writings of Solon, a Greek legislator and poet who heard the story from Egyptian priests during his travels in Egypt around 500 B.C.E—about one hundred fifty years before Plato.

"According to Plato, Atlantis was a utopian civilization and a great power. They worshiped Poseidon, and their residents were half-human, half-god. Their great navy permitted them to travel the world, and they mined precious metals and kept exotic animals. The city was located somewhere in the vicinity of, or beyond, the Straits of Gibraltar. The story is vague in that respect. Their home city was made up of a series of concentric islands separated by canals, with a great temple in the center. Atlas ruled as their high king, though sources name multiple kings of Atlantis and indicate there were as many as ten Atlantean cities, with Plato's being the motherland.

"I could go on all day, but for brevity's sake, I'll fast-forward to the end. Plato said the Atlanteans fell into moral decay and were eventually destroyed by a great deluge as their city sank into the sea in a single night. Virtually every scholar considers it a cautionary tale, but I believed that, even if Plato's story wasn't accurate in every detail, there was a true story there somewhere. So, I dedicated years to digging into the myths, legends, and theories. Finally, my work led me to Spain."

"So, did you find it?" Bones grinned at Sofia. Here were two of his favorite things: a crackpot theory and a beautiful woman. Avery shot a dark glance in his direction but kept silent.

"Yes." Sofia beamed and her smile seemed to brighten the room. "Near Cadiz, we found the remains of an ancient city. Its architecture bore resemblance to that of ancient Greece with elements of Egyptian architecture as well, as did its writings. The city itself was laid out in accordance with the Atlantean legend. We found a series of circular canals and, at the center, the temple of Poseidon." She glanced at Tam. "Do you want to show them the pictures?"

Tam clicked the remote and a snapshot of an ancient temple, half-buried, appeared on the screen. The architecture was striking, the details fascinating. The room fell silent as image after image flashed before them: an ancient temple, a statue of Poseidon, an altar reminiscent of Stonehenge, a pyramid-shaped structure. It was overwhelming. When Tam stopped on an overhead shot of the dig site, showing the concentric circles that surrounded the temple, no one spoke.

Sofia looked up and down the table, her eyes narrowed as if she feared they would scoff.

"Why haven't we heard anything about this?" Kasey asked. "If you discovered Atlantis, your find would be one for the history books."

Sofia took a deep breath. "Shortly after we opened up the temple, Mister Bishop showed up. He brought armed men with him and they killed everyone. Well, almost everyone. I escaped, obviously."

"I'm not seeing the connection to our situation," Dane said.

"What if I told you that, after this Mister Bishop slaughtered Sofia's team, a freak tsunami flooded the dig site, destroying everything?" Tam raised an eyebrow. "But it was no ordinary tsunami. It struck the area of the dig site and left the areas on either side unaffected."

"Sounds familiar to me," Willis said.

"But our business is the Dominion," Bones said. "Where's the missing link?"

"Mister Bishop…" Dane said. "Do you mean Bishop Hadel?" Bishop Frederick Hadel was the leader of the Kingdom Church in Utah, and purported to be the leader of the American branch of the Dominion.

"I don't know anything about this Dominion, or about Bishop Hadel," Sofia said, "but when I saw what happened to Key West, I immediately recognized the similarities to what happened at my dig."

"Sofia told her story to the people at the US Embassy. That's when I became aware of her," Tam explained. "I get pinged when certain words or phrases come up in government communication. We know the Dominion is interested in Archaeology of ancient mysteries. That combination, along with the name

Bishop, was enough to bring her to my attention. Her description of him matches Hadel to a T."

"Odd, isn't it? The Dominion usually takes an interest in items of religious significance. How does Atlantis fit in?" Dane asked.

"I think they wanted the machine." Sofia bit her lip. "We found something strange in the center of the temple."

Tam clicked the remote again, and a bizarre, silver contraption appeared on screen.

"You think they used this machine to cause the tsunami?" Dane ran a hand through his hair. This was a great deal to take in.

"Yes. I also found a codex. The translation is incomplete, but what I found indicates the Atlanteans possessed machines that were capable of such things. I believe the Dominion used it to destroy both my dig site and much of Key West. I also believe a machine like this was used to destroy Atlantis, or at least the city I excavated."

"Hold on a second." Dane raised a hand. "If you found Atlantis, and this machine was still in the city, then who was responsible for the attack?"

"As I said, my translation of the codex is incomplete, but it seems that Atlantis was, in fact, made up of more than one city. A conflict arose, maybe a civil war. According to the codex, the city I excavated was unable to defend itself due to a lack of crystals, whatever that means."

Out of the corner of his eye, Dane saw Bones sit up straighter.

"If you're correct, the Dominion can use this machine to attack any coastal city it chooses, with no one the wiser." Greg's brown eyes bored into the image on the screen.

"While Bones and I were trying out the submarine, we experienced a brief power outage just before the tsunami hit," Dane said. "It didn't last more than a moment. Perhaps this machine creates a wave of energy of some sort."

"So they could strike anywhere," Greg said.

"I don't think so." Bones rocked back in his chair and propped his feet on the table.

"What makes you say that?" Tam asked sharply.

"I don't think they have any more crystals. You guys probably wouldn't know anything about this, since most people don't exactly share my taste in reading material, but there's been a rash of crystal skull thefts in museums around the world." Bones' love of legends, conspiracy theories, and cryptids was well known to his friends.

"Crystal skulls?" Avery didn't bother to hide her skepticism.

"Seriously? You can say that to me?"

"Be professional, you two," Tam snapped. "Go ahead, Bones."

"There are four well-known crystal skulls: the Mitchell-Hedges skull, the Paris skull, the British Museum skull, and the Smithsonian skull. Over the course of the last few months, three of the four have been stolen, plus a bunch of other skulls that everyone knows are fake. The Paris skull is the only one that hasn't been taken." He looked at Sofia. "Does that more or less coincide with the timeline of your dig?" Sofia nodded. "Sounds to me like, once Bishop knew Sofia was on to something, he gave the order to acquire the skulls."

"But how would he know he needed the crystal skulls unless he had a copy of the codex?" Greg asked.

"Who can say for sure? Maybe he has information

we don't. Or it might be a hunch. The crystal skulls have been associated with Atlantis myths for a long time; maybe he was hedging his bets." Bones shrugged.

"It's too big a coincidence to ignore." Tam turned to Greg. "I want you and Kasey in Paris tonight. Take Bones along." She ignored Kasey's exasperated sigh. "Keep an eye out for anybody trying to take that skull. Hell, steal it if you can." Greg nodded. "Anything else for us, Sofia?"

"I've got copies of the codex for everyone, along with what I've translated so far." She took out a plain manila folder and passed it around. Inside were several sets of stapled sheets, each with an enlarged photograph of a clay tablet etched with glyphs. Sofia had jotted her translation in the margins.

"Where are the originals?" Joel asked.

Sofia's face fell. "I was betrayed by the man who was helping me translate it. We went back a long way and I thought I could trust him, but he tried to sell it to black-market antiquities dealers. They killed him."

"Any chance these dealers were connected to the Dominion?" Dane asked.

Tam nodded. "Let's assume so, just to be on the safe side."

"There's something I really don't get," Matt said. "Why Key West? We're not important in the big picture. Washington, New York City, those I could see, but Key West? It doesn't make sense."

"I bet we were a practice run." Willis scowled down at the translation of the codex in his hands. "Just to make sure they have their act together when the real fun starts."

"So they chose some place vulnerable," Kasey said, "a tourist town where they weren't likely to be caught."

"I'm sure they didn't mind that we're an inclusive

town with a significant gay population here," Willis added. "They made sure their people were safe, and then they went around killing off anybody they could find who doesn't fit their mold. Imagine if they can plot something like this on a large scale."

"The Coast Guard needs to be on alert. Have you notified anyone?" Greg asked Tam.

"I've shared my suspicions as much as I can, but we're still talking about the government here. If I go to the wrong person with a story about Christian terrorists using Atlantean weapons to run their own little genocide, we'll find ourselves pushing pencils on the bottom rung of the CIA. We need proof." She clapped her hands once. "We need to think like the Dominion. What are they up to?"

"If Sofia is right," Dane began, "there are more Atlantean cities to be discovered, and more weapons. If I were them, I would assemble an entire arsenal so I could hit all the major coastal cities at once. A freak tsunami here and there would cause problems, but would also raise suspicions and put the country on alert. But if I could knock out all the big cities, the major ports, offshore mining operations all at once, I don't think America could cope with the disaster. Considering the shape our economy's in and the tendency of so many people to believe any wacko conspiracy about the government, no offense, Bones, the government could collapse."

"Especially if the disaster is accompanied by genocide." Kasey grimaced. "They could destroy the economy and the social order."

"So, we need to find these other Atlantean cities first." Bones rubbed his hands together. "Screw the crystal skulls. Who's with me?"

"Hold your horses," Tam said.

"Is that supposed to be some slur against Native Americans?"

"No, I would've said, 'Hold your fire water.' Corey, whenever Maddock doesn't need you, you're going to work on translating the rest of the codex. Sofia will get you started." Corey nodded. "You too, Avery. And you can dig into possible Atlantean locations. Sofia will point you in the right direction. Bones, if you have any suggestions, pass them along. Sofia, do you have any ideas on where we should look first?"

"The author of the codex, a man named Paisden, gives what I think are clues to the locations of Atlantean cities. I think he hoped someone might gather the weapons stored there and fight back. Combining what I've translated so far with what I know of potential Atlantean settlements, there is one place in particular that I think is worth investigating right away."

"Fine. Give Maddock and Willis a full report." She turned to Dane. "This should be right up you dummies' alley. Tell me what you need and get a move on."

"Avengers assemble!" Bones raised a fist.

"What about us?" Joel inclined his head toward Matt.

"You two just found religion." Tam smiled at their puzzled expressions. "I want you to infiltrate our favorite local church."

"I'm an atheist," Joel objected.

"You're also an actor. Make it happen. Do it however you see fit, but I have a feeling Matt can pull off the role of a disgruntled ex-soldier with a grudge against the government. You'll have to be more creative." Joel smiled and nodded.

"What if I'm recognized?" Matt asked.

"I don't think there's much chance of that. The only men who got a look at you are dead, but shave that crap off your face, and put on some nice clothes, just to be safe. If somebody does recognize you and tries anything, take him down and bring him to me for interrogation."

"Shave my beard?" Matt raised a hand to his cheek. "But it's just now filling out."

"Shave it," Bones said. "It looks redneckish."

"I like it," Kasey said. "It makes you look tough." She shot a defiant glance in Bones' direction.

"All right people," Tam said, "let's do this. And don't forget, we might not have much time."

CHAPTER 10

Key West Church of the Kingdom was a rectangular brick building with white columns at the entrance and a tall steeple that loomed high above the other buildings in the area. The morning sun shone on the stained glass windows and the golden cross atop the steeple. Matt thought it was an oddly happy image for a place suspected of such dark deeds.

Since the water had damaged the sanctuary, the worship service took place in a large, crowded room on the second-floor. Organ music wafted through the stairwell, guiding Matt and Joel upward. They entered just before the service began and settled into folding chairs on the back row. Joel, who seemed to know a lot about church for an atheist, explained that church visitors usually liked to remain inconspicuous on their first visit. That way, if the church wasn't a good fit for them, they wouldn't have to deal with awkward visits from the pastor or church members. Matt was happy to remain inconspicuous. He ran a hand across his smooth cheeks. He had gotten used to his facial hair, and now he felt naked without it.

Everything about the service was ordinary: hymns, prayers, and a sermon about repentance, followed by an altar call. By the closing hymn, he wondered if they were in the right place. He glanced at Joel, who nodded. Apparently he wasn't concerned. After the benediction, they took their time leaving. A few people sitting nearby greeted them and shook hands, but most stared at them with varying degrees of suspicion.

After a few minutes, they joined the crowd making

its slow way downstairs and out onto the street. When they reach the front steps, a sandy haired, middle-aged man in a three-piece suit greeted them.

"Welcome." He shook hands first with Joel, and then with Matt. He had a firm grip and a tight smile. "Is this your first visit?"

"Sure is. Me and my brother here just moved to the area." Joel inclined his head toward Matt. "We are opening a business, and thought it would be a good idea to start getting to know some of the people in the community." Matt had to hand it to Joel. With just a few subtle changes in his posture, facial expressions, and vocal inflection, he had adopted an entirely new persona.

The man's features relaxed when Matt was introduced as Joel's brother. "I forgot to introduce myself. I am Davis Franks. So, what sort of business are you all in?"

"We'd like to open a pistol range. Maybe sell handguns and ammo. Matt here is ex-military and a pretty fair instructor. Of course, with the way the winds are blowing, it might not be the best business to get into."

"Gotta love the government." Matt rolled his eyes, playing the role of disgruntled soldier. "It's like they've never heard of Constitutional rights."

"Amen to that, brother." Franks nodded sympathetically. "What branch of the service were you in?"

"Army." Matt didn't say anything else, letting Franks guide the course of the conversation.

"I take it you didn't like it very much?"

"I liked the Army fine. It's the federal government I don't love." Matt looked around, then lowered his voice. "I guess that's not a popular opinion around here, is it?"

"No, not in Key West, but you'll find sympathetic ears in this church. If you don't mind my asking, why did you decide to settle here? Most of the locals aren't exactly firearms enthusiasts."

Joel gave an embarrassed smile. "The worst reason in the world. I love Jimmy Buffett. I've wanted to live down here for twenty years. We just hope we can get the required permits and find enough like-minded people to keep our business afloat. If not, we'll figure out something else." He shrugged as if to say, "*What are you going to do?*"

"Well, you've already found one," Franks said. "I love to shoot, and so do a lot of the fellows here. We've got to keep in practice. You never know when you'll be called to stand up against tyranny." He paused, thinking. "Listen, we have a men's group meeting tonight at six o'clock. If you two would like to visit, I'll give you directions. I think you'd enjoy it. Lots of potential customers in that group."

After they accepted his invitation, he introduced them around. The church members were much friendlier now that Matt and Joel had been accepted by one of their own, and by the time they left, they'd already fielded and politely declined three invitations to lunch, explaining they needed to start scouting around for possible places to open their business.

"Good work today," Joel said as they headed back to their car. "We'll make you an undercover agent yet."

"Do you think we're on the right track?"

"Can't say for sure, but I bet we'll find out tonight."

CHAPTER 11

"This place is freakish." Bones couldn't help but stare at the frontage of the Quai Branly Museum. Set in the shadow of the Eiffel Tower and a stone's throw from the Seine, the building was, in itself, a work of art, with its tall, glass panes and protruding blocks of varying size and color. "It looks like a living cubist painting."

"I don't think you understand cubism." Kasey made a face and looked to Greg, who ignored her, apparently having decided to tune out the bickering.

"Tell me that doesn't remind you of *Factory, Horta de Ebbo*." Bones pretended not to notice Kasey's surprise. "Obviously, there's no glass in that painting, but the way Picasso represents the sky…" He gestured toward the building and then watched out of the corner of his eye as she gave a reluctant nod.

"I see your point." Kasey tugged at her ear, something she did, Bones noticed, whenever she felt annoyed.

Bones nodded. Truth was, he didn't know much about art, but he'd picked up a few things here and there, mostly back when Maddock was dating Kaylin Maxwell, who worked as a professor of fine arts and was a painter herself. As with many other subjects, he knew just enough to carry on a conversation, or even take someone by surprise with his knowledge.

"You should see the green wall," Kasey said.

"At Fenway Park? Been there, done that."

"No, it's a section of the museum's exterior." This time, she even sounded amused. "Imagine an office building with big, modern windows, but the rest of the building looks like it's made of jungle. They call it a vertical garden. I've seen it in pictures, but never in person."

"Sounds pretty cool, actually. How big is it?"

"Two hundred meters long, twelve meters high."

"I could climb that easy. How about we grab a bottle of wine and race to the top?" Bones winked.

Kasey lowered her eyebrows and pursed her lips.

"Or we could do the Eiffel Tower. Your choice."

"Okay, time to get to work." Greg remained on his usual, even keel. "We'll split up. You two go in first, I'll follow in a few minutes. Keep in touch." He tapped his ear, indicating the communication devices with which they'd all been outfitted.

"Why do I have to go in with *him*?" Kasey stressed the last word.

"Because you two argue like a couple that's been together forever. Nobody will look at you twice."

"Chicks always look at me twice, sometimes more," Bones said.

"I don't know why karma has it in for me." Kasey sighed and took his hand. "Come on, you big ape. If we're going to do this, let's do it right."

"You know something? You and my sister would get along."

"You have a sister?" Kasey winced. "Give me her address. I want to send her a sympathy card."

The interior of the museum provided an odd juxtaposition of modern architecture and displays of artifacts from primitive cultures. Sinuous, shoulder-high partition walls snaked across the floor, and many of the exhibits were encased in glass on all sides, giving visitors an oddly distorted view of people and objects in the distance.

"Pretty creepy." Bones looked around at the

primitive displays. "I didn't expect such funky stuff in a snooty place like Paris."

"Their subject matter is interesting. That's for sure." Kasey paused to inspect a sculpture of a Maya warrior. "This guy is imposing."

"Looks a lot like my grandmother, except she had a beard."

"Let's just find the crystal skull." Kasey sighed and resumed walking. They wandered through the exhibits, feigning interest in the items on display. They moved a little slower than Bones would have liked, but they didn't want to draw attention to themselves.

They reach the crystal skull display and stopped short.

"Lovely. Can't say I'm surprised." Kasey shook her head.

The pedestal where the skull normally stood was now bare, save for a sign reading, in French and in English, THIS EXHIBIT IS TEMPORARILY OFF DISPLAY. Kasey pressed a finger to her ear and spoke softly. "Greg, are you there?"

"I'm here. What have you got?" Greg sounded as if he were standing right next to them. Kasey told him about the skull. *"Okay. I'm working on getting into their server right now. You two wander around and keep your eyes open. Be ready to move when I give the word."*

"I don't know about all this cloak and dagger stuff," Bones said. "Normally, I'd just look around for a sign that reads *Do Not Enter*, and walk on through."

"It might come to that, but let's see what Greg can learn before you go blundering into a bad situation."

"We're in a museum, and one full of Frenchmen at that. How bad a situation could we possibly get into? I guess they could throw wine and cheese at us."

"You know, the more time I spend with you, the

better I understand why Tam calls you a dummy." Though she stood a foot shorter than he, Kasey somehow managed to look down her nose at him. "Have you forgotten who else wants the skull?"

"Oh yeah." Bones scratched his head. "I actually *had* kind of forgotten. The company of a beautiful woman does that to me."

Just then, Greg's voice sounded in his ear. *"Could you two turn off your mics when you start in on each other? You're giving me a headache."* Kasey shot a dirty glance his way and Bones shrugged. *"You guys need to make your way to the southwest corner of the museum. When you get there, look for a door with a sign that reads* Do Not Enter."

"See? Told you."

Kasey pointedly ignored his gloating smile. Despite his longer legs, he was forced to quicken his pace in order to keep up with her as she strode through the museum, not slowing down until they reached the corner of the museum. She paused in front of a display of primitive musical instruments, turned, and jabbed a finger against his chest.

"I want you to follow my lead when we get in there. You understand?"

"Yeah, but I have to warn you, I'm only good at following orders up to a point. Sometimes instinct kicks in and then…" He made a wry face.

She exhaled, long and slow. "Well, do the best you can." As she walked away, he heard her mutter something about Tam and choosing her own partners from now on.

Bones grinned and followed along behind her. Keeping an eye on the few visitors wandering the exhibit, they slipped around a display and out of sight. Kasey took one last look to make sure no one was watching, gave him a warning frown, opened the door, and stepped through. Give her time, he thought. Sooner or later, she'd come to appreciate him.

CHAPTER 12

The waters of Guanahacabibes off of the western tip of Cuba sparkled in the morning sun. Dane sucked in a deep breath of the damp, salty sea air and smiled. Being out on the water felt like a reunion with an old friend. He never tired of it.

"So, this is supposed to be a sunken Atlantean city? I've never heard of it."

Sofia leaned against the rail and looked out over the water, her brown eyes glassy. She perked up at the sound of his voice.

"No one has really taken the theory seriously. About ten years ago, a research crew made sonar scans of the area, revealing what looked like roads, walls, buildings, even pyramids. Another researcher used remotely-operated video equipment to collect footage of the site, but all she got were some poor quality images of stone blocks and some formations that might bè man-made structures. When she couldn't produce more definitive proof, skeptics concluded there was nothing to get excited about. The mild interest the discovery stirred quickly died down, and now the place is all but forgotten.

"The so-called experts don't like theories and discoveries that run contrary to their beliefs. Most of them have a lot more in common with religious fundamentalists than they'd like to admit."

Sofia raised her eyebrows and cocked her head. "You surprise me. You don't find many people who think that way. Except, of course, on the internet forums where the loonies congregate."

"Bones' second home." Dane grinned. "I've seen some things over the past few years that have opened my eyes. I'm still a skeptic at heart, but I no longer dismiss theories out of hand just because they seem unlikely. There's more to this world than the average person would ever suspect."

Sofia nodded. "That's one of the reasons I haven't shared my findings from the dig site. All I have are photos and the codex, and the scientific community would point out that either could be fakes. When it's safe, and if the Spanish government will let me, I'll go back some day and re-excavate. Hell, I might live-stream the dig so everyone will know it's real." She spoke the last sentence with bitterness in her voice.

"You don't think the government would let you come back?"

"Who knows? I tried for months to get a dig permit and they stonewalled me. It took Bishop Hadel, or Mister Bishop as I knew him, getting involved to make it happen. When he killed my crew, he had a police officer with him. Somebody he bought off, I expect. Clearly, he's got connections at more than one level of government." She looked down at the blue-green water rushing by, and her eyes fell. "Governments can be weird, in any case. Look at how much trouble people have researching Noah's Ark."

"That's one I have trouble buying into. I have enough trouble spending a few days cooped on a boat with Bones. Add a wife, kids, daughters in-law, and a ton of animals to the mix? No way."

"Don't be so sure." She nudged him with her elbow and smiled. "What did you just tell me about dismissing the improbable?"

"I'm not dismissing it. I'm just skeptical."

"Fair enough." Sofia's voice took on a tone of

forced casualness. "Speaking of improbable, how is a handsome guy like you still single? No wedding band, no tan line where a ring should be. What's your deal?"

"I was married a long time ago, but she died." He left it at that. Melissa's death no longer haunted him, but he'd never feel comfortable talking about it.

"Sorry. I tend to say whatever comes to mind. When you work in a male-dominated field, you can't be passive."

"No problem. Bones is the same way and he and I are like brothers." Sofia smiled and the warmth in her eyes made him uncomfortable. "In fact, I'm dating his sister." He took out his phone and showed her a photo of himself and Angel.

"She's beautiful." Sofia laughed. "When you mentioned his sister, I imagined Bones in a dress."

Tam's voice rang out above the hum of the engine and rush of the sea breeze. "Bones in a dress? I'd pay to see that."

"You and no one else." Dane returned his attention to Sofia. "So, what makes you think this place is worth our time?"

"I've had my eye on it since its discovery. A passage in the codex describes a sister city "across the waves to the west," with details that match photos of the sunken city. It was supposedly ruled by Azaes, a king of Atlantis who is associated with this part of the world."

"I don't know that name." Dane had done his share of reading about the legendary lost city, but Sofia was miles ahead of him in that department.

"He's better known in this part of the world as Itzamna."

"Ah! The man who brought the arts and sciences of a destroyed civilization to the people of the Yucatan." Dane had heard this story before.

"The old, bearded, white man who escaped a flood that destroyed his civilization," Sofia added. "Sound familiar?"

"Yeah, sounds like Noah."

"You're funny. Seriously, though, the Gulf of Mexico used to be much smaller and shallower. In fact, Cuba and the Yucatan Peninsula were once connected by a land bridge which included this area. A few years ago, archaeologists found three well-preserved skeletons in deep, underwater caves off the coast of the Yucatan. The remains dated back 11,000 years. It fits." Sofia sounded like an attorney making her closing argument.

"You think this was Azeas' home and, when it flooded, he fled to the Yucatan and started over?" Dane couldn't deny the potential connection.

"I think it's a strong possibility."

"Corey says we're almost there," Tam called from the doorway leading into the cabin of Dane's boat, *Sea Foam*. She wore shorts, a tight-fitting tank top, and an eager smile. "I've got to tell you, Maddock, this discovery stuff is fun. I spend too much time these days sitting at a computer going through files."

"You're sure you and Corey can handle things up here?"

A roll of her eyes was Tam's only reply.

"Corey says we're right over the spot." Willis appeared on deck. "I finally get to try out the sub. Let's do this!"

Dane, Willis, and Sofia took their places inside *Remora*. They didn't bother with wetsuits, as they'd not be exiting the sub. When everyone was secure and Willis reported all systems were go, Dane took *Remora* into a steep dive.

The waters turned from a bright aquamarine to a

deep sapphire as they descended below the sunlight zone and into darkness where the sun's rays seldom penetrated. Dane switched on the front lights and let the nav computer guide them to their destination.

"It's so dark down here." Sofia spoke in a reverent whisper. "It's creepy."

"This ain't nothing," Willis said. "Get down below 3,000 feet, that's the midnight zone. It's like diving in ink. You don't know which way is up."

"I've done some diving, but I've never been so far down."

"You won't dive this deep, girl. You've got to be in a sub if you don't want to get squished."

"Approaching one thousand feet." Dane kept his voice level in spite of his excitement. The images Sofia had shown him of this city were remarkable, and he couldn't wait to see them for himself.

"Will the sub be all right this far down?" Sofia's casual tone didn't quite mask the concern in her voice. "Isn't the water pressure substantial at this depth?"

"It's rated for two thousand feet, so we'll be fine." Dane hoped the rating was accurate.

Just then, a shape appeared in the distance. He slowed *Remora* and approached with caution. In a matter of seconds, they found themselves gazing at a massive structure of stacked, square blocks.

"It's a pyramid. Looks kind of like the ones the Mayans built," Willis said. "Except for the top. It looks more Egyptian. See how it's pointed?"

"Maya, not Mayan," Sofia corrected.

"Whatever. Hey Maddock, let's circle this bad boy and let me take sonar readings."

"Roger that. Corey, are you picking up on our feed?"

"Loud and clear. Audio and video. Tam says she wants you

to scout the city before you zero in on any single structure."

"Sorry, you dropped out. I'll ping you again after we scout the pyramid." Dane smiled when he heard Tam curse in the background.

"That girl is going to have serious cash in her cussing jar if she keeps working with us."

"You have got to stop calling her 'girl.' It's a dangerous habit." Dane piloted the sub around the pyramid's base. Thousands of years of undersea currents had worn the sharp corners smooth, but it was still a remarkable structure, with well-proportioned levels and the remnants of steps still visible on the lower half of one side. As Willis noted, it looked like an amalgam of Maya and Egyptian architecture, with the stepped lower portions giving way to a classic pyramid structure at the top.

"This is amazing! Seeing this firsthand, I can totally believe the stories of an outside influence on Yucatan culture. I wish I could touch it, walk on it." Sofia sounded as if she were ready to climb out of the sub for a closer look.

"Scan's complete," Willis said. "Let's move along."

Not wanting to try Tam's patience, Dane followed the route he and Sofia had plotted out earlier. They passed the remains of buildings, some largely intact, and three more pyramids. Streets paved with flat, square stones ran throughout the city. No vegetation grew here, so far from the sun, and strong currents kept the streets clear of silt. It felt like a sunken ghost town which, Dane supposed, it was, after a fashion. By the time they completed their circuit and found themselves once again in front of the first pyramid they'd discovered, Dane had no doubt that these structures were wrought by human hands.

"What now? Want to run a grid over the whole

area?" Willis asked.

"We need to go to the center of the city. There's something we need to find." Sofia's excited voice rose as she spoke.

"Works for me. Time permitting, we can scout the rest of the complex afterward." Dane redirected the sub, ignoring the navigation program and instead following the street that ran ramrod-straight through the city. Minutes later, a high hill, ringed by several canals, appeared up ahead.

"Rings of canals," Sofia said. "You can't deny the connection to Atlantis."

"It's impressive." Dane was forced to admit he was captivated by this lost city that, all these years, had lain so close to his home.

"Looks like we're coming up on the target area," Willis said. "What's that dark shape up there?"

"We'll check it out." Dane accelerated and they swept over the canals like a bird in flight. As they drew closer, the shadowy figure swam into focus. It looked like some sort of monster out of legend.

"What is that?" Willis whispered.

"Corey, are you guys getting this?" Dane's heart pounded.

"We've got it." Dane was surprised when Tam's voice sounded in his ear. *"I got tired of using nerd boy as a go-between. Approach with caution."*

"I always do."

"Right, I keep forgetting Bones isn't with you."

Dane smiled, but keenly felt his best friend's absence. He found he actually missed Bones' constant chatter. Doubtless, if he were here, Bones would be spouting theories about aliens until he was blue in the face.

"What do you think Bones would make of this

thing?" Dane asked, but no one replied. All of them had fallen silent at the sight that lay before them.

The fine details had worn away over the years, but there was no mistaking the giant sphinx that sat atop the hill overlooking the city. Unlike its Egyptian counterpart, which lay in silent contemplation, this sphinx sat up on its haunches, its mouth open wide as if eager to devour anyone or anything that might intrude upon its watery domain. Dane marveled at the size of the sculpture.

"This thing could eat us for lunch." Dane found himself transfixed by the stone beast.

"We should call him Jared." Willis waited a few seconds. "Aw, come on. Eating a sub? Jared? If Bones had said it, you'd all be cracking up."

"We *want* it to swallow us," Sofia said. "Maddock, can you take us inside?"

"Are you serious? That seems… dangerous."

"Do it," Tam said in his ear. *"She and I have already discussed the plan."*

"Didn't bother to clue us in, did you?"

"I'm the boss of you, and don't you forget it. Take it slow, and don't get yourself into trouble."

"If you say so." Dane shifted in his seat, sat up straighter, and steered *Remora* into the sphinx's gaping maw.

Inside, a wide pit ringed with stone steps plunged straight down. Cold sweat rising on the back of his neck, Dane took them down into the inky blackness.

"Okay, so maybe this wasn't such a great idea." Sofia's breathy words were barely audible.

Indeed, it felt like they were descending into Tartarus. The pit seemed to go on forever, with only the steps hewn in the wall breaking the monotony. It felt like they'd never reach the bottom, but, at long last, their instruments indicated they were drawing near to solid ground.

When they reached the bottom, Dane halted their descent and slowly turned the sub about. The walls of the pit were blank.

"Dead end. Guess we need to head back up." Willis sounded relieved.

Run a few scans and see what you can find." Dane searched the stones in front of him. There had to be something here. "Maybe we're missing something."

He heard Willis' fingers tapping buttons on his console. A minute later, his friend cried out in triumph.

"That's what I'm talking about! At ten o'clock, there's a break in the wall that's partially blocked."

Sure enough, they had overlooked an opening. It was almost large enough for *Remora* to pass through, but a pile of rubble and silt barred the way.

"I supposed we could use the arms to clear an opening, but it could take a while." Dane scanned his monitors. They had an hour before they'd have to draw on their reserves of power and oxygen. He didn't want to cut it that close, especially since they and the sub were still getting to know each other, as it were.

"No need," Willis said.

Before Dane could ask what his friend meant, a bright flash blinded him, debris pelted the plexiglass bubble, and a dull explosion reverberated through the pit. Sofia screamed as the sub pitched to the side.

"What the hell?" Dane shouted, trying to blink the spots out of his eyes and struggling to right the craft.

"Sorry, y'all." Willis sounded sheepish. "It was one of the little torpedoes. I didn't go for one of the big ones."

"You have got to be kidding me. Even Bones wouldn't have done that." Dane knew it was a lie, but he didn't care. "What if you'd brought the whole place down on us?"

"My bad. I'll ask next time. But, check it out! I got the tunnel open."

Sure enough, the rubble was gone—blasted away by the torpedo. Through a curtain of silt, the sub's lights revealed a short tunnel and a large open space beyond. Hoping the blast hadn't destabilized the rock, Dane plunged *Remora* through the passageway.

The space beyond proved to be almost a match for the temple Sofia had discovered in Spain: a column-lined chamber a good thirty meters long. A statue stood in the center, encircled by an altar resembling a tiny Stonehenge monument.

"I remember that old dude." Willis said as Dane directed the lights upward.

"Poseidon," Sofia whispered. "It's just like the temple I excavated in Spain. This is proof that the Atlantean civilization spread across the ocean."

"I want to make a record of this place." Dane tapped the console and a camera began snapping still pictures of the chamber. "Where to next?"

"Check around behind the statue. That's where the adyton should be."

Dane stole another glance at the sub's readings. They still had time, but the window was closing. "You think there's a weapon down here?" He asked, navigating *Remora* to the back of the chamber, careful not to hit Poseidon or the altar.

"There it is! Straight ahead. See it?"

Inside an alcove beneath a pyramidal facade, something silver reflected the sub's light.

"It's a machine like the one Bishop Hadel took from the temple in Spain."

Dane moved the sub in to get a closer look at the

gleaming contraption. It was identical to the pictures they'd seen of the weapon Sofia had found: a metallic dish suspended beneath a pyramid-shaped frame, topped by a grasping hand.

"All right. Let's see if we can get this thing out of here in one piece." Dane considered the instruments he had at his disposal and formed a strategy in his head.

"Man, you got to be kidding! This little sub can't handle that thing."

"It only took a few men to carry the one in Spain," Sofia said. "It must be deceptively light."

"We've got to give it a shot," Dane said. If the Dominion had one of these things, it could only help them to study it and hopefully learn how it worked and what it could do. It also would be a good idea to keep it out of the Dominion's hands. If this machine truly could create a tsunami, the enemy could double the devastation should they obtain it.

He brought the sub as close as he dared, extended the robotic arms, and took hold of the device. "Watch out for old ladies crossing the street behind us."

"Beep! Beep!" Willis chimed in as Dane reversed the sub.

Slowly, he dragged the Atlantean machine from the chamber and out into the temple. As Sofia had predicted, it was light and moved easily.

"Now for the tricky part." He released the machine and used the robotic arm to hook a cable around their prize. It took three tries and a rain of taunts from Willis before he got the job done, but finally, towing the machine behind the sub, he was able to lift it and carry it toward the exit.

"Be careful not to hit the…" Willis began, but before he could finish his sentence, the sub jerked to a stop.

"What was that?" Dane glanced at the screen displaying the feed from the rear camera. The cable was snagged on Poseidon's trident, and the statue now lay atop the device, which appeared undamaged, but was pinned to the temple floor. What was worse, there was no way he could reach it with the robotic arms.

They were stuck.

CHAPTER 13

Silence fell as Bishop Frederick Hadel entered the boardroom. His eyes passed over the men assembled there, taking in their expensive suits and gaudy watches, the trappings of a materialistic society. One of the many things he would change when their plans came to fruition. Wealth was a means to an end, but not an end unto itself. Until that day, he would play their game, operating his headquarters from this opulent retreat center in the Wasatch mountain range, and deliver his weekly sermons from a gilded pulpit in a lavishly-decorated church. What was it about common people that obscene displays of wealth inspired them, even when the religion they purported to follow taught against the accumulation of material possessions?

He smoothed his flyaway gray hair and slid into an oversized chair at the head of a table of dark wood polished to a high sheen, and forced a smile. Everyone beamed at him, puppies eager to be scratched behind their ears. Those assembled weren't entirely worthless. All had some degree of power and influence in the secular world, but the men of true worth in the Dominion would not be found here, save one or two. Those men understood his vision and didn't mind getting their hands dirty to achieve their purpose.

"My friends," he began after a sufficient pause, "I am pleased to report that our first attempt was successful, and we are making plans for the next stage."

The men exchanged nervous glances before Utah Senator Nathan Roman cleared his throat.

"Bishop," he began, "we are all wondering about

this next stage. Will it be similar to the last one?"

Hadel stared at the senator until the man broke eye contact. "If you are asking if we are targeting another city, the answer is yes."

"Do you think that is wise?" Roman stared at a spot just above Hadel's head. The others wouldn't notice, but the bishop could tell. "Another unnatural disaster and the feds might take notice."

"Do you think me a fool?" Hadel's voice was like ice, though the senator's question did not bother him in the least.

"Of course not." Mitchell Sanders, president of one of Utah's largest banks, spoke up.

"Then, by definition, my decisions are wise, are they not?" Hadel waited for a challenge he knew would not come. "Let them take notice. In fact, when the time is right, I intend to let the world know who we are and what we can do. I want the people frightened, with no confidence in their government's ability to protect them." A few heads nodded. "Look at what happened after the terrorist attacks of 2001. Yes, the United States changed the regime in Iraq, but to what end, and at what cost to the people? Americans rushed to surrender their liberties in exchange for the promise of security, surrendering freedoms the terrorists could never have taken from them. The terrorists might lose the battles, but in one sense, they are winning the war. We will capitalize on that fear, and that eagerness to be cared for at any cost."

"What happens then?" Roman shifted uncomfortably in his seat and adjusted his tie.

"I am not ready to reveal the subsequent stages, but we have solid plans and ample resources."

"What I would like to know is how we caused the destruction in Key West." Steven Ellis was a dean at

Southern Utah University, and had a sharp mind, though it was slanted a bit too heavily toward the world of academia. "I assumed it was a bomb, but descriptions of the phenomena contradict that."

"I fear I am not qualified to explain the science behind it, but our researchers are preparing a report for the board, which I hope to have available at our next meeting. Suffice it to say, we have at our disposal, a weapon unlike any in the world. Indeed, it is so remarkable that I can credit only the grace of God that we discovered it." The frowns around the table indicated a degree of dissatisfaction, but no one pressed him.

"Why are we spending so much money on archaeological expeditions?" Sanders jumped back into the conversation with a question from his domain. "I can only describe these expenditures as exorbitant, with little to be gained."

Hadel smiled. If they only knew the real number, which was much higher than the one reported to the board. "As I have explained to you before, there are a number of reasons. First, the search for Biblical relics, the discovery of which would strengthen the devotion of our flock, draw new followers to our ranks, raise our profile in the Christian world, and prove to the skeptics the truth of Scripture.

"Second, we are a church, and it is important that we act like one, or else we risk unwelcome scrutiny from the outside. Supporting missionaries and, yes, Biblical archaeologists, and the Archaeology departments of Christian universities, are some of the things that churches like ours do. I also have other, more personal reasons, that I do not wish to share at this time." He steepled his fingers and stared at Sanders. "Repeating myself is not a good use of my time. I trust I will not be expected to answer the same questions at every meeting?"

Duly cowed, Sanders shook his head and lowered his eyes.

"We apologize for making you repeat yourself, Bishop. Understand, our motives are sincere." The speaker was a square-jawed man with intense, green eyes. He seemed uncomfortable in his finely-cut suit, but perhaps it was merely the juxtaposition with his powerful build and GI haircut. Jeremiah Robinson was the only board member whom he had considered bringing into his inner circle. To the outside world, he was a National Guard recruiter, but he was also one of the highest-ranking members of the Dominion's paramilitary branch. The other members of the board underestimated him, which made him a perfect mole. "Would you mind telling us which city is the next target?"

Hadel pretended to consider this. He and Robinson had, of course, planned this ahead of time. "San Francisco," he said. "We considered New Orleans, but we want to send the message that our power extends beyond the gulf." He made a show of checking his watch. "I thank you for your time, gentlemen. Members of my staff will meet with you individually to give you your instructions. I bid you a good day."

They all rose as he stood and left the meeting room. Some of the instructions the board members would receive were important, but most were inconsequential, serving only to convince the board members of their value to the Dominion.

He retreated to his private office. It was not the "secret" office known only to board members, which was, in fact, a red herring, but a conference room hidden in plain sight, where picture windows offered mountain views that calmed his nerves and reminded him of God's majesty.

Thirty minutes later, Robinson let himself in and locked the door behind him.

"Were you successful?" the bishop asked.

"I was able to speak with each of them individually, giving every one of them a different city as the "real" target. If one of them is leaking information, we'll know it soon enough." He declined the Bishop's offer of a chair, instead standing with his hands clasped behind his back.

"How are we progressing on the skulls?"

"As expected, the Smithsonian skull is a forgery, and thus, is completely useless."

"And the Paris Skull?"

"Our man on the inside failed, and the skull has been taken off display. A team is on its way as we speak to acquire it."

Hadel rubbed his chin and watched a golden eagle ride an updraft. An omen of the Dominion's rising, perhaps? It was superstitious nonsense, of course, but pleasant to contemplate.

"So we will have but a single bullet in our gun, should the Paris skull be genuine."

"We have analyzed the skulls but, so far, have failed to synthesize them. We think we might have found an alternate source for crystals. A research team discovered a cave…"

Hadel held up his hand. "I don't need every detail. Put it in a written report. Now, what about the rest of the operation?"

"Sofia Perez has gone to ground in Spain. We've had her passport suspended, so she can't leave the country. We'll find her. Until then, we have people working on translating the codex."

"And the Revelation Machine?" Despite his best efforts at remaining calm, the bishop's heart raced.

"No more clues than what we've had for a year now, but we hope the answer lies in the codex."

"Very well." The bishop sighed. "Move forward with stage two, and keep me abreast of developments."

Robinson's right arm twitched as if he were about to salute. He settled for a sharp, "Yes, Bishop," turned, and strode from the room.

The bishop returned to watching the eagle and contemplating the future—a future in which he controlled the fate of the United States and, perhaps, the world.

"Lord, haste the day," he whispered. "Lord, haste the day."

CHAPTER 14

"Upstairs or downstairs?" Bones whispered. They stood on a landing behind the door through which Greg had sent them.

"Downstairs," came Greg's reply. *"When you hit the ground floor, turn left. You want the fifth door on your right. You'll pass some private offices. I haven't gotten access to their security system yet, so I'm blind. Be wary and try not to let yourself be spotted."*

"Don't worry about me," Kasey said. "I just wish you hadn't made me bring a bull into this china shop."

"Tell you what. If I give us away, you can make me a steer."

Kasey gave Bones a withering look before descending the steps on silent feet, Bones creeping along behind. The hallway was silent and empty.

"Remember," Kasey whispered, "I take the lead."

Bones winked and she sighed. *"Until you screw up,"* he mouthed at the back of her head. Kasey glided along like a shadow, peering through each office window as she went. The girl moved well, and looked good doing it.

They reached their destination without incident, and found the door locked.

"Need me to pick it?" Bones offered.

"It's electronic, genius." Kasey drummed her fingers on the door frame. "What's the holdup, Greg?"

"Something odd's going on. I'm being blocked, but it appears to be from the outside. Someone else is hacking into the system." Bones heard the sound of furious tapping on a keyboard. *"You might want to duck out of sight until I get it."*

Bones looked around, for what, he was not sure. The office closest to them was empty, but the door was ajar and the lights were on. He figured the occupant was likely to return soon. Shelves lined the walls, and modest desk and chair, with a jacket draped across the back, faced the door. "Hold on," he said. "I got this."

He stepped inside, unclipped a security badge from the jacket, and brought it to Kasey. "I swiped it so you can swipe it."

"Oh my God, do you ever stop?" Kasey sighed. "But it *was* a good idea." She held the badge up to the sensor. A green light flashed and, with a click, the door unlocked. "We're in," she said for Greg's benefit, and they stepped inside and flicked on their Maglites.

Bones had expected a vault, or something equally imposing, but instead found himself in a simple storage closet. Bundles and boxes, all labeled, filled the metal shelves on his left and right, and a few more items lay on a trestle table.

He kept watch while Kasey searched the room. The hall remained empty, but his senses were on high alert, and Greg's next communication only stoked his nervous energy.

"I think we're almost out of time. Have you found the skull?"

"Not yet," Kasey said. "Why?"

"The outside hacker just called up the skull's location in the museum's database. Two guesses who's behind it."

Bones gritted his teeth. "Is there another way out if they come down the stairs?"

"Checking."

"I've got it." Kasey appeared at his side, clutching a fist-sized bundle. "Let's get out of here."

They hadn't taken more than a few steps when footsteps echoed down the hall.

"That's got to be them. In here, quick!" Bones shoved Kasey inside the open office, turned out the light, and closed the door."

"We'll be trapped in here."

"Trust me. I've got a plan." He turned on his Maglite and played it across the desk. The beam fell on a coffee mug. Bones dumped the contents on the floor and stuffed it into his jacket pocket.

"Not that there's ever a good time for stealing, but now? A coffee mug?" Kasey asked.

Bones ignored the comment. "Greg, you got an escape route for me?"

"Far end of the hall, opposite the direction you came. Turn right. There will be a stairwell on your left."

"Roger." Bones turned to Kasey. "I'll lead them away. When they're gone, you get out of here. I'll connect with you when I can." Before she could argue, he kissed her hard on the lips, turned out his Maglite, and ducked out the door.

Three men, casually dressed, strode down the hallway. All were tall, fit, and moved with single-minded determination.

"Pardonnez-moi," one of them called. His accent was atrocious, but his attempt at French indicated he had taken Bones for one of the museum staff.

"Oui?" Bones called over his shoulder.

"You're an American." The man looked hard at Bones. "What've you got in your jacket?"

"Naked pictures of your old lady."

"He's got the skull!" The man shouted. "Come on!"

Bones turned and dashed down the hallway, keeping one hand clutched to his jacket pocket to maintain the ruse that he carried the skull inside. He turned the corner and slowed his pace a bit. If he lost them too soon, one or more of them might double-back and then Kasey would be in trouble. He stole a glance back to make sure all three were still behind him, and then sped up again.

He found the stairwell and took the steps three at a time. His footfalls thundered in the empty space.

"Bones, what's happening?" Greg asked.

"I'm heading up the stairs and I've got all three guys after me. Kasey, get out of there!"

"Way ahead of you," came her breathless reply.

Bones hit the first floor landing, shouldered through the door, and emerged in the middle of a display of primitive dress from around the world. All around him, faceless figures encased in glass stood sentinel. Before he could get his bearings, the glass pane before him exploded and he caught the faint pop of a silenced pistol.

"I thought they had gun control in France," he muttered as he took off through the maze of glass cases.

"Stay alive, Bones." Greg's voice remained implacably calm. *"I'm on my way."*

The shots continued, and screams filled the air as museum patrons made a beeline for the exit. All around him, glass shattered and bullets tore through the silent figures. He didn't know where, exactly, the shooter was, but the man was between Bones and the front door. He'd have to find another way out.

The three men who had been chasing him added their voices and bullets, to the cacophony. Bones dove behind a marble pedestal and assessed the situation. The walls of glass, and their scant protection, were literally crumbling all around him. He was almost out of time.

"Spread out! One of us is bound to find him."

The voice was only meters away and coming closer. Bones tensed, ready to spring, and waited. He could now see the man's blurred form through one of the few standing displays. The man held his pistol at the ready, and moved at a steady walk. Knowing he needed as much of the element of surprise on his side as possible, Bones took the coffee mug out of his jacket and tossed it over his shoulder.

The man heard the clatter and crash, fired a shot in the direction from which the sound had come, and took off running. Bones stuck out a leg as the man sprinted past, tripping him up and sending him falling hard to the floor. His breath left him in a rush, and his consciousness followed a few seconds later when Bones hammered two vicious elbow strikes to the temple. Helping himself to the man's weapon, a nickel-plated Beretta 92FS, he grinned. The odds were not yet in his favor, but he'd shortened them considerably.

"Stevens! Did you get him?" someone cried out.

"He's headed back toward the stairs," Bones called in a nasal voice. He had no idea what Stevens sounded like, but if silence had greeted the question, the men might have jumped to the correct conclusion. This way, there was a slight chance he could throw them off the trail. He counted to ten, and then moved quietly in the direction of the front door.

No joy. A figure stepped out in front of him and opened fire. Bones dove to one side, came up in a crouch, and fired off a single shot that just missed. His target dropped to the floor and flattened out behind a pedestal covered in broken glass and the shredded remains of a display. Cursing the unfamiliar feel of the Beretta, Bones rolled behind a still-standing display, wondering when the others would arrive.

The man behind the pedestal opened fire. As

broken glass rained down on Bones, the shots ceased.

He's reloading, Bones thought. *Time to move in.*

He raised up, Beretta at the ready, just in time to see a tall, lean figure move like a shadow across his field of vision. The man on the floor managed a cry of surprise that melted into a gurgle as Greg struck him in the throat, then put him to sleep with a chokehold.

Footsteps, more gunshots, and Greg melted into the shadows.

Two men appeared, looking around wildly. Bones recognized one as the man who had spoken to him downstairs. They spotted him at almost the exact moment he saw them. They raised their pistols, but Bones was quicker. He squeezed the trigger.

And nothing.

The Beretta was empty.

"Of course," he muttered. "Now what?" His eyes fell on the figure above him—a Maori warrior, clutching a tao, a traditional short spear. "Any port in a storm." He snatched the spear, gave the dummy a shove, and ran.

The ruse only fooled his pursuers for a moment. Bullets shredded the dummy, and then the men were on the move again.

Bones zig-zagged around the few displays that remained standing, bullets whistling all around him. They had to run out of bullets sooner or later… he hoped.

Up ahead, a broad staircase led up to the second floor gallery. Mounting the steps, he ducked his head as he climbed, regretting his height and broad shoulders. Shots pinged off the marble banister, one ricocheting inches from his head.

"If one of these bullets rips my jacket, I'm going to be pissed."

At the top of the stairs, he turned left and ran along the balcony overlooking the second floor. The men weren't shooting now. Though he hoped their magazines were empty, it was more likely they were merely conserving their bullets until one of them got a clear shot at him.

"Greg, where are you?"

"I'm following along behind you guys, but I don't have a weapon. The guy I took out had fired his magazine dry."

"Any idea where I'm headed?" Bones dashed along the balcony, wondering when the next hail of lead would fly. "All I see up here is a set of double-doors."

"Conference rooms, I think. No idea if there's a way down."

"Lovely." A bullet whizzed past his ear and struck one of the doors with a thud. Acting on instinct, Bones dodged to the side, whirled, and flung the spear at the man in the lead. It flew true, taking the surprised man in the thigh and sending him tumbling to the ground. His partner stopped short, gaping at the fallen man. Seeing his chance, Bones dashed through the double doors as bullets flew again.

A short hallway led to a conference room, where windows framed in the thick vines of the so-called green wall, overlooked the street below. There were no other exits. He was finally cornered. The last pursuer was closing in. Time was almost up.

A wooden podium stood at the far end of the room. Bones ran to it, picked it up, rushed toward the nearest window, and struck it, battering ram-style.

The glass cracked, but did not shatter.

"Seriously?" Bones dropped the podium and lashed out with a series of side kicks. Glass flew, falling to the sidewalk below. He finally cleared a hole large enough for him to fit through, and clambered out the window just as the conference room door flew open.

Down on the street, people cried out, and sirens wailed in the distance. Bones gripped the thick vines, his feet finding holds in the green wall's tangled foliage. Moving with the agility of a monkey, he clambered not down, but up and to the side. He'd just come level with the top of the window when his pursuer leaned out, looking down at where he expected Bones to be.

Bones was ready. He lashed out with a powerful kick, catching the man square on the chin. Stunned, he wobbled, and Bones caught him with an up-kick across the bridge of the nose, and then drove his heel into the base of the man's skull. The man flopped unconscious, half in and half out of the window, like a wet blanket draped over a clothesline, his gun falling to the ground two stories below.

Bones slipped back through the window to find Greg entering the conference room.

"That's the last of them."

"Good," Greg said. "Kasey's got the car and will pick us up. Let's get out of here before the police arrive."

Bones laughed. "If only I had a dollar for every time I've said that very same thing."

They circled the museum at a fast walk, and hurried down Avenue de la Bourdonnais to Rue de l'Universite, where they joined a crowd of tourists headed for the Eiffel Tower.

"That thing is huge." Bones gazed up at the famed landmark. He knew the iron lattice structure rose more than a thousand feet in the air, but he was unprepared for just how impressive it was, its bronze surface gleaming against the cornflower sky. "Dude, I would love to climb that thing."

"You could take the elevator," Greg said.

"The hell with that. I'm a climber."

"Let's hope it doesn't come to that. You'd be treed like a cat."

They strolled beneath the tower and wandered along the manicured green, reminiscent of the National Mall in Washington D.C., until they reached the Champ de Mars.

"Kasey should be along any minute." Greg glanced at his watch, then checked his phone. "No messages. I guess she's okay."

Bones looked up and down the street. "Either that, or she can't text while she's being chased."

"Why would you say that?"

Bones grimaced. "Wait a few seconds and see for yourself."

CHAPTER 15

"Why aren't we moving?" A note of panic resonated in Sofia's voice.

"We just hit a little snag, that's all," Willis reassured her. "Maddock, how you want to handle this? Release the cable?"

"I'd hate to have come all the way down here and leave without the device." Dane carefully brought the sub about. "With all the gadgets we've got on board *Remora*, surely one of them will do the trick."

"Whatever you're gonna try, you'd better make it quick. Oxygen's starting to run low."

Dane glanced at the panels in front of him. Willis was right; time was growing short. He tried pulling the device free. It was not so much a serious attempt, but a matter of eliminating the simplest solution first. No luck.

He brought the sub about, unable to maneuver well with the cable still attached, and moved closer to the fallen statue. Poseidon gazed up at them through dead eyes of stone, a faint echo of the life that once teemed in this sunken ghost city.

"Should we call to the surface for help?" Sofia asked.

"We lost contact with them a while ago," Willis said. "Too far below the surface and too much rock in between."

"There's nothing they could do anyway. We've got the only sub." Dane extended the sub's mechanical arms, grabbed hold of the statue, and lifted, but the statue didn't budge. The point of the device was stuck between Poseidon's left arm, held down by his side, and his hip. Dane tried again, but to no avail.

"New plan. Let's see if we can cut it free."

"You're not going to cut the statue!" Sofia protested. "It's thousands of years old."

"You'd prefer to leave the device down here?" Dane asked. When silence met his question, he extended the sub's cutting blade and set to work on the statue. The stone was solid and the blade's first stroke scarcely made a scratch. Gritting his teeth, Dane set to cutting again. Silt and bits of stone clouded his view, and he used a water jet to clear his view. Soon, he'd managed to cut more than halfway through.

"Will you get it before our air runs out?" Sofia's forced casualness lent a stiff tone to her voice.

"No problem." Dane didn't know if that was necessarily true, but he saw no reason to worry her. "Not much more to go." He set to cutting again, the blade now chewing up the rock. Just a few seconds more…

"Maddock! Stop for a minute." Willis, usually unflappable, sounded concerned.

"What is it?"

"I'm picking up some odd vibrations. Hold on." Willis activated the sub's external microphones and turned them up. "You hear that? It sounds like…"

"Falling rock." Dane's mouth went dry. "We've got to get out of here. He turned the sub about and gunned the engines. It strained against the cable. Dane's finger hovered over the release switch that would free the sub from its tether. He didn't want to lose the strange, Atlantean device, but his desire to live was stronger.

Just as his finger touched the switch, they broke free, and the sub lurched forward, dragging the device behind it. Willis and Sofia cheered as *Remora* zipped toward the exit tunnel.

Up ahead, chunks of stone fell like giant snowflakes from the ceiling of the passageway. Dane had no choice but to try to make it through, or else they'd be trapped in the pyramidal chamber.

"Guess those torpedoes were a bad idea," Willis said.

"We're about to find out." Dane gritted his teeth as the mini sub entered the tunnel. Falling rock pelted the sub's exterior, but the little craft surged ahead. "Hang on!" Dane barked, steering the sub hard to the right as a huge chunk of stone broke free and fell right in front of them.

They almost managed to avoid it.

The falling rock struck *Remora* on its port side, causing it to pitch to the starboard side, where it banged into the tunnel wall.

"Oh God!" Sofia cried.

Dane struggled to regain control of the sub. The craft rolled, righted itself, and plowed forward again. The shower of rock continued unabated, debris now collecting on the tunnel floor, narrowing their window of escape.

"We're never going to get out," Sofia groaned.

Another huge chunk of rock fell in their path. Dane took the sub hard to port…

…and then they were free.

He angled the sub upward, climbing the shaft as fast as they dared. A quick glance told him they had fifteen minutes of air remaining, and a long way to go before they reached the surface. As they emerged from the mouth of the Sphinx and began their ascent, they regained contact with *Sea Foam*.

"Maddock! Do you copy?" Tam sounded as agitated as Dane had ever heard her.

"I copy. We've got the device and we're on our way back right now."

"We've got company up here," Tam said. *"The Cubans have located us. We're bugging out."*

"Wait! We've only got a few minutes of air left."

Five seconds of silence greeted this proclamation. Finally, Tam replied in her trademark, patronizing tone.

"Why don't you turn on the carbon dioxide scrubber, sweetie?"

Dane felt his cheeks warm, Tam's words rendering him mute and more than a little bit embarrassed. During their training exercise in *Remora*, he'd focused on piloting and working with the various mechanical appendages, leaving most of the other details to Bones.

"Aw, hell," Willis finally muttered. "Okay, I got it."

"You think you boys can get Doctor Perez back safely? I mean, now that you can breathe again?"

"We'll be fine," Dane said, "but what about you and Corey?"

"We've got a good lead on them, but it's going to be close. I don't know if we can make it back to international waters before they catch us. If we make it back in one piece, I'm arming this boat."

Dane considered the situation. "I've got a better idea. We're going to ping you. Corey, bring her about and head for our location."

"Got it," Corey said.

"Just what are you planning, Maddock?" Tam sounded suspicious.

"I'm planning on atoning for my stupidity."

He brought *Remora* to the surface, and hovered just below water level. "Corey, have you got a reading on us?"

"Affirmative. We're closing on you fast. What's the plan?"

"I want you to pass right over me and keep going

in a straight line. Make sure you're followed."

"That's not a problem."

The seconds crawled by, stretching into an eternal minute.

"What are you gonna do, Maddock?" Willis whispered.

Dane didn't reply. As *Sea Foam* closed in, Dane took *Remora* deep enough for the craft to safely pass above them. When the ship had jetted past, he swung the sub a few meters to port and brought it up to surface level.

"Cuban ship's closing fast," Willis said.

"I've got it." As the craft shot toward them, Dane activated the targeting system and made ready to fire. "Now it's my turn to try out the torpedoes."

The Cubans were almost on top of them when Dane fired. The torpedoes cut through the water and struck the ship on its starboard bow. Willis whooped at the sound of the explosion.

Dane took them deep and made a beeline toward Miami. The ship wouldn't sink, but it wouldn't be following *Sea Foam*.

"Nice one, Maddock," Tam said. *"But you know you've got to write up an expense report when we get back. Torpedoes are pricey."*

Dane couldn't help but laugh.

"Will do, and you're welcome."

CHAPTER 16

A sleek, silver BMW 4 series wove in and out of traffic and screeched to a halt in front of Bones and Greg. The passenger side window lowered a few inches and Kasey called out to them. "Hop in fast, boys, and don't you," she said to Bones, "make any cracks about women drivers."

"Wouldn't dream of it." Bones stuffed his bulk into the back seat. "Some of the hottest drivers I know are women."

"Whatever." Kasey floored it, and the BMW screeched out into the sparse traffic. "In case you haven't noticed, I think someone's following us.

Bones stole a glance through the rear window where a white sedan bore down on them.

"They've been behind me for several blocks. They tried to play it off casual-like, but they just happened to make too many of the same turns as I did. I blew a few lights and got a lead on them, but it didn't last. She yanked the wheel hard to the right, sending Bones crashing into the driver's side door. Blaring horns and screeching tires drowned out Bones' protest. Moments later, they rocketed across a bridge spanning the Seine.

"Nice view." Bones gazed out over the water. "Kasey, once we shake these jokers, how about you and I go out for a romantic dinner?"

"No, I hate French food."

Bones chuckles and looked back again. The sedan closed in on them again. They came down off the bridge and took a hard right, the BMW fishtailing as they rounded the curve, and soon they were flying along the banks of the Seine. Bones took in the serenity of the scene, where couples walked hand-in-hand by the slow-moving water, unaware that a deadly chase played out meters away from them.

A shot rang out, a bullet clanged off the wheel well closest to Bones. Kasey cursed and yanked the wheel hard to the left, and their car bounced over the low median and hurtled into the oncoming lane. A pair of smart cars parted like the Red Sea as the BMW shot between them. A horn blared and Bones looked up to see the grill of an oncoming box truck filling their windshield. Kasey cut the car back to the right, narrowly missing the truck. They bounced back over the median and onto the right side of the road.

"Holy crap, chick!" Bones shouted. "Nice maneuvering." He looked back to confirm they'd gained ground on the sedan, but for how long?

"We've got to make it out of town if we're going to catch our flight out of here." Greg remained as calm as ever.

"Do you seriously think I don't know that?" Kasey glanced at the rear view mirror and frowned when Bones caught her eye and winked. "I'm just trying to keep us alive."

"And you're doing a fine job. Keep it up."

Another bullet struck the car, this one shattering the corner of the rear window.

Bones' hand went to his hip, reaching for his Glock, which, of course, wasn't there.

"Greg, remind me why we didn't bring guns."

"Because we were supposed to be burglars, not armed robbers. Also, getting them into the museum would have added another layer of difficulty."

"Next time, I vote we take our chances with museum security. They don't worry me nearly as much as the Dominion does." Bones' eyes remained glued on the pursuing car. Kasey was doing a good job keeping traffic between them, but she couldn't manage to shake them.

"You're forgetting the most important reason of all," Greg said, his tone still serene.

"What's that?"

"Tam said no."

"Everybody grab what you've got!" Kasey cried.

Bones turned to see a massive stone arch barring their way. He had only seconds to take in the sheer size and spectacular artistry of the Arc de Triomphe before Kasey took them into the midst of the congested traffic circle that rounded the famed monument. He cursed as they barely missed sideswiping a Renault. Then, mostly to feel like he was doing something, he flipped off the driver of the car behind them, who blared his horn.

Kasey whipped the wheel back and forth until it was all Bones could do not to close his eyes as Kasey navigated the dense traffic. Greg even gripped the dashboard and pressed his brake foot against the floorboard. All around them, alarmed and angry drivers cursed and blew their horns as they tried to get out of the way of the BMW. Bones found himself holding his breath until, as quickly as they had entered the circle, they were out again, shooting south down the Champs Elysees.

The white sedan wasn't so fortunate. Bones watched as the driver, stuck in the inside lane, tried to force his way out. His vehicle struck another car, fishtailed, and smashed headlong into one of the concrete pilings supporting the chain that ringed the Arc de Triomphe, coming to an abrupt halt amidst a cloud of steam and smoke.

"Sweet!" Bones gave Kasey's shoulder a squeeze.

"The Dominion might as well give up. We're too much for them."

Kasey managed a smile which melted away in a flash. "Nice going, Bones."

"What did I do?"

"I think you just jinxed us." Kasey didn't need to elaborate. Up ahead, a two man helicopter hovered ten meters above street level. It turned broadside to the BMW and the man in the passenger side of the helicopter leveled a rifle at them and fired.

A bullet pinged off the BMW's hood and Kasey veered to the right, crossing back over the Seine and into the southern part of the city. She gunned the engine and the BMW leapt forward. Bones found himself fearing a crash almost as much as the Dominion helicopter, which followed behind them.

The chase went on for what seemed an eternity, Kasey barreling through Paris at a breakneck speed, weaving in and out of traffic, screeching around curves and even taking out a mailbox-- an obnoxiously bright, yellow number that, in Bones estimation, had gotten exactly what it deserved. Meanwhile, the helicopter kept pace, sometimes deviating its course to avoid buildings, but always taking up the chase again. Periodically, the shooter sent a bullet their way. When the rear window exploded in a shower of glass, Kasey cried out in alarm and changed directions again, and the chopper temporarily disappeared from sight.

"If either of you has an idea about how to get out of here," she said "now would be a good time to mention it."

Brushing glass out of his hair, Bones looked around. They flashed past a familiar-looking sight: a statue of a lion. Where had he seen it before?

And then he remembered.

"If you can find a safe place nearby to stop, do it."

Kasey steered the car onto a narrow street and stopped halfway along the block. The helicopter would never make it through, but, without cover, they remained sitting ducks for the shooter.

"What now?" Greg asked, craning an ear toward the sound of the approaching chopper.

"Hop out and follow me." Bones sprang out and took off down the narrow street, eyes peeled, and hoping his memory of a particular episode of one of his favorite paranormal shows was accurate. If he was wrong, they were dead.

"Are we looking for something in particular?" Kasey called from behind him.

"A manhole cover. Here!" He dropped to one knee next to the heavy steel plate, worked his fingers into the slot in the center, and wrestled the cover free.

"You're stronger than I thought," Kasey said.

"Thanks. I'll do some muscle poses for you later. Now get down there!"

The drone of the helicopter nearly drowned out his words. The Dominion had caught up with them again. As if announcing their presence, a bullet clipped the sidewalk inches from where Bones knelt.

Kasey blanched, but kept her composure as she disappeared down into the tunnel.

"You next." Bones held the manhole cover like a shield while Greg climbed into the hole. A bullet deflected off the solid steel plate, vibrating Bones' arms all the way up to the elbow. Out of time, Bones clambered into the tunnel and dropped the cover back into place as a third bullet missed his hand by a hair's breadth.

Daylight vanished, and they descended in total darkness. Time lost all meaning, and he was surprised when his feet hit solid ground. Finding his balance, he dug the Maglite out of his pocket and clicked it on, partially covering the beam with his fingers so as not to blind himself or his companions.

The thin slivers of light shone down a long stone corridor. The air was cool and heavy with the scent of stale water.

"This doesn't look like a sewer," Kasey whispered.

"It isn't," Bones said. "We're in the catacombs."

CHAPTER 17

"**They call this** place an island?" Joel scanned the shore of Bottlenose Island, a tiny patch of sand and palm trees off of Key West's northwest coast.

"I've seen smaller. But if this place is privately owned, somebody greased a lot of palms to get hold of it." Matt guided their boat toward the gleaming white sand beach where three empty boats sat beached.

"Sounds like the Dominion to me. They're never short on resources." Joel looked around and stiffened. "There's Franks. Time to get into character."

David Franks had traded his three piece suit for cargo shorts, flip flops, and a Ted Nugent concert tee shirt one size too small for his thick middle. He raised his hand in greeting and waited for Matt and Joel to drag their craft onto shore.

"Glad you found the place." Franks shook hands with each man.

"It's not hard to find. That is, if you know what you're doing," Matt added, remembering his adopted persona. "Anybody ever get lost trying to make their way here?"

"Once or twice. Anyone who can't make it here doesn't have what it takes to be a part of our group." Franks indicated they should follow him, and led them toward the edge of the wooded area.

"Is this some kind of sailing club?" Joel flashed a wicked grin. "Maybe orienteering?"

Franks' expression went stony. "It's a *men's* club, and we expect our members to live up to the name."

"Amen to that." Matt made a show of checking out

his surroundings. "Lucky the tsunami didn't hit here."

"God is good," Franks said.

"Does this place belong to one of the group members?" Matt tried to make the question sound casual.

"It belongs to the church. We use it for small group meetings. It's not much, but it gets us away from the noise of the city… and prying eyes."

"There are a lot of things in the city I don't mind getting away from," Joel added.

"Definitely." Franks pointed up ahead. "It's just through those trees."

A faint scent of wood smoke hung in the humid air, and soon Matt heard low voices and a crackling fire. Nine men sat on benches around a campfire. They all fell silent when Franks, Matt, and Joel emerged into the clearing. Franks introduced them, first names only, and invited them to take a seat.

Franks waited for silence and then opened the meeting. "Brothers, we gather once again to reflect on the Lord's wisdom, and His perfect plan for this sinful world. Brother Bill, I believe you have the devotion."

Bill, a stocky man with thinning ginger hair, stood, opened his Bible, and cleared his throat.

"Hear the words of the Lord from the book of Ezra.

"When these things had been done, the Jewish leaders came to me and said, "Many of the people of Israel, and even some of the priests and Levites, have not kept themselves separate from the other peoples living in the land. They have taken up the detestable practices of the Canaanites, Hittites, Perizzites, Jebusites, Ammonites, Moabites, Egyptians, and Amorites.

"For the men of Israel have married women from these people and have taken them as wives for their sons. So the holy race has become polluted by these mixed marriages. Worse yet,

the leaders and officials have led the way in this outrage."

He closed the Bible, looked around at those assembled, and proclaimed, "The word of God for the sons of God."

"Thanks be to God," the group intoned.

The meeting began with a perfunctory discussion of the Tsunami recovery efforts. It seemed the church was taking up a collection to assist members whose homes had suffered damage in the flood, while the men's group, which didn't seem to have a name, had helped clean up Key West Cemetery.

The discussion then turned to the topic of illegal immigration. Every man assembled stood opposed to anything short of removing non-citizens from American lands and beefing up border security, but their comments were much less incendiary than Matt would have expected. Some alleged a correlation between rising unemployment and an influx of foreign workers, while others discussed the impact on prisons, schools, and public services. Matt couldn't help but think the men were all tempering their comments until they had the measure of himself and Joel.

Finally, Franks chimed in. "Such worldly issues are important, no doubt, but God is the ultimate authority."

"There's Deuteronomy, chapter 32," Brother Bill offered. "He separated the sons of man, He set the boundaries of the peoples according to the number of the sons of Israel." Everyone, even Matt and Joel, nodded.

Joel surprised Matt by chiming in. "What about Deuteronomy 28? *The foreign resident among you will rise higher and higher above you, while you sink lower and lower. He will lend to you, but you won't lend to him. He will be the head, and you will be the tail."*

"Amen!" several men chimed.

Franks turned to Matt. "You've been quiet so far. What are your thoughts?"

"I admit I don't know the Bible as well as my brother." Matt spoke slowly, racking his brain for a believable answer. "But I seem to remember we're taught to stay in our places." He held his breath, hoping he'd remembered that detail correctly. Everyone stared at him, the silence so complete that he thought they must be able to hear his heart beat over the crackling campfire.

Finally, Franks nodded. "The Apostle Paul, in particular, taught that one should remain in his condition upon entering the church."

"And Proverbs tells us not to move land markers. The borders should not change and the people should not mix," another man added.

Matt's tension melted away. First hurdle cleared.

Franks checked his watch, then clapped his hands once.

"Brothers, our time is almost at an end. We need to set this week's fishing schedule."

Matt and Joel exchanged frowns. Matt enjoyed fishing, but this sounded like an awfully strong dedication to the sport.

Brother Bill went around the circle, assigning a pair of men to each night of the week. "I'll take tomorrow night." He looked at Matt and Joel. "Are the two of you up for some fishing?"

"Absolutely," Joel said. "But we don't have any tackle."

Everyone laughed and exchanged knowing looks.

"No need to worry on that account." Franks smiled broadly. "The Lord will provide."

(HAPTER 18

The Catacombs of Paris were comprised of 1,500 miles of caverns, sewers, and crypts that lay beneath the storied city. Formed from centuries-old limestone quarries, the caverns housed pockets of French resistance and German bunkers during World War II. A section of these passages had been converted to an ossuary containing the bones of six million Parisians, making it the world's largest necropolis. The ossuary was now a popular tourist destination, while the lesser-explored tunnels were the domain of cataphiles—people who illegally roamed the passageways.

Bones breathed in the faint scent of mold on the chill, damp air, and shone his light around. His breath rose in clouds to the ceiling, where moisture clung to the old stone. Droplets of water clung to the ceiling. This was one of the mining tunnels and not part of the actual ossuary, yet it was quiet as a tomb here, with only the occasional drip of water onto the floor to break the silence.

"Do you think they'll follow us down?" Kasey whispered.

"The pilot won't, but I'll bet the guy with the rifle will." Bones looked up, wondering how soon they could expect pursuit.

"Unless they call in reinforcements," Greg said. "No telling what kind of manpower they can call upon here. The helicopter was unexpected, so we'd better assume they've got more nasty surprises coming our way."

Kasey took out her own flashlight, a tiny keychain

number with a high intensity beam, and shone it along the wall. "How did you know we could get down here through the manhole?" she asked Bones.

"*Casebook: Paranormal* did a show down here not too long ago. They contacted the spirit of a German soldier who died in a secret bunker."

"Really? What did he say?"

"I don't know. He spoke German."

Kasey sighed. "You don't buy into that stuff, do you? Ghosts, I mean."

"Let's just say I don't dismiss things out of hand just because they don't seem likely."

"Down here, I can almost believe it." Kasey shivered and rubbed her arms. "It seems like the kind of place a ghost would hang out."

"The Empire of the Dead," Greg said. "At least, that's what the sign above the front entrance reads. Saw it in National Geographic."

They all turned and looked up when the scrape of metal on stone pierced the veil of silence.

"Here they come," Bones said. "Let's move."

They hurried along the tunnel, moving as quietly as possible and keeping an ear out for the sounds of pursuit. They passed a pillar of stacked boulders that appeared to be supporting the ceiling.

"It's best if you don't touch anything," Bones whispered. "Sections of these tunnels have collapsed in the past, sometimes taking entire houses with them."

"So glad you brought us down here." Kasey looked up at the ceiling as if might fall on them at any moment.

They went right at the first fork in the tunnel and followed it around a series of curves. Along the way they passed occasional holes big enough for a man to wriggle through, had he sufficient determination.

Maybe as a last resort, Bones thought. He didn't want to find himself trapped down here, so finding an exit topped his list. They rounded a sharp curve and Bones stopped short, throwing out his arms to hold Greg and Kasey back. Before them, a pit barred their way.

"That's a long way down," Greg remarked as Bones shone his light into its depths.

"Yeah, I forgot. Lot of wells and pits in the floors."

"Any other potentially fatal details you forgot to tell us about?" Kasey thumped him on the chest.

Bones scratched his head. "Nothing fatal, but if we're unlucky, the tunnels might flood with sewage."

Kasey bit off a retort. The sound of running feet echoed through the chamber. The Dominion was closing in on them.

"We can't cross here." Greg turned around. His eyes scanned the dark passageway behind them.

"I saw a side passage back there," Bones said. "Come on."

A few paces back around the corner, they found a dark hole in the wall just below waist height. Bones shone his MagLite inside, revealing another, smaller tunnel. Kasey wriggled in first and Greg squeezed through behind her.

"Get in here," Greg whispered.

Bones considered the narrow opening. "I'll never fit."

"We'll pull you through." Kasey held out her hand.

"And get me stuck like Winnie the Pooh in the honey tree? No thanks." The footsteps came louder now and he saw the faint flicker of a flashlight beam. "I'll be okay. You two stay hidden. If we get separated, go on without me."

Before they could argue, he turned out his light and felt his way back around the corner to the edge of the pit, where he pressed against the wall and listened to the sound of the Dominion's approach.

Footfalls. Heavy breathing. Closer and closer.

This had better work, Bones thought.

A beam of light slashed through the darkness and then someone cried out in surprise. The man stopped at the edge of the precipice, just as Bones had. In that instant, Bones struck.

It wasn't the stuff of action movies or heroic epics. Instead, he kicked the man in the backside with all his might. That was all it took to send the Dominion's agent plummeting down into the darkness, his cries ending with the wet splat of flesh hitting stone at terminal velocity.

Bones paused, listening for more pursuers, but heard none.

"You guys can come out now." He spoke in a conversational tone, but it sounded like a shout in the stillness.

Kasey wormed her way out of the passageway and tried, in vain, to brush the grime from her clothing. "What happened?"

"I kicked his ass."

"Whatever. So, do we head back to the car, or do you think the chopper's still hovering around?"

"I doubt it, but I'll bet they've disabled our car and maybe even set someone to watch it." Greg knuckled the small of his back. "I'm too old for spelunking."

"Walking is good for that," Bones said. "Let's find a way out."

They retraced their steps, making it back to the first fork in the tunnel they'd encountered, before trouble found them again. Someone called out to them in French and shone a light in their direction.

"The police patrol this place regularly," Greg

whispered.

Just then, a shot rang out, the bullet zinging off the tunnel wall.

"That's not the police!" Kasey took off running, with Bones and Greg bringing up the rear.

"You didn't manage to relieve that last guy of his weapon, did you?" Greg huffed.

Bones held out his empty hands in reply.

"Whoa!" Kasey froze and shone her light all around the room they had just entered.

The walls were lined with bones. Layers upon layers of skeletal remains were stacked to the ceiling, broken every meter or so with a ring of skulls, their eyeless sockets casting dark gazes on all who entered.

Bones ran a hand over one of the skulls and it came away covered in a fine coating of bone dust. He rubbed his fingers together, feeling the fine powder. "I wish we had time to look around, but I don't think that's a good idea. Sounds like our friend's getting closer."

They took off again. Chamber upon chamber of dry bones and leering skulls flashed by in a blur. Here and there, the floor fell away in a yawing chasm or dark pool. They hurdled the smaller ones and rounded the larger, all the while hoping the man chasing them would stumble, but he kept coming.

By the time they came to the intersection of two passageways, Bones found himself thoroughly disoriented.

"We should split up," Greg said. "Kasey, give Bones the crystal skull."

Kasey handed it over without a word of protest, and Bones tucked it into his jacket.

"It's our turn to play decoy. You just get the skull out of here, and don't even think about trying to rescue us if we get into trouble."

"No way, dude."

"It's our job. Now go." Greg gave Bones a gentle shove to set him in motion.

Bones took the tunnel to the left, cursing Greg under his breath. There were times when running away from danger was the right thing to do, but not when friends were in danger. He had to admit, though, Greg was right. It was imperative that they keep the skull away from the Dominion.

He kept his eyes peeled for the iron rungs that would indicate a way back up to the surface. So far, he hadn't seen a single one. He soon left the ossuary behind, and found himself back in old quarry tunnels. The darkness seemed to sharpen his other senses, and he caught a whiff of the rank smell of sewage. Nice.

The tunnel began to narrow and occasionally he was forced to duck to avoid a low section of ceiling. Beneath his feet, the tunnel floor grew rough and uneven. This must be one of the older sections, which meant the probability of finding a shaft leading up to the surface was small. He'd have to double back.

The thought evaporated at the sound of someone approaching. Apparently, Greg and Kasey hadn't managed to draw the Dominion's agent off his trail. That made him feel better. Now, the entire burden was on his shoulders—just the way he liked it.

He stole a glance back over his shoulder and, thankfully, did not see the flashlight glow that would tell him the Dominion agent was almost upon him.

A flash of red burst across his vision, hot pain shot through him, and, an instant later, he found himself on the ground, gazing up at a pile of rubble. The ceiling had collapsed here.

"You've got to be freaking kidding me." He looked around, his heart now racing, and his eyes fell on a tiny side passage. It would be a tight squeeze, but it was better than running headlong at an armed man. Holding his MagLite in his teeth, he forced his bulk through, and found himself in a small rubble-strewn antechamber, staring at an iron door.

"Now, where do you lead?" He tried the handle and was surprised when it turned. He slipped through and closed the door behind him. "Dude! What is this?"

Rodent droppings covered the moldering remains of burlap bags at the base of the wall to his left, while the rotted remains of wooden crates lay on the right. Rifle barrels and heaps of ammunition jutted up from the debris like islands in a sea of ruin. But it was what lay right in front of him that held his gaze.

Before another iron door, a skeleton lay curled in the fetal position atop a pile of dust and dirt that had perhaps been a blanket. Nothing remained of his clothing, but his dagger identified this as a Nazi bunker.

Bones picked up the dagger, feeling thrilled and repelled in equal measure. The history buff in him was amazed to have stumbled across a previously-undiscovered bunker, but the image on the dagger—an eagle, its spread wings forming the quillon, clutching a swastika in its claws, turned his stomach. Nonetheless, he needed a weapon. He tucked the knife into his belt, and then moved to inspect the old rifles. As he'd feared, the dampness had been unkind to them. Even if the seventy year-old ammunition was still good, the rifles were too fouled and rusted to fire.

"Too much to hope for," he muttered.

He would have liked to inspect the bunker further, but just then, he heard movement outside. His pursuer had found the antechamber, which meant he'd be coming through the door at any second. Bones thoughts raced. Fight or flight?

He decided to take his chances with door number two. He forced it open, and found himself in a rough, dank tunnel. He looked around for an alcove, or any potential hiding place from which he could ambush the agent, but the passageway ran straight ahead, gently sloping upward into the darkness. Cursing his luck, he took off at a sprint.

He heard the door behind him open. Instinctively, he dodged to the side, just as gunfire erupted and bullets deflected off the stone walls. Something needed to give, and fast.

The tunnel curved and sloped downward, and the sewage smell dissipated, replaced by the moist smell of clean water. The beam of his light glinted on a pool of water and he skidded to a halt on the slick stone floor. His breath caught in his chest as he stared out at a sight that many believed to be a myth.

Fed by an underground river and made famous by *The Phantom of the Opera*, the subterranean lake beneath Palais Garnier was, in fact, a cistern built by construction workers when they found themselves unable to remove the water from the ground where the foundation of the famed opera house was to be built. Now, the space was almost forgotten, though it was occasionally used by firefighters to practice swimming in the dark.

Bones shone his light up at the grate in the ceiling—his sole path to freedom, and knew he didn't have a chance of getting there before the Dominion's agent caught up with him. He had one hope.

The tunnel sloped downward at a steep angle and the way grew slick with moisture. Eric slowed his pace. It wouldn't do to fall and crack his skull or lose his weapon. He no longer heard the big Indian's running footsteps, which meant that the man had given up on running, and decided to turn and fight. Or, more likely, he was hiding in the shadows, waiting to spring.

Eric had gotten a good enough look at the man to know hand-to-hand combat was unlikely to favor him. He needed to locate the Indian before he attacked, and put a bullet through his heart. He shone his light all around, but saw nowhere the man could hide.

Up ahead, the tunnel opened onto a larger space. One filled with water! What was this?

"Where am I?" Eric whispered. He stood on a ledge looking out at a body of dark water of indeterminate depth, inside a concrete vault. He played his light around, inspecting the walls and ceiling. Aside from this tunnel, a single grate appeared to be the lone means of egress.

The Indian was nowhere to be seen. He must have gone into the water.

The thought had scarcely passed through his mind when a strong hand seized him by the ankle and yanked him into the water.

Eric lost his grip on his flashlight, and it clattered to the ground and bounced into the water. He managed to squeeze off a single, wild shot as he fell, but it went wild. In the muzzle flash, he caught a strobe-like glimpse of dark eyes and bared teeth, and then icy black water enveloped him.

He kicked and flailed, trying to get back to the surface, but wasn't a strong swimmer, his sodden clothing weighed him down, and he didn't know which way was up in the black water. His assailant seized him by the hair and, for an irrational instant, he thought the Indian would pull him free of the water. But then the truth hit him like a dagger to the heart—the man was holding him beneath the water.

Panic overrode rational thought, and he clawed at

the hand that held him down, but the man's grip was like iron. His lungs burned and lights swirled before his eyes. His time was almost up. Desperation welled up inside him and he fought harder to dislodge the death grip. His lungs began to cramp, and he thrashed about like a fish on the line. He opened his mouth to scream and icy water filled his lungs. He jerked once and then relaxed in the face of his inevitable demise.

At least I gave all to the service of the Lord.

Something thin and sharp pressed against his throat, and he relaxed as death made him its own.

(HAPTER 19

"What do we think?" Dane ran his hand along the smooth, silver surface of the thing they'd taken to calling, simply, the Device. They'd brought it back to headquarters, where it now sat on supports beneath a bank of fluorescent lights, looking like an inscrutable piece of modern art.

"I think it's dangerous," Tam said.

"Shouldn't we send it to a lab somewhere to be analyzed?" Willis eyed the Device like it was a rattlesnake coiled to strike.

"What lab and where?" Tam's face tightened and then relaxed. "Remember, we don't know who we can trust, and our little group doesn't carry any weight, or even credibility. Yet." Her features hardened and she raised her chin.

"Our group needs a name," Bones said. He, Greg, and Kasey had returned from Paris in the middle of the night, having managed to keep the skull out of the Dominion's grasp. "Something that doesn't sound like a coffee klatch."

Tam ignored him. "I've got someone coming in to look at it. He's an engineer from NASA. I've known him for a while and I'm sure he's not connected to the Dominion."

"How sure?" Dane asked.

Tam's shoulders sagged. "As sure as I can be."

"I don't see what there is to figure out. You put this," Bones hefted the crystal skull, "in the hand, point, and shoot. Boom! Instant tsunami!" He strode over to the device and stepped up onto the framework that held it off the floor."

"Don't you dare!" Tam sprang forward and snatched the skull out of Bones' hand.

"Chill. I just wanted a closer look. Does it have a trigger?"

"You see that faint outline that looks like a handprint?" Corey pointed to a spot below the silver hand. "I think that's it."

"Sweet. I can't wait to fire this thing." Bones held his hand above the trigger point. "Those Atlanteans had small hands. Sucks for them."

"Your paws are just freakishly large." Dane turned to Tam. "We should fire it. Hear me out." He took the skull from Tam and turned it over in his hands, feeling its cool, smooth surface. "Not here, and not alone. You say our group doesn't have any buy in from the powers that be. Fly some movers and shakers down here for a demonstration. They'll have to believe us then."

"And snatch it away from us while the military squabbles over who gets to study it first? Not yet. Not until I'm ready."

"I get it." Dane chose his words carefully. "Bones and I have trusted the wrong people before, and paid for it. But this is a national security threat. I don't think we should keep it to ourselves."

"I've already notified my superiors, plus a few contacts in other agencies. They know what we suspect—the Dominion has a weapon that can cause a tsunami."

"They aren't taking the threat seriously," Dane argued.

"I don't know how they're taking it, and neither do you," Tam said.

"But…"

"Don't push me on this, Maddock. It's my

decision, and I say no. At least, not right now."

Dane, Bones, and Willis exchanged dark glances. Dane knew Tam was on the right side, and she'd given him some much-needed help a few months before, but he still didn't trust her. Technically, he and his crew were working for her voluntarily, but she'd gone to a great deal of trouble to investigate their pasts, and now she held their misdeeds over their heads like a guillotine blade.

"If any of you have further objections, now would be a good time to keep them to yourselves."

"You know better than that," Bones said. "You buy the muscle, the mouth comes along with it. It's a package deal."

"I can live with that, so long as you remember who is the chief and who are the Indians."

Bones covered his mouth and pretended to sneeze. "Racist," he huffed.

The corners of Tam's mouth twitched. "Fine. I'm Achilles and you're my Myrmidons."

"I like that." Willis stroked his chin thoughtfully. "The Myrmidon Squad."

"I'll have some t-shirts printed up." Tam smirked. "Maddock, you and Bones come with me. You've got a new assignment."

They followed her to the conference room, where Sofia and Avery waited. Sofia smiled at them, while Avery drummed her fingers on the table and tapped her foot.

"About time. You're getting slow in your old age." Avery winked at Dane before shooting Bones a dirty look. The three new arrivals took seats at the table and Avery began. "We think we've found another Atlantean site." She handed Dane a manila folder, then offered one to Bones, but when he reached for it, she tossed it onto the floor with a flick of her wrist.

"Professionalism," Tam chided. "But I understand."

"Don't let them fool you," Bones said to Sofia. "Women really do love me."

"I'm sure." Sofia opened her own folder and got down to business. "Translating the codex has involved a great deal of guesswork. In some cases, it's pure trial and error. Last night, Avery matched one of my possible translations to an actual site—one I hadn't given serious consideration due to its location."

"Yonaguni." Dane read the heading on the first page of Avery's report.

"I've heard of that place," Bones said. "It's in Japan. Sunken pyramids and stuff. But people dive there all the time. If there was anything there, wouldn't someone have found it by now."

"Not if they don't have the codex." Sofia tapped her folder.

"Yonaguni features some very distinctive rock formations," Avery added. "We've matched what initially seemed to be string of nonsense lines in the codex to these formations. We think they will lead to the temple."

"The codex mentions a temple?" Dane asked, turning pages filled with underwater photographs of strange formations.

"No, but it stands to reason. The two Devices that have been uncovered so far were found in the temple, which appears to have been the center of Atlantean life." Sofia turned to Tam. "I'd like to go along. I'm an experienced diver, and no one knows Atlantis better than me."

"I need you here working on the codex," Tam said. "Losing a few hours on the Cuban site is one thing.

Going to Japan is another. I've got an experienced archaeologist lined up on the other end. With her help, I trust Maddock not to screw this up."

Dane wondered if she'd intentionally omitted Bones' name.

"You two pack your bags. You leave in," she checked her watch, "four hours."

"Who do you have lined up on the other end?" Bones asked. "Not some crusty old bone picker, I hope."

"Hardly. You know her quite well, in fact."

Dane noted a hint of forced nonchalance to Tam's demeanor. His mind ran through what she had just said. Archaeologist. Japan. You know her quite well. The pieces fell into place and he sprang to his feet, upending his chair.

"You can't be serious." He clenched his fists, trying to control his anger.

"I'm dead serious." Tam met his scowl with an impassive gaze.

"No way. Play your mind games with someone else, Tam. I'm not joining in."

Tam's expression remained serene as Dane's rage broke over her. "As I have told you before, the people I can say with one hundred percent certainty are not connected to the Dominion are few and far between. She's one of those people. Trust me, she wasn't any happier about it than you are. You know what they say about a woman scorned."

"Then send someone else. Willis, Matt, Greg…"

"I want you. Don't forget, you agreed to work for me."

Their eyes locked, and Dane wondered if Tam referred to the implied threats she'd made months ago on board a ship in Baltimore's Inner Harbor.

"Oh, this is going to be all kinds of fun." Bones closed his eyes and rubbed his forehead.

"Wait. Are you talking about Jade Ihara?" Avery asked. "Maddock's ex-girlfriend?"

"The one I broke up with not too long ago."

"Good old, reliable, Maddock." Bones chuckled. "You can count on him for two things: courage under fire, and cowardice in the face of an angry woman."

Sofia failed to cover her grin and Avery laughed out loud.

"I'm not afraid of women." Dane's face burned as he spoke. "I just prefer to avoid conflict if I can help it." Seeing no one else was buying his explanation, he excused himself and left the meeting room.

It was a short walk from headquarters to his condo, and Dane had only been home a few minutes when his phone vibrated. It was Angel.

"Hey." His voice sounded falsely cheerful to his ears, and Angel picked up on it immediately.

"What's the matter?"

"I'm good. Just a little stressed out." Grabbing a Dos Equis from the refrigerator, he headed out onto the deck overlooking the Gulf of Mexico, settled into his favorite chair, and began to fill her in on the events of the past few days. He told her as much as he was permitted to about his escape from the sunken city, Bones' run-in with the Dominion in Paris, and their pending trip to Japan.

"Japan sounds fun. I wish I was going with you."

"Me too. You don't know how much I wish you were coming along."

"Aw, that's so romantic," Angel said. *"Which is how I know it's a load of crap. What's really going on?"*

"No, it's true. If you weren't in the middle of training, I'd take you in a heartbeat."

"Of course you would, but that's not the point. You're not telling me everything."

"You know I can't do that now that I work for the government."

"We both know I'll get it out of you sooner or later. I'm very good at that." Angel's gentle voice sent a wave of tingling heat coursing through him, and he wanted nothing more than to be lying on a beach with her somewhere far away. *"Spill it. I'll thank you properly the next time I see you."*

"You might want to wait until you hear what it is before you make that offer." Before he could reconsider, he told her about Jade.

The line went silent for so long he thought they'd lost the connection.

"Are you there?"

"Are you freaking kidding me? Tell Tam you won't go."

"It's not that simple."

"Only because you make everything complicated. Most things in life are simple: I love you and you love me, but how long did it take you to figure that out? You always have to look at every little angle so you can make the decision that you think will piss off the fewest people."

"If you'd let me explain. Tam has…"

"You're not hearing me, Maddock. This isn't one of those things that requires an explanation. It's the wrong thing to do, so you shouldn't do it."

Dane flung his bottle of beer, still full, against the wall, where it shattered with a satisfying crash. The shower of beer that now soaked the front of his shirt, however, was not so satisfying. "Why don't you trust me? I'd never cheat on you, and you know it."

"That's not it at all, and the fact that you don't get that is a

real problem." Angel sighed. *"Loving you is tiring, you know that?"*

Dane managed a grin. "Just trying to make things interesting. I'm always hearing that women love a challenge."

"You know what they say—don't believe everything you hear, especially if my brother says it." She paused. *"I've got to go. Call me when you can."*

As if on cue, Bones stuck his head through the sliding glass door as Dane hung up.

"I heard the crash and figured you needed another beer." His eyes fell to Dane's sodden shirt. "And a poncho."

"I didn't hear you come in."

"You think Indians are only quiet in the forest?" He handed a beer to Dane. They clinked bottles and drank deeply, Bones punctuating his swig with a loud belch.

"Nice." Dane finished his drink in silence, savoring the smooth, malty flavor. "I guess we should get packing." He glanced down at his shirt. "After I shower."

"After you, bro."

Dane had decorated his condo to reflect his love of the sea. The walls were painted a rich, Mediterranean blue, and trimmed in white. Paintings of old sailing ships hung in the living area, while his first-floor study was adorned with anchors, a ship's wheel, an antique compass, and an old cutlass. Nets hung from the ceiling, giving the room a comfortable, yet cocoon-like feeling. The upstairs was done in the same fashion.

"You probably ought to get your own place now that we're headquartered here," Dane said over his shoulder as they mounted the stairs.

"You need me here," Bones said. "You're too

reclusive when I'm not around. It's unhealthy."

"True, but it's going to be awkward when Angel comes to visit."

"Not awkward at all. You two can get a room somewhere." Bones hesitated. "Was that Angel on the phone?"

"Yep." Dane really wasn't in the mood to talk about it.

"And you told her about Jade?"

"Yep."

"Maddock," Bones groaned. "You really don't know anything about women."

CHAPTER 20

"Permission to come aboard?" Matt asked Brother Bill, who waited aboard a sleek Wellcraft Sportsman fishing boat. The craft, a roomy twenty-footer with the most powerful engine one could get with that model, looked brand new. He hoped Bill would give him some time at the wheel.

Bill pursed his lips and his forehead crinkled. "I thought you were an Army man."

"I am, or was. Why?"

"The way you talk. That, and you're looking at my boat like you want to marry her." His face split into a gap-toothed grin.

"Can you blame me? She's a fine craft."

"That she is. Can't properly call her mine, though. The men's club bought her for our fishing trips and the like." He scratched his belly and his unfocused gaze ran from bow to stern. He seemed to remember himself, jerked back to full wakefulness, and invited the two men on board.

"Does she have a name?" Matt asked.

"We call her *Domino*."

"Somebody must love pizza," Joel said.

Bill grinned. "It was a compromise. Some of us wanted to call her *Dominion*, you know, for the dominion of the Lord, but others thought that wasn't a fitting name for anything short of an aircraft carrier."

A chill ran down Matt's spine. It wasn't confirmation of the connection between the church and the shadow organization, but it was close.

"I'll say this much," Joel began as Bill steered

Domino toward deep water, "so far, this seems like my kind of men's group. Most church groups are nothing but coffee and conversation. No offense."

Bill waved the apology away with one beefy hand. "I've been in my share of those."

To the west, the last rays of the setting sun colored the sky a blood red that faded to purple overhead and indigo to the east. Matt breathed the cool salt air and thought this would be a perfect night to wet a line and relax under the stars. If only they weren't on duty.

When the scattered lights on shore were but a memory, Bill cut the engine and let Domino drift. "Time to fish." He rubbed his hands together. "Should be a good night for it. Clear skies and calm water." Three fishing rods sat in holders at the stern, and he picked one up, freed the hook, and cast the line into the water.

"Don't you need bait?" Joel asked.

Bill paused. "That would look better, wouldn't it?" He opened a cooler, shifted the cans of beer aside, and pulled out a container of frozen jumbo shrimp. "You two want to bait your hooks, or do you need daddy to do it for you?"

Matt forced a laugh, and he and Joel each picked up a rod, baited the hook, and cast it into the water.

"That'll do for appearances in case the Coast Guard shows up." Bill returned the bait to the cooler and handed each of them a beer. "Drink slow, fellows. We need to stay sharp."

"What are we fishing for?" Matt asked.

"I'll give you two guesses." Bill took out a key, unlocked a large locker, and raised the lid. Inside lay three Colt AR-15 semi-automatic rifles.

"Sharks?" Joel guessed.

"Nope. Something much nastier. At least, some of

them are."

Matt felt another chill as Bill passed him a rifle. It felt like dead weight in his hands as he contemplated the implications.

"Now, you fellows know anything about marine radar?" He tapped a screen next to the wheel.

Matt nodded.

"Good. We're going to cruise nice and slow-like. You keep an eye on the radar, especially for small targets. And I do mean targets."

Joel glanced at the radar. "I expected something that would find schools of fish."

"That's what this does," Bill said. "Only, the fish we want swim on the surface." With that cryptic comment, he returned to the wheel and took the craft into deeper water.

"Tell me about your time in the Army," Bill said after they'd cruised for an hour without catching a single fish or spotting a single boat.

"Not much to tell. I fought in Desert Storm, came home, got no help from the government when I got back. Been trying to make it ever since."

"Government," Bill spat. "At least you got a chance to put them Islamics in their places."

Matt shrugged.

"How about you, Joel?"

"No military service for me. I don't follow directions too well. I've mostly worked for private security firms. We're really hoping our new business venture will pan out. I mean, who doesn't like to shoot?"

"Too many people in Key West." Bill grimaced and shifted in his seat. "If you do open a shooting range, though, I can promise you'll get plenty of business from the men's group."

"I've noticed we don't fit in with many of the locals," Joel said. "But the men's group seems different. You all seem to be the out-of-doors type, like us."

"You two do much climbing? Caving?" Bill asked.

"Hell, yes," Matt said truthfully. "Been doing it since I was a kid."

"We've got a retreat coming up that the two of you just might like. Nothing's firm, yet. We just got word from the home church a few hours ago. If you're interested, I'll talk to Franks, put in a good word for you."

Just then, a blip appeared on the radar. Bill noticed it at the same time as Matt.

"We just might have a fish."

He zeroed in on the blip on their radar and, minutes later, they came upon three dark-skinned men floating on an inner tube raft. They paddled with old planks, but stopped when they spotted Domino. The two groups of men gazed at one another in silence until Matt spoke up.

"What's the plan? Turn them in to the Coast Guard?"

"Hell, no. You know what happens when we do that? They get processed and then turned over to their families in Miami or wherever. They never get sent back where they came from."

"And they stay here either living off the government dole or stealing jobs from Americans." Joel had managed to remain in character, while Matt fought to keep his dinner down. He'd killed men in his day, but never a cold-blooded execution.

"I'll give you the first shot." Bill said it as if he were bestowing upon Matt a great honor.

Matt thought fast. If he hesitated, he, at best, lost any chance of having his ticket punched to the men's group's inner circle. Worst case, he might rouse suspicion, thus putting the mission, and perhaps himself and Joel, into danger. But he couldn't kill the men on the raft, who had noticed the rifles and were frantically, and uselessly, struggling to paddle their raft away.

"Take us a bit farther away. I like a challenge, and this isn't it."

Bill considered this. "How far?"

"Fifty yards is good considering the limited light. Daylight, I'd make it farther." He made a show of examining his rifle while Bill took them farther away from the terrified refugees. He'd only delayed the inevitable for a few moments. He looked at Joel, who appeared completely at ease. "You aren't going to try to talk me into giving you the first shot?"

"Not at this distance. You're the marksman in the family."

Matt shrugged. "It's your call." He didn't dare emphasize the last word, lest Bill notice, but he raised his eyebrows as he spoke.

Joel winked. Message received.

"This far enough?" Bill asked, cutting Domino's engine.

"It'll do." Heart racing, stomach churning, Matt took aim. He had to make this shot perfect. Gently, he squeezed the trigger and felt the rifle buck against his shoulder. The shot boomed like thunder in the quiet night, the muzzle flash like lightning, and the men on the raft cried out in fear.

"You missed." Bill sounded disappointed.

"Look again. I hit what I was aiming at.'"

Bill leaned across the rail and squinted. "You were trying to hit the inner tube? What for?"

"Just watch." Matt took aim again, taking as much

time as he dared, and fired again. Another inner tube exploded. By the time he'd taken out three of the inner tubes, both Bill and the refugees understood his plan. The men were now desperately trying to paddle their raft away.

Bill, for his part, laughed and cheered Matt on. "Listen to them squeal!"

The sounds, both the laughter and the cries, sickened Matt. He bit down on the inside of his cheek, letting the pain distract him. A few more shots and the refugees would be in the water, either to drown or be finished off by Bill or Matt.

Another shot, and now the men clung to the few inner tubes that remained inflated. Matt understood enough Spanish to understand they were now begging for their lives.

"That's what you get!" Bill shouted. "This ain't your country!"

Matt considered turning the rifle on Bill, knowing that doing so would ruin everything, but he would not kill these helpless men.

"Someone's coming!" Joel barked, tapping on the radar screen. Sure enough, a boat was approaching. Joel's call had gotten through.

"Damn! Could be the Coast Guard." Bill took the wheel and turned Domino toward shore. "Sorry you didn't get to finish the job," he said to Matt. "But it was a good time."

"How'd you do it?" Matt whispered.

"Texted Tam and Corey. One of them must have pulled the right strings."

"Good work." Matt replaced his rifle in the locker, grabbed another beer, and took a seat. He took a drink and tried to relax, but couldn't. They'd avoided the close call with the refugees, but what might they encounter on the so-called retreat? Right then, he keenly felt Maddock's absence. Matt hadn't realized just how much he relied on his friend's leadership and calming presence. Now he was on his own. He supposed he'd better be prepared for anything.

CHAPTER 21

"Maddock and Bones! Long time, no see!" The tall, lean man stepped out of the crowd at baggage claim in the Yonaguni Airport and approached Dane and Bones.

"Professor?" Dane couldn't believe it. Pete "Professor" Chapman was an old Navy buddy with whom he and Bones had shared a few adventures during their days in the SEALs. "What are you doing here?"

"I've been sent to pick you up." Professor glanced down at the ground. "I work with Jade Ihara. Well, I work for her."

"Now that's one heck of a coincidence." Bones shook hands with Professor.

"I don't know about that. She looked me up a few months ago and made me an offer I couldn't refuse. She said the two of you spoke highly of me. And I needed the money." Professor shrugged.

"Okay, so not a coincidence, but I'm glad to see you all the same." Dane slung his duffel bag over his shoulder and he and Bones followed Professor to their waiting car.

They spent the drive catching up with their old friend, though they avoided the subject of Jade. Professor had lived up to his nickname, earning his PhD after leaving the SEALs and working at the university level. "I never managed to secure tenure. They always blamed in on budget constraints, but I suspect it's my demeanor."

"What? You were the mellowest guy in our

platoon," Dane said.

"I was mellow by SEAL standards. The average college kid doesn't respond well to my... need for structure." Professor grimaced. "You should have read my end-of-course evaluations. *Intimidates students. We don't feel free to express ourselves.* What a bunch of crap. Every one of my students was free to express him or herself, provided the opinions expressed weren't stupid."

"There's the Professor we know and love," Bones said from the back seat.

They made small talk for the remainder of the drive, lapsing into silence when Professor parked the car in front of a small cottage.

"Home, sweet home." Professor cut the engine. "There are just the two bedrooms, so I'm afraid you two will be bunking on the floor."

Dane's reply froze on his lips. Jade stood in the doorway, hands on hips, her expression hard.

She was as beautiful as ever. She wore her lustrous black hair in a thick braid slung over one shoulder, and her shorts and tank top accentuating her trim, athletic figure. She was half Japanese, but in this setting, she looked like a native.

Jade maintained her blank stare a few seconds longer, then smiled and hurried forward, arms extended. Dane stepped forward to meet her, but she brushed past him as if he weren't there.

"Bones!" she cried. "It's so good to see you again." She caught the big Cherokee in a tight embrace which Bones, surprised but clearly pleased, returned. "Come on inside. I need to bring you up to speed so we can get started. You aren't too tired from your flight to do a little diving, are you?"

"Never," Bones assured her.

She led the way inside, once again pretending Dane wasn't there.

"Brrr!" Bones shivered and rubbed his arms. "Good thing I brought my jacket."

Professor whistled between his teeth. "Not fun when she gets like this. She'll warm up. Just give here a few minutes to get used to seeing Maddock again."

"A few minutes?" Dane smirked. "You don't know Jade like I do." For all her good qualities, and there were many, Jade had always been short-tempered and could hold a grudge like few people Maddock had ever known.

Inside, Jade had hooked her laptop to an HD television set. The screen now displayed a three-dimensional rendering of what looked like a series of staircases, terraces, and block-shaped structures atop a rectangular mound. When everyone was seated, she launched into a description of the Yonaguni site.

"The Yonaguni Monument was discovered in 1986. It lies about five meters below the surface. As you can see, it has several distinctive features, including steps, terraces, roads, and odd-shaped stones. Theories abound in regard to its nature. Some connect it with Lemuria, others say it's a civilization destroyed by Noah's flood. There's never been a serious scientific study, but it's a fascinating place."

"I did a bit of reading about it on the way here. Some say it's nothing more than fractured sandstone, sections of which just happen to look man-made," Dane said.

Jade didn't even look at him, but instead glanced at Professor.

"That's certainly at play here, but we believe human hands have worked many spots here. Check out this staircase." He tapped the touch pad and an image of a narrow staircase, with walls on either side, filled the screen. "What are the odds that this happened due to fracturing?"

"It's too perfect." Bones rested his chin on his fist and stared thoughtfully at the screen. "I've seen fracture patterns that sort of looked like steps, but for a staircase-shaped section to pop out of the middle of a huge block of stone, with the sides still intact? That's a heck of a coincidence."

"We think so too." Jade took up the discussion again. "There are also engravings that seem to be wrought by human hands. These glyphs, for example." She clicked over to a close-up picture of a wall covered in what looked like writing. "The photos available online leave much to be desired, so we'll want to try and get some high-resolution images while we're down. Professor will take care of that."

Dane tried again to engage her in conversation. "Do you think there's a connection between these glyphs and the Atlantean writing Sofia Perez is working on translating?"

Again, Jade ignored him. After an uncomfortable pause, Professor jumped in.

"Possibly. Some of the images are similar to Kaida script, an old writing system found only in this part of the world, but others resemble Atlantean."

"If Yonaguni were an Atlantean city, the writing could have evolved over time," Bones said.

"That's what we're thinking." Pete glanced at Jade.

"This place looks like it's made of solid rock," Bones said, "but we're searching for something that could hide a weapon—an underground chamber or something. Has anyone ever found something like that?"

"No one's ever looked for it. Very few people take

Yonaguni seriously as a site of historical interest. We're hoping the clues from the codex will lead us to just such a place."

Dane struggled to keep his annoyance in check. Jade couldn't ignore him forever. They had to work together. "Even if the Dominion hasn't deciphered this section of the codex, we have to assume they're keeping an eye on any site that's reportedly Atlantis-related."

Jade turned to Professor. "You finish up with Bones. I need to get some things ready. We leave in an hour." Still refusing to meet Dane's eye, she stalked out of the room.

Dane rose from his seat and made to follow her.

"Are you sure you want to do that?" Bones asked.

"Definitely." He strode out into the warm sun to find Jade standing alone, staring out toward the sea.

"You're going to have to talk to me sooner or later. You know that, don't you?"

"I *don't* have to do anything." Jade's cheeks turned a delicate shade of pink, clearly annoyed that Dane had gotten her to break her silence.

"So you do know how to talk. I mean, to someone other than Bones."

Jade turned her back on him, fists clenched.

"You knew when you agreed to this job that you'd be working with me. Why don't you stop being a child and…"

Jade's full armed slap cut him off in mid-sentence. She'd caught him right across the ear, the loud pop setting off a clanging in his head that nearly drowned out all other sound.

Jade's eyes widened and she covered her mouth. "Sorry."

"No, you're not."

"You're right. Of course, it didn't feel as good as I'd hoped it would."

"I'm just glad you went with the open hand."

"I'd planned on a roundhouse, but I was afraid I'd fracture a toe on your thick skull." Amusement flickered in her eyes, but died again just as quickly. "I never wanted to see you again, Maddock."

"Then why did you take the job?"

"Because I hate the Dominion even more than I hate you."

That stung. He knew she was angry with him, even furious, but what had he done to earn her hate?

"Jade, I never cheated on you. You and I weren't even seeing each other when Angel and I got together." Jade didn't say anything, so he went on. "Let's face it. It seemed like you and I could never keep things going for more than a few months at a time. You started working in China, and then Japan, and we never saw each other."

"Why do you think I went to China in the first place?" Her eyes glistened with unshed tears. "I wanted you to come and get me."

"What?" This was the last thing he'd expected her to say. If there had been one thing in their relationship he thought he could count on, it was that Jade didn't play games. Yes, she was jealous and short-tempered, but she also told him exactly what was on her mind.

"I thought if I was on the other side of the world, you'd realize you needed me and would ask me to come back." Jade forced a laugh. "The first and last time I played a head game like that."

"I didn't know," Dane said. "I didn't want to be one of those boyfriends who tried to hold you back. After a while, I just figured I wasn't that important to you."

Now Jade looked him in the eye for the first time since he'd arrived. "Listen to us talking like a couple of lovesick teenagers. This is stupid. I'm not going to waste my time with someone who didn't feel for me what I felt for him." She glanced at her watch. "Let's go. We've got work to do."

Dane watched her as she returned to the cottage. All the anger had melted from her stride, and she moved with her usual, catlike grace, her braid swinging and her hips…

Dane closed his eyes and gave his head a shake. "Get a grip," he muttered to himself. "You already have enough problems with women. Don't go creating another one." Cursing inwardly, he followed Jade inside, wondering how he could avoid screwing things up.

CHAPTER 22

"**Who's first?**" **Bones** sat perched on the rail, ready to take the plunge into the sparkling, blue water.

"You two lead the way. I'll bring up the rear." Dane knew his friend was eager to dive, having missed out on the Cuban excursion.

"Excuse me. My boat, my expedition." Jade threw a challenging look in his direction. At least she was finally speaking to him. "Bones first. Me second. Maddock third." Spotting Dane's perplexed smile, she added, "I know sense when I hear it. Now, let's go."

"Wish I was coming with you." Professor had a wistful look in his eyes.

"Do you usually dive alone?" Dane asked Jade.

"We haven't dived since I brought Professor in." She adjusted her SCUBA tank. "I have grad students who could have held down the fort, but I didn't want to bring more people into the circle than necessary."

Dane nodded. He doubted any of the students was a Dominion plant, but word of this mission didn't need to get out.

"Speaking of Professor, how'd you come to hire him?"

"He had the qualifications I was looking for and his name rang a bell. You two always spoke well of him."

"I'm surprised my recommendation carries any weight with you," Dane said.

"It does in some areas. I wouldn't take relationship advice from you." Jade paused, cocked her head to the side, and smiled. "Are you jealous, Maddock? Or maybe you thought I hired him to get back at you in some twisted way?"

"The thought never occurred to me," he lied. "Just wondered. I haven't kept in touch with him, so I was surprised to see him, that's all."

"You have a habit of discarding the people you used to care about." Jade turned her back on him and clapped her hands twice. "Let's do this."

"As you wish." Bones checked his mask one last time, winked, and flipped backward into the water, Jade a few moments behind.

A feeling of comfort enveloped Dane the moment he plunged into the water. He'd loved diving for as long as he could remember, and the prospect of adventure was icing on the cake.

Dane knew the monument lay just below the surface, but he was unprepared for it to fill his vision the moment he hit the water. He gazed at a pair of columns that almost reached the surface and marveled that so remarkable a place had lain forgotten until modern times. The staircases, passages, and multiple levels put him in mind of a step pyramid.

"Dude, this place is wicked." Bones' voice sounded in Dane's ear. "Too bad we can't stay all day."

"Maybe we'll come back some day and bring the crew," Dane said.

"I'll bring the beer."

"If you two can focus, we need to look for the first clue." Jade's voice cracked like a whip.

"Remind me what it is again?" Bones asked.

"*Behind the watcher's starry eye.* There's a sphinx-like sculpture, called the totem, somewhere in the complex, but I couldn't find anything online that pinpoints its location."

"Do we want to spread out?" Bones asked.

"We'll stay together for now. Let's start at the

bottom and work our way up." Jade pointed to the base of a steep staircase.

They circled the base of the monument, inspecting its smooth walls and sharp angles. They made three circuits, rising as they went. The stairs and terraces were bare, and they reached the top without spotting anything that could be called a watcher. At the top, they swam through narrow passageways, past walls constructed at perfect right angles, and around octagonal stone pillars, but still no watcher.

"No way this place is a natural formation," Bones said. "It reminds me of ruins I've seen in South America. Saksaywaman?"

"It definitely reminds me of the sunken city in Cuba, but there's one big difference. There aren't any ruins here. It looks like it was all carved out of one solid block."

"It's assumed that what we see here is the foundation upon which temples and the like were constructed. Look there." Jade indicated a row of perfectly round holes bored in the stone.

"Postholes," Bones said.

"That's the assumption. Whatever was here must have been washed away in whatever deluged submerged this place."

Something moved in the corner of Dane's vision and his hand went to the small spear gun he wore at his hip. "What's that?"

The three divers stared as a half-dozen shadows approached. Dane tensed, on the verge of sending Jade back to the boat while he and Bones attacked. The shapes grew larger and more alien as they drew closer. Long, thick bodies, wide flat heads with bulbous eyes on the sides emerged from the distance.

"Hammerheads," Dane breathed.

"I forgot to tell you," Jade said, "this place is teeming with them."

Dane relaxed. Like most creatures, the hammerhead was more than happy to leave you alone provided you extended it the same courtesy. In fact, they were his favorite sharks. While some people found their appearance frightening, he considered them ugly ducklings, and always looked upon them with a degree of affection and something like sympathy.

"They are awesome," Bones said, reaching out to almost touch one as it passed him by. "Weird that people are so afraid of them."

"That could work to our advantage," Dane said. "If the Dominion sends divers in, maybe the sharks will put a scare into them."

"We can hope. Let's keep looking." Jade didn't wait for them, but kicked hard and swam over the edge of the monument and down toward the smaller structures.

Dane couldn't help but fondly remember all the dives he and Jade had made together. She'd always taken the lead, trusting he'd always be right behind her. For the briefest moment, he fought down the urge to chase her down and catch her up in a rough embrace, just like the old days.

"Did you find something?"

Bone's voice yanked him back to reality.

"No, just taking a last look around," Dane lied. "Let's catch up with her before she does something reckless."

"Wouldn't want that to happen," Bones said. "Reckless is my domain."

When they caught up with Jade, she was hovering over an odd-shaped rock formation.

"The turtle." Jade indicated the five-pointed, hump-backed formation atop a stone platform. "It's one of the features mentioned in the codex." She took out an underwater camera and snapped a few pictures before continuing on.

They searched for nearly an hour, working in a grid pattern around the monument. They passed through more channels beneath archways and around blocks of stone that might have been remnants of old structures, and discovered hieroglyph-like carvings of which Jade made a thorough photographic record, but no totem. It was a shallow dive, and the three of them were experienced divers, so none of them had expended much more than half her or his supply of air, but they decided to surface for fresh cylinders, not knowing what they'd encounter once they located the totem. After fending off Professor's attempt to switch places with Bones, even trying to bribe him with beer, they returned to the water.

Their search of the final quadrant bore fruit almost immediately. They passed through a deep stone channel and exited to find a stone face staring back at them, and they swam in for a closer inspection. The currents had eroded its sharper features, but the long face, sunken eyes, and protruding forehead were easy to make out.

"You know what this thing looks like?" Bones asked.

"Moai."

Dane's first thought upon seeing the totem was its resemblance to the moai, the statues made famous by Easter Island. He ran a hand across the huge, stone brow, wondering what it could mean. Was there a connection between Yonaguni and the island on the far side of the Pacific? Considering what they and Sofia had found so far, the possibility did not seem far-fetched.

"What now?" Bones asked.

Dane recited the clue from the codex.

"Behind the watcher's starry eye, at the center of the trident, the crone points the way to Poseidon."

"Open up and try not to blink," Bones said to the statue as he shone his light inside the eye socket. "Lots of gunk in here. Let's see if it's covering anything." He took out his dive knife and began scraping. Dane did the same to the right eye.

It wasn't long before he uncovered a rectangular stone bar set in a grooved track.

"I found what looks like a lever."

"Me too," Bones said. "Should we pull them both and see what happens?"

"No!" Jade said. "Think about the clue. The watcher's starry eye, not eyes. I think we're just supposed to pull one of these handles."

"How do we know Sofia translated it correctly?" Bones asked. "Do hieroglyphs have plurals?"

"I don't know about that," Dane said, "but why make specific mention of the 'starry' eye unless the word is important?"

Bones flitted his light back and forth between the eyes. "No stars here. If the clue refers to a constellation the figure faced back when this place stood above water, we're screwed."

Dane had a different idea. "Jade, where is the turtle formation from here?"

"Just over there." She pointed to their left. "Why?"

"Except for the rounded back, I didn't think it looked much like a turtle, did you?"

"You're right. Some people call that formation 'the star.' Let me check it out." Again, Jade swam away without waiting for a partner, returning in less than a minute. "It points directly at the totem. The right eye, to be exact."

"You're sure?" Dane asked.

"Only one way to know for sure." Bones thrust a hand into the eye socket.

"Hold on," Dane said. "Remember what happened to Matt?" On a dive at Oak Island, their crew mate had tried something similar and almost lost his arm.

"There's one big difference," Bones said.

"What's that?"

"I always come out on top." Before anyone could stop him, Bones pulled the lever. Everyone swam back as a rumbling sound broke the silence and the totem sank out of sight. "Score!" Bones shone his light down into the hole the totem had revealed. Not only the statue, but a square ten feet across had sunk into the earth, and an angled passageway of the same shape and size lay before them. "A word of advice. Never play me in Russian roulette."

The passageway sloped downward for about fifteen feet, then leveled out, heading straight for the main monument. Whatever lay at the end would likely be found beneath the mountain of stone.

The passageway through which they traveled was perfectly square. The block walls and slab ceiling were made of the same rock as the monuments, while the floor was lined with huge paving stones.

"Reminds me of the Bimini Road," Bones said.

"Is there anything that doesn't remind you of a conspiracy theory or far-fetched legend?" Jade asked.

Dane didn't disagree with Jade, but he came to his friend's defense nonetheless. "You can say that to him after all the things we've seen?" In fact, Jade had been by their sides during some of their most remarkable discoveries.

"Don't be so touchy, Maddock. You're like a soccer

mom or something."

Dane bit back a retort and kept his eyes straight ahead.

"Looks like we've reached the proverbial fork in the road." Bones slowed down and shone his light around. Here, the tunnel split into three seemingly identical passages. "Three roads diverged in a creepy tunnel."

"When you make it to the afterlife, I'll bet Robert Frost will be waiting for you with a shank and a baseball bat," Jade said.

"And miles to go before I'm appreciated," Bones sighed. "So, which tunnel?"

"I think this tunnel is the trident the clue mentions," Dane said. "A straight shaft, splitting into three at the end."

"Sounds good to me, dude. The center, then?"

A short way in, Dane noticed a change in the passageway. "No more bricks and slabs," he noted. "Just a smooth tunnel carved in stone."

"We must be under the monument," Jade said.

"And it's about to get weirder. Look up ahead." Their lights glinted on the surface of the water up ahead. "There's a pocket of air down here. Maybe a big one."

They broke the surface together and looked around. They were in a pool in the center of a thirty foot-high chamber. Dane climbed out of the pool and offered Jade a hand up, which she ignored, and hauled herself up to the stone floor.

"Wonder what the air-quality is like in here?" Bones said.

"No telling." They were wearing full masks so their communication devices would work. "I don't care to find out, though."

Dane turned his attention to the far end of the room where three statues of Greek goddesses, each at least three meters tall, stood on a ledge above three tunnels. Each figure pointed downward at the tunnel beneath her feet, which was partially obscured by a curtain of water pouring from her mouth.

The goddess on the left exuded strength and vigor. She was posed in mid-stride, looking to the side and reaching back for the bow slung over one shoulder. The figure in the center wore a cylindrical crown, held a piece of fruit in her right hand; a mature beauty seemed to emanate from her solemn face. The figure to the right held a torch aloft, and spikes radiated from her crown.

"I guess this is where the crone points the way, "Jade said. "But which one is she?"

Dane looked the statues up-and-down. Each was a woman from Greek mythology, but he thought he knew the answer right away.

"It's Hecate, the one on the right."

"Are you sure?" Bones asked.

"Definitely. The one on the left is Artemis. You probably know her as the hunter, but she was also known as the maiden. Hera, in the center, is the mother, and Hecate, on the right, was the crone. What's more, she's associated with crossroads and entryways."

"Sounds like a winner to me." Bones moved in for a closer look. "You're right about the center passage. Check it out."

Dane and Jade stepped around the water falling from Hera's mouth and shone their lights down the passageway. In the distance, at the very edge of their dive lights' glow, a skeleton lay impaled by a broken spike.

"I'll bet it was designed to go back into the floor so it could catch the next person," Dane said. "It must have broken when it caught this poor fellow."

"Or lady," Jade added.

Dane ignored her comment. "Hecate was my suggestion, so how about I lead the way?"

Jade made a show of mulling this over before agreeing.

Dane led the way up the corridor. He felt certain he had chosen the right path, but the knowledge there were booby-traps in this place made him cautious. The gently sloping passageway soon opened up into a temple much like the others they had discovered. The now-familiar Poseidon stood watch over his domain.

"Whoa!" Bones exclaimed, staring at Poseidon. "Awesome."

While Bones marveled at the sights and Jade snapped pictures, Dane moved to the chamber at the back of the temple. His heart fell when he shone his light inside and found it empty.

"What do you see?" Bones asked.

"Nothing. If there was anything here before, it's gone now." Dane's stomach twisted into knots. They had come all this way and worked so hard for nothing.

Hearing his words, Jade hurried over. When she saw the empty chamber, she seemed to deflate, disappointment marring her beautiful face.

"What do you think happened?"

"I don't know." Dane shrugged. He shone his light on the floor and spotted a line of scrapes and gouges in the flagstone. "It looks like something heavy was dragged through here."

"The Dominion?" Jade asked.

Dane considered this, remembering the entrance to the passage that had led them here. "I don't think so.

We had to clear away a lot of silt and growth on the levers. Unless there is a back door, and I don't see one, whoever got here first beat us by several years."

"Great," Bones said. "Now we just have to figure out who it was."

Dane nodded. "Another mystery."

CHAPTER 23

"That's it." Sofia pushed away from the desk and gazed at the computer screen. She had finally completed her translation of the codex.

"Let me take a look." Avery rolled her chair next to Sofia's and read aloud.

"Our only hope lies in our collective strength. Few of us remain, but we must continue to resist, lest we leave this world on its own to face the great city and its deadly power."

Avery rested her elbow on the desktop, cupped her chin, and gazed at the screen. "Not a very cheerful message, is it?"

Sofia shook her head. As she read these words she could not help but wish she had never sought Atlantis.

"It sounds like the tsunami machine is nothing compared to whatever the so-called great city had at its disposal."

"And by great city you think they mean…"

"Atlantis. The true Atlantis. The capital or mother city, if you will, of the Atlantean civilization." She sighed. "It's funny. A few weeks ago, I would have given anything for definitive proof that Atlantis was more than a myth. Now I wish I could somehow undiscover it. This is all my fault." The back of her throat pinched but she forced herself not to cry.

"If it hadn't been you, it would have been someone else. If I've learned anything from my brother and his cohorts, it's that the Dominion is relentless. They'd have kept on until they achieved their goal." Avery gave her a tight smile. "I'm glad it was you. Another scientist might have given up, or worse, joined their cause."

"They didn't give me a chance to join. They tried to kill me as soon as I found the temple." Sofia winced at the memory.

"Because they knew you'd have refused. Evil is not in your character. Believe me; I've known some very bad people in my lifetime." Avery gave Sofia's shoulder a squeeze. "Okay, enough feeling sorry for yourself. We've got work to do."

Sofia sat dumbstruck for a moment, but then she broke into laughter. "Some bedside manner you've got there."

"It's the Maddock in me coming out. But I'm right." She winked, and Sofia laughed again.

"This is so frustrating." Sofia ran her fingers through her hair. "The author of the codex seems to think the location of the mother city was common knowledge, but directions to the other cities were needed."

"His breadth of knowledge is impressive. So much specific detail. It makes you wonder if they had some sort of advanced communication device." Avery forced a smile, uncertain how Sofia would react to that comment.

"They had a machine that could create a tsunami, so I don't think that would be so far-fetched an idea."

Avery took a deep breath. The idea was a test balloon to see how Sofia would react. She'd been hesitant to make any suggestion that might seem too "out there." She already felt like an imposter amongst this group of accomplished agents and experienced soldiers. Even Corey, who might not have a resume to match that of Maddock or Bones, had played an important role in their adventures. And Sofia was as smart as she was beautiful, which would have rankled if she weren't also annoyingly kind and congenial.

Though Avery didn't doubt her own skills and knowledge, she feared that the others viewed her as little more than Maddock's little sister.

"Speaking of far-fetched ideas, I have one." She paused, trying to read the expression on Sofia's face, but the archaeologist merely looked at her with polite interest. "We can surf websites filled with crackpot theories about Atlantis all day long."

"And we have," Sofia added with a grin.

"Touché. Anyway, everyone has his or her own theory about the location of Atlantis: Mediterranean, Antarctica, the middle of the Atlantic, you name it. The one point of agreement, however, is that once upon a time, a record of Atlantis' true location did exist."

Sofia's jaw went slack. "You're talking about the lost library of Alexandria."

"Exactly." Avery felt her cheeks warming and she hurried on. "Hear me out. No one questions that the library existed, and though it was destroyed, scholars generally agree that most of its knowledge was dispersed long before its final destruction. Considering what we now know about the power Atlantis wielded, I can't help but believe that information about it would be considered highly important. Surely, someone, somewhere preserved some part of it." She swallowed hard and waited for Sofia's response.

Sofia sat in silence for several seconds. "It's an angle I considered. In fact, I had just begun researching it when I was diverted by the dig in Spain." Her eyes fell. "Anyway, I agree with you. I think the knowledge is out there somewhere, but I doubt we're going to find it in any of the traditional sources of information."

"So what do we do?" Avery was grateful to be taken seriously.

"In my research, I kept turning up one name: Kirk

Krueger. He's an author and researcher who has devoted his life to tracking down the knowledge from the Great Library."

"Are you sure he's not a crackpot?" Avery asked.

Sofia grinned. "I can't say for sure, but he doesn't act like one. For one, he doesn't seek the spotlight. He's a recluse who never makes public appearances and doesn't make guest appearances on those wild theory-based television shows. He hasn't even written any books, for that matter."

"He's definitely not trying to profit off his research, then," Avery said.

"Exactly. Which is why I suspect he might be reliable. He published the occasional essay, or makes a post on the discussion board. On even rarer occasions, he'll speak with a fellow researcher, but never on the record."

"Great! Where does this guy live?"

"That's the problem," Sofia said. "I tried to track him down, but he seems to have disappeared."

"You think the Dominion had something to do with it?"

"Considering he disappeared right about the time they hired me, yes."

Avery probably should have found this news discouraging, but instead it only made her more determined. "In that case, I think we need to start a manhunt, and I know a great person to help us."

CHAPTER 24

"Another round?" Bones didn't wait for an answer, but headed to the bar and returned with four bottles of Asahi Black.

"Cheers, Bones!" Professor clinked bottles with Bones, Jade, and Dane, and they all filled their mugs with the dark, liquid.

Dane watched the foamy head dissolve, then took a gulp. The beer wasn't as cold as Dane would have liked, and was a touch on the heavy side, but it had a strong flavor that reminded him of coffee beans with a hint of dark chocolate. They were lucky to have found any sort of bar on this tiny island.

"I didn't think we'd find a bar on this island, much less a dive like this," Bones said, echoing Dane's thoughts. "My kind of place." There was nothing about the place, save the clientele, to remind them they were in Japan. This bar, with its musty air seasoned with the sour aroma of spilled beer, uneven wood floor, chipped Formica-top bar, and cheap neon beer signs, would have fit in any number of places back in the States.

"It's for the tourists, as few as they are." Jade picked at the wrapper on her bottle. Her attitude toward Dane had warmed, but the air between them crackled with unease.

They sat in discouraged silence, watching the beams of afternoon sunlight journey across the mats that lined the floor.

"What do we do now?" Jade finally asked. "Go door-to-door asking if anyone has seen an alien-looking machine that might have belonged to the Atlanteans?"

"It's a small island," Professor mused. "Maybe we start with the recreational divers. Surely somebody knows something." He took a sip of beer and glanced at Jade.

"I don't know. I'm still too stunned to think straight. Who would have thought we'd find an Atlantean temple only to find someone's beaten us to it?" She sighed and ran a finger down the side of her untouched mug.

"I don't suppose there's a library or local newspaper we could check out?" Dane doubted it, but he had no better idea. He glanced at Bones, who sat with his chair rocked back on two legs, grinning broadly. "What are you smiling about?"

"You guys are thinking about this all wrong." Bones took a long, slow drink, dragging out the moment.

"So, enlighten us." Jade put a foot on the front stretcher of Bones' chair and slammed it down to the floor.

"Careful, chick. You almost made me spill my drink." Seeing her angry look, he hurried on. "A tiny place like this where pretty much everyone has lived in the same place for generations, what you want is a storyteller." He frowned at their blank looks. "You know, the revered old dude who knows everyone and all their secrets. Every small community has at least one. That's where we should start." He took another drink, a self-satisfied expression on his face.

Jade considered this. "It's not the worst idea. I'll see what I can learn." She rose from the table and approached the only other occupied table. The three men, all middle-aged Japanese men with weathered faces, watched her approach with unconcealed eagerness.

Dane felt his fists clench, wondering if he'd have to intervene, but Jade remained unfazed, pulling up a chair without waiting for an invitation, and chatting away.

"I thought Japanese men didn't appreciate assertive women," Bones said.

"See the way they're looking at her?" Professor smiled. "She can do anything she wants. Clever and beautiful. It's a dangerous combination."

Dane shifted in his seat and took a sudden interest in the world outside the dirty window by the front door.

After a brief conversation, Jade returned to the table, smiling. "I've got a name and directions. Let's go."

Daisuke Tanaka lived in a shack overlooking the sea. Wrinkled and graying, he sat on the ground, a bottle of beer in one hand, and watched their approach with suspicious eyes.

Jade stopped a few paces away and bowed low. Dane and the others awkwardly followed suit. Finally, the man inclined his head, and they straightened. At the advice of the men in the bar, Jade had brought along a half-dozen bottles of beer, and Daisuke's eyes immediately wandered to them.

"Daisuke-San," Jade began, but the old man waved her into silence.

"Please, just Daisuke. I'm too disreputable for *San*."

Jade smiled. "Daisuke, we're archaeologists, and would like to learn more about Yonaguni, specifically the monument, and we were told you are the man to ask."

"I see you brought payment." He pointed to the ground in front of him and Jade laid the beer down.

"Sit."

There was nowhere to sit but the ground, so they settled down in a circle.

"Your English is excellent," Bones said.

"So is yours." Daisuke drained his beer, opened another, and took a long drink. "Almost as good as this beer."

Dane waited to see if he would offer his guests a drink, but no luck. Daisuke made short work of the second beer and opened a third. Dane was just beginning to wonder if they'd have to wait for him to finish the entire six-pack when Daisuke finally spoke again.

"It begins with the dragons."

"Dragons?" Jade asked.

"Many call this," he gestured toward the water, 'The Dragon Sea.' It is haunted by the spirits of the dragons that protected Japan in ages past."

Dane and Bones exchanged surreptitious glances. This could get weird.

For the next hour, Daisuke regaled them with stories of sudden storms, lost ships, and spectral apparitions. By the time full dark was upon them, Dane was convinced they were in the midst of another Bermuda Triangle.

"What can you tell us of the monument?" Dane asked when it seemed Daisuke had run out of steam.

The old man thought for a moment. "I dove there many times when they were first discovered. I probably know them better than anyone." He took a drink. "It was once the home of an ancient people who are now gone."

"Who were they?" Bones asked.

"No one knows, but they left behind the curse of the dragons to protect their city. That is why the storms claim so many ships. To keep them from uncovering what they should not."

"Not good for tourism," Jade said. "I understand Yonaguni hopes to become a popular destination for divers."

"Tourists." Daisuke virtually spat the word. "Fouling the island and the waters. I think the dragons hate them too. Lots of their little boats find our sea inhospitable." His laugh was coarse like sandpaper.

"Have many divers explored the monuments?" Dane asked.

"Not too many. The dragons chase them away." Daisuke laughed again.

Jade bit her lip and glanced at Professor before asking the question that lay foremost in their minds. "Have you heard tell of anyone bringing back any artifacts from the monument?"

"Artifacts?" Daisuke asked sharply.

"I mean… relics of whatever civilization lived there." Jade continued. "Any rumors at all? It might have been years ago."

"No." He returned to his beer, turned his gaze back to the sea, and his eyes went cloudy.

After a few minutes of silence, they made a few more attempts at conversation, but the old man had clammed up. They might as well have been invisible for all the acknowledgment they received from him. Finally, discouraged, they returned to the house where Jade and Professor were staying.

Dane sat staring at the moon and turning his cell phone over in his hands. He had tried calling Angel, but she was still letting his calls go to voicemail. Since they'd last spoken, his only communication from her had been a couple of curt text messages saying she was busy and they would talk later. He sighed deeply and gazed down at the blank screen, wondering if he should give it one more try. A gust of cool air, moist with the damp of the sea, made him shiver, but he didn't go inside. Right now, he needed the quiet.

"Somebody's being antisocial."

He looked up to see Jade standing behind his chair.

"I figure it's more comfortable for both of us if I give you space," he said.

"Don't be like that, Maddock." She laid her hands on his shoulders and began kneading the taut muscles as she had done so many times in the past. "I know I gave you a hard time when you got here, but can you blame me? You know what they say about a woman scorned."

Dane closed his eyes and felt the tension drain away. Jade had the perfect touch—just enough pressure to work out the knots but soft enough to turn a man to butter. It was one of the things he'd always loved about her. His eyes popped open and he stiffened again. "You know it was never going to work between us, don't you?"

Before she could reply, Bones called out from the doorway.

"Hey you two, Professor thinks he's on to something."

Jade jerked her hands away as if she'd been burned, and Dane sprang to his feet.

"Great," he said. "Let's see it."

He followed Jade back to the house. When she disappeared through the front door, Bones grabbed Dane's arm.

"What the hell is going on out here?"

"Nothing." Dane yanked his arm free. His first

instinct was to tell Bones to mind his own business, but his friend deserved an explanation. "I was trying to call Angel, and Jade came out and started talking to me."

"She was doing a little more than that." Bones raised an eyebrow.

"She just started rubbing my shoulders and, before I could say anything, you stuck your big head out the door and interrupted us. You've always had bad timing."

Bones folded his arms and looked down at Dane with the air of a disapproving schoolteacher. "You have any witnesses to back up your story?" And then he grinned. "Maddock, if I didn't know you were one of the good guys, I'd probably kick your ass right now, but I guess you've at least earned a little bit of trust over the years."

Dane relaxed a little. "There's nothing going on. You've got my word on it."

"But will it stay that way if Angel keeps ignoring your calls? If it takes us a while to find whatever was taken from the temple, you and Jade are going to be working at close quarters. Can you handle it?"

For all his clowning and buffoonery, Bones could be insightful when he made the effort.

Dane met his friend's eye and gave a single nod.

"Good enough for me. Let's see what Professor has for us."

Inside, Professor paced back and forth, almost bouncing with scarcely contained excitement. He held a roll of papers and slapped them into his open palm.

"I think," he began, grinning at Dane and Bones, "that our friend Daisuke knows more than he is letting on."

CHAPTER 25

"**What do you** mean?" Dane asked, now interested.

"I did some checking on Daisuke. He was in the papers all the time, back when the monument was first discovered. Basically, there were two camps: one sought to use the discovery as a way to bring in more divers and tourists, and draw attention to Yonaguni; the other wanted exactly the opposite."

"No need to hazard a guess as to which one Daisuke belonged," Dane said.

"Definitely not. In fact, he was the most extreme of his group. He wasn't only opposed to tourism; he didn't even want researchers to visit the site. He wanted it completely closed off."

"I can't totally blame him," Bones said. "Even the best of the academics can disrespect sites that others hold sacred. Just ask my people."

"That's an interesting angle considering some of the things you and Maddock have done." The corner of Jade's mouth twitched.

"I'm a complex man, my dear." Bones winked. "And, as I recall, you were along for a few of our hijinks."

Jade fixed him with a disapproving look and then turned back to Professor. "But what makes you think he knows something about the missing device?"

"I've been researching the Dragon Sea and I've learned that most of the problems he talked about: the storms, shipwrecks, lost sailors, happened in the past twenty five years."

The others absorbed the information for a

moment.

"So?" Bones asked. "What does that mean for us?"

"By itself, nothing." Professor unrolled the papers he was holding. "This is a map of the Dragon Sea. I've plotted the locations of the various incidents. What do you see?"

"They're pretty much all in a single place. Or at least, very close together." Jade rested her chin on her hand and nodded.

"So you think the missing Atlantean device is causing all these problems?" Dane asked.

"I've heard crazier." Bones tugged absently at his ponytail. "I mean, the device the Dominion found, and presumably the one you recovered, causes tsunamis, so why not another device that affects the seas?"

Dane glanced at Professor and saw he was grinning. "There's something you haven't told us yet."

"What if," Professor began, "I told you that this spot right here," he uncapped a ballpoint pen and made a dot on the coastline, "is Daisuke's house?"

Bones and Jade looked puzzled, but Dane immediately saw where Professor was headed. "You think he's got the device?"

Professor nodded sagely.

"Wait. What?" Bones looked from one man to the other.

"You might be right," Jade whispered. "He said he was one of the first to discover the monument, and he…"

"… hates tourists with a bitter passion," Bones finished. "Let's kick his ass."

"Maybe we should leave you here," Dane said to Bones. "Professor's idea makes sense, but it's still pretty far-fetched. We need to investigate, not come down on the guy like an avalanche."

"Show of hands. Who votes avalanche?" Bones raised his hand and looked at the others. "You guys suck."

"Don't worry about it. This way, you get to use some of that famous Native American stealth you're always bragging about." Dane turned to Jade and Professor. "All right, folks, it's time to devise a plan of attack."

Two hours later they anchored off the coast a short distance from Daisuke's home. This time, Jade had drawn the short straw, and would wait with the boat while the others made the dive. To Dane's surprise, she had acquiesced with only the slightest protest when he pointed out that, of the four of them, the three former Navy SEALs were most likely to be able to complete their task without being seen.

After a brief, invigorating swim, they found themselves on the cliff below the house. As they had planned, Bones stripped off his fins and quickly scaled the rock wall. He would keep a lookout while Dane and Professor searched. Dane had reasoned that the device would not be inside the old man's home, but hidden somewhere nearby, in a place with a good view of the sea. Using his map, Professor had determined what he considered to be the likely starting point: a central point from which the old man, or an accomplice, could have used the device on unsuspecting ships.

Maglite in his teeth, Dane ascended the cliff. He was an experienced climber, so he would take the high ground while Professor would cover the area just above the shore. His fingers dug deep into the cracks and crevices and his feet searched for toeholds as he made his way up. He tried to bear the weight mostly on his legs, but in a few places, he had to swing from one spot to another with only his arms holding him up. He soon felt the burn in his neck, shoulders, and lower back, but it was a good feeling. In the early days of their friendship, when they still had not learned to trust one another fully, he and Bones had bonded over their mutual interest in climbing. The first time he had met Angel was when Bones took him back to North Carolina on a climbing trip. She had just finished high school then, and a relationship with her had been the farthest thing from his mind. In fact, he found her abrasive and annoying. A lot had changed over time. The memory made him smile.

"Find anything yet?" Bones whispered question startled him.

"Did I say I found something?"

"Touchy. The house is dark, so I'm going to scout along the cliff. I figure, if he comes down here regularly, he might have worn a path, and he definitely would need a way to climb down."

"Definitely," Dane agreed. "Of course, it's hard to imagine Daisuke scaling a cliff."

"Don't be so sure. My grandfather kept climbing well into his sixties, until my grandmother put her foot down."

"I imagine you'll be a lot like your grandfather. Now, shut up and let me work."

Dane turned his attention back to his climb, ignoring the obscene gesture that he knew Bones was directing his way. Down below, over the gentle rush of the surf, he heard Professor picking his way through the rocks.

"Somebody's forgotten how to be quiet," Dane said, just loud enough to be heard.

"I figured, if you two Marys could have coffee and

conversation, there wasn't much need for stealth," Professor replied. "You do remember we have communication devices, don't you? He tapped his ear.

Dane shook his head, though he doubted his friend could see him in the dim light. Was everyone going to bust his chops?

He continued to work his way along the cliff face. Although he wanted to find Daisuke's hiding place, if it existed, he was enjoying himself nonetheless. What if he gave up treasure hunting altogether? He could move to North Carolina with Angel and they could spend their free time up in the mountains doing what he loved. For a moment, he imagined them sitting on the porch of a mountain cabin watching the sun set.

So distracted was he by the daydream that he almost fell when his right foot came down in empty space. He cursed and dug in his fingertips. Idiot! He'd been climbing instinctively, and lost his focus.

He turned his light downward and saw that he had stumbled across a recessed area over a rock ledge. Inspecting the area above, he could just make out what looked like handholds carved in the rock. His heart skipped a beat. Could this be it? Cautiously, he dropped down onto the ledge and looked around. It was a narrow space, not much wider than his shoulders. He could see how it could easily be overlooked by passersby. But, when he shone his light back, he was disappointed. There was nothing here but a rock wall.

His shoulders sagged, and he let his hands fall to his sides. He'd been so sure. And then something on the ground caught his attention. A glint of metal. He dropped to a knee and brushed aside loose gravel and sand, revealing an iron ring. Smiling, he took hold of cold metal, and pulled.

A hinged trapdoor, one meter square, swung up

and to the side until it rested against the rock wall. He shone his light inside, revealing a padlocked door. Smiling, he called for Bones and Professor, this time remembering to turn on his mic and speak in a low voice. His companions joined him a few minutes later.

"Bones, do you think you can pick that lock?" Dane knew that Bones had some skills in that area, developed during his teenage years.

"Easy as picking my nose," Bones assured him. Flashing a roguish grin, he slid down through the trapdoor and went to work on the lock.

"He really hasn't grown up at all over the years, has he?" Professor asked.

"Would we really want him any other way?" Dane chuckled and considered his own question. The truth was, he wasn't always sure of the answer.

"We are in," Bones called a minute later.

Dane and Professor followed him through the door and froze. They were inside a small cave. The walls and ceiling showed signs of past habitation. Soot stained the ceiling, storage niches were carved in the walls, and an array of broken tools and household items lay scattered across the floor. But it was the thing in the center of the room that rendered them speechless.

Their triple beams of light shone on what could only be an Atlantean device.

"What the hell is it?" Bones finally asked.

"It definitely looks like a weapon of some sort," Professor said.

Dane had to agree. Standing on a makeshift bamboo tripod, the device looked to him like an oversized titanium telescope. On one end, he saw a trigger and what looked like an eyepiece, perhaps for sighting in a target. On the other end, four crystals came together in a point. He reached out and ran his hand along its perfect surface. Even after seeing the other device, it amazed him that the Atlantean's could have done such precise metalwork so many millennia ago.

"What kind of metal is this?" Professor ran the beam of his Maglite up and down its length. "Titanium?"

"They're still running tests on the device we recovered," Dane said, "but my money is on something previously unknown."

"A previously unknown metal? What are the odds?"

Dane and Bones exchanged looks. Once before, they had encountered such a metal. What if there was a connection? It was too much to consider at the moment.

"What are these things?" Bones pointed to a row of depressions running along the top of the cylinder near the eyepiece. They were of varying shapes and sizes. Clearly they served a purpose.

"Maybe it's where they put the crystals that powered it."

"But if this thing runs on crystal power, how did Daisuke use it?" Bones mused.

Dane looked around and found the answer almost immediately. Nearby lay an old dive bag, and when he opened it and shone his light inside, he found what he was looking for.

"This is how." He reached inside and scooped out a handful of crystals. The shapes, sizes, and colors were varied, as were the quality. Some were finely shaped gems, while others were raw stones in smoky hues of blue and green.

Bones took one and held it up, shining his Maglite so that the beam refracted in tiny slivers of red all over the cave. "This one looks like it was made to go into this first slot. Should I try it?"

"No!" Dane and Professor exclaimed in unison.

"Just kidding." Bones tossed the crystal back into the bag. "Where do you think he got all these?"

"I'll bet he found them in the temple. He was probably the first person to discover it, so I imagine he cleaned the place out."

"And then he used it as his own high-tech, *Keep Out* sign." Bones shook his head. "I'd love to see his face when he comes down here and finds it gone."

Dane put his arms underneath the device and checked its weight. It was astonishingly light. They would have no problem getting it out of here. He replaced it on the tripod.

"Let's call Jade and let her know we found it. Then, we need to touch base with Tam and have her make arrangements to get this thing home. I don't think we can put it in our checked luggage, and I'm not sure it will fit in the overhead bin."

"Wait a minute." Professor frowned. "Shouldn't we notify the authorities? If he's been using this thing to cause ship wrecks, and who knows what else, he should be made to pay."

"Good idea," Bones said. "As soon as we get back to the house, you can call the police and let them know that a local drunk found a weapon from Atlantis, and used it to turn the Dragon Sea into the Bermuda Triangle."

Professor's jaw went slack as he considered Bones' words. Finally he laughed. "Okay. I'll defer to your judgment. I don't have as much experience as you with this sort of thing."

"Stick with us." Dane clapped his friend on the shoulder. "You'll have all you can stand."

CHAPTER 26

"Are you sure we're in the right place?" Sofia looked doubtfully at the bookstore facade. Perched in front of a four-lane highway, the big, square building with large glass panes across the front looked like an old grocery store.

"Jimmy says his debit card is swiped in the coffee shop here every weekday around this time," Avery said. Jimmy Letson was an accomplished hacker and an old friend of Maddock's. He'd done a little searching on their behalf, and discovered that Kirk Krueger was living in Rachel, Nevada under the name James Ronald. Tam had sent Avery, Sofia, and Willis to search for him.

"So this road is seriously called the Extraterrestrial Highway?" Willis asked.

"It's the town closest to Area 51," Avery said. "It's small, but it draws a fair number of tourists."

"Kind of weird, a conspiracy theory nut living this close to Area 51, of all places, don't you think?" Willis ran a hand across his shaved scalp.

"Perhaps he's hiding in plain sight?" Sofia offered. "I guess we can ask him when we find him."

"How about we get going?" Avery said. "We'll go in separately and do some browsing. If one of us spots him, text the others."

"Look at the little girl taking charge." Willis smiled indulgently.

"You have a problem with that?"

"No, girl. It's just the Maddock in you coming out."

"Whatever. Remember, I don't want you approaching him," she said to Willis. "Sofia and I are a bit less intimidating. You just hang back in case we need you."

Willis nodded.

"Okay, let's do it." Avery waited until first Willis, then Sofia, entered the store, then followed a minute later. The bookstore was packed with rows of overstuffed shelves teeming with books, DVDs and CDs. New and used items were shelved together. She inhaled the aroma of slightly scorched coffee beans and smiled. This was her kind of place.

She spotted Willis' head bobbing along above the shelves in the movie section. Sofia was nowhere to be seen. Avery thought for a moment. Where might an expert on the lost library browse? She approached the register and asked the sleepy-looking cashier to direct her to the section on ancient mysteries. He waved her toward the back corner of the store and slumped back onto his stool, a defeated look on his face.

The ancient mysteries aisle was empty of customers, so she selected a book at random and wandered toward the coffee shop. Krueger wasn't there. She bought a cup of house blend, one sugar, no cream, in a to-go cup, and resumed her wanderings. She hadn't gone ten steps when her cell phone vibrated. It was a text from Sofia.

Seating area beside the magazines.

Avery rounded the magazine display and found a circle of sofas, chairs, ottomans, and side tables. Sofia was curled up in an overstuffed armchair reading a magazine. Avery couldn't help but notice, and envy, the way Sofia did everything, even sit in a chair, with such natural grace. She wondered, with a touch of resentment, how long it would be before Bones got his hooks into the beautiful archaeologist. Pushing the juvenile thoughts aside, she refocused.

You're here to find someone, she thought. *Where is he?*

And then she spotted him. Directly across from Sofia sat a slender, fair-skinned man with blue eyes. He wore his shockingly blond hair in a flat top cut, and he was clad in jeans and an Oxford cloth shirt. He was flipping through the sports section of the Roswell Daily Register, his coffee untouched on the table beside him.

His eyes barely flitted in her direction as she sat down in the chair next to his. She smiled and he made the faintest of nods before returning to his paper. She took a sip of coffee, opened her book, and pretended to read. She'd inadvertently grabbed a book titled Mysteries of the Ancient World, and now wondered if Krueger would notice and fear something was amiss. Way to be heavy-handed, Avery.

Out of the corner of her eye, she spotted Willis loitering in front of the magazines—the Playboys, to be exact. The guy had spent too much time with Bones. She glanced at Sofia, who looked meaningfully at Krueger and nodded once. Avery took a deep breath.

"Excuse me, could I borrow the front page?"

Krueger looked up at her, surprised, and then held out the front page section. As Avery accepted it, she leaned in close and whispered, "We need to speak to you, Mister Krueger."

Krueger sat up straight. "I'm sorry," he mumbled. "You have the wrong person."

"Please," Sofia said, unfolding her legs and leaning toward him, urgency in her eyes. "We need your help."

"There's nothing I can help you with." He folded his paper and made to rise, but Avery stood and blocked his way.

"Too many people have already died. We need your

help to stop it."

"People you've killed," Krueger retorted. "I don't know how you found me, but I promise you, I won't go down without a fight." He reached down and grabbed the cuff of his jeans.

Avery's stomach lurched as she caught a glimpse of a small revolver, and then Willis was there. He seized Krueger's wrists from behind and held him still.

"No need for that. Whoever you're running from, we ain't them."

Alarmed, Krueger looked back at Willis and then, strangely, relaxed.

"You're right. You aren't."

Willis released Krueger and sat down on the arm of the chair on the side of Krueger opposite Avery. From there, he could be on the man in an instant should he make another try for his weapon.

"I'm glad you can see that," she said. "Do you know who's after you?"

"I don't know who, exactly, they are, but I know what they want and why. Best I can tell, they're no better than Nazis. They probably saw my surname, saw a picture of me, and figured I'd be a sympathizer." He smirked at Avery. "I could believe you were one of them, but a Latina and a black man? Not a chance. Tell your friend to relax." He tilted his head toward Willis. "I'm not going to run, and I definitely won't try for my gun again."

"Glad to hear it." Avery waved at Willis, and he slid down into his chair, though he still appeared as tense as a runner waiting for the starting pistol.

"So, who are you and what do you want?" Krueger asked.

"We're part of a team dedicated to rooting out the people who are after you," Sofia said.

"Who are they, exactly?"

"We're not supposed to talk about that." Avery bit her lip, wondering how he would respond.

"If you want my help, you're going to have to trust me, at least a little bit." Krueger's gaze was rock hard.

"Fine. They're called the Dominion. They claim to be a Christian group, and they have roots in many churches, but they've also infiltrated branches of government. We're new to the team and aren't privy to all the information our director has, but their leanings definitely tend toward Nazi beliefs." Avery paused while Krueger mulled this over.

"What are their aims? Overthrow the government?"

"More like take it over organically," Avery said. "For some time now, they've been building their power in the shadows, both in the religious and secular spheres. But something they did very recently leads us to believe they're either changing their strategy or, more likely, expanding it."

Krueger frowned at her.

"Did you hear about the Tsunami that struck Key West?" Kruger said he had, and Avery filled him in on what they knew, and what they thought they knew, about the disaster.

Krueger stared at her for a full ten seconds, and then he laughed.

"Atlantis? Right. Tell you what, I'll let you get back to your book," he tapped the book on ancient mysteries, "and your whacked-out ideas. I need to find a new town and create a new identity."

"Would you like to see some pictures of the weapon?" Sofia asked softly.

Krueger froze, half in, half out of his chair.

Sofia took out her iPad and flipped through a series

of images, all showing the Atlantean device they had recovered off the coast of Cuba. Next, she showed him several images of the temple, all screenshots taken from the submarine's video feed. Finally, she showed him the pictures she had taken of the temple in Spain before its destruction.

"Mister Krueger," she began, "I'm not a crackpot conspiracy theorist. I don't believe in Bigfoot or Nessie."

"Don't let Bones hear you say that," Willis interjected.

Sofia rolled her eyes and continued. "I've already found two cities that we believe were part of the Atlantean civilization. We've seen the devastation wrought by a single Atlantean weapon, and the codex hints that the mother city holds an even deadlier weapon. We must get there before the Dominion."

"Why do you need me?" Krueger asked weakly.

"You know why." Avery looked him hard in the eye and he seemed to melt under her gaze.

"I suppose I do. If Atlantis was real, and it seems that it is," he glanced at Sofia's iPad, "that means it's likely that the Great Library contained information about it."

"Can you help us find it?" Avery held her breath while Kruger looked at the three of them in turn, a lingering look of disbelief in his eyes. Finally, the last remnants of skepticism appeared to fall away.

"I think I can."

CHAPTER 27

"Mexico." **Matt looked** down at the fresh stamp on the fake passport Tam had provided for him. "This wasn't what I expected when they invited us on a camping trip."

"Not much to see out here." Despite the situation, Joel managed to sound bored.

Matt gazed out the window of the van in which they rode. The dull brown of the hilly landscape was speckled with a touch of green here and there, but there was no forest to be seen. Since they'd left the Villalobos Airport in Chihuahua, they'd seen little more than dust and dirt.

"I'm told the camping isn't the best." Bill glanced at them in the rear-view mirror. "But the caving is supposed to be out of this world."

"Caving, huh? Sounds like fun." Joel's eyes widened and his voice held a tone of forced bravado.

"Claustrophobic?" Matt whispered, but his friend didn't answer.

"I don't care for it myself. I don't fit too well into small places." Bill barked a laugh and Matt and Joel joined in. "I'll be staying back at the campground, running things."

"What's there to run?" Matt asked. He didn't miss the glance Bill stole at Greer, another member of the men's group, who was seated in the passenger seat. It was just the four of them, and a ton of equipment. The remaining seven members of their party rode in a second van.

"Just camping stuff," Bill said. "Planning the meals

and the Bible study and stuff."

"Has your group done much caving?" Matt asked, more to alleviate boredom than out of any interest.

"This is the first time. The mother church is sending a man down from Utah to be our guide. He'll have special equipment for us."

Matt perked up at the mention of Utah. "What's the name of the mother church?"

"The Kingdom Church." Bill looked like he was about to say more, but Greer silenced him with a tiny shake of his head.

Matt considered this new information. According to Tam, the Kingdom Church, led by Bishop Hadel, was believed to be, if not the headquarters of the Dominion in America, one of its strongest outposts. She had been trying for some time to gain evidence of Hadel's connection to the organization, and hinted that she was coming closer by the day.

They rode in silence through a small town called Naica, and stopped in the foothills to the west of the city. They climbed out and looked around. There was nothing to distinguish this flat patch of brown dirt from the rest of the landscape, but Bill called it a "campground," and began unloading the van. By the time a forest green jeep bounced up the dirt road and parked alongside the van, they had set up camp. Matt and Joel, as the new guys, had been tasked to dig the latrine, and both were coated in dust and sweat by the time they finished.

The newcomer, who introduced himself as Robinson, had them pile back into their vans and follow him to a mining operation. While everyone milled around the vans, Robinson went to speak with someone. Pretending to look at the mountains, Matt wandered out of sight of the group and fired off a quick text to Tam.

Caving in Naica, Mexico. Man from Kingdom Church is here.

As soon as he'd sent the text, he deleted it from his Sent Messages folder, pocketed the phone, and returned to the group. Robinson emerged from a dilapidated-looking office building a few minutes later and led them into the worksite.

A man in a hardhat, who introduced himself as Rivera, with a light on the front led them down through the mine until they finally stopped in a hollowed-out chamber of gray stone. Conduit ran along the walls and down the middle of the ceiling above, where lights hung every twenty feet or so. When Bill had said they were going caving, Matt had expected cool, even chilly caverns, but it was hot in here. Uncomfortably hot.

Rivera stopped in front of a metal door and turned to face them. He was a tall, thin Latino man with a wispy mustache and a thin beard that didn't quite cover his pockmarked face.

"On the other side of this door is the Crystal Cave of Giants," he began in lightly accented English. "It was discovered by accident during mining operations in the year 2,000. Inside, more than three hundred meters below the surface, you will find the largest crystals known to mankind. The largest more than ten meters long and weigh up to fifty five tons." He paused to let that sink in.

He went on to describe the makeup and formation of the crystals, and give them a brief description of the caverns, including the dangers.

"Footing can be treacherous inside, and many of the crystals are razor sharp. If you slip, you can find yourself impaled on a razor sharp selenium spike. In fact, one of the chambers is called the Cave of Swords because the walls are coated with dagger-like crystals. But that is not the greatest danger the cavern poses."

The group members exchanged glances. A cave brimming with crystal swords ready to slice you apart seemed dangerous enough to them.

"Because the cave rests above a magma chamber, the air temperature is more than fifty degrees Celsius, or more than one hundred-twenty degrees Fahrenheit. The relative humidity of ninety percent makes the air feel more than double those temperatures. Without proper protection, you will quickly lose your higher brain functions, which increases the chance of a fatal fall." He smiled, as if pleased by the thought. "In as few as fifteen minutes, your body will begin to shut down, and death follows soon after. No one lasts more than thirty minutes."

The words scarcely registered with Matt. As soon as Rivera said the word "crystal," he knew why they were here. Somewhere in these caverns, the Dominion believed they would find crystals that could power the Atlantean machines, and they'd sent the more than expendable members of the men's group into this deadly environment. He looked at Robinson, who wore a revolver on his hip and an expression of calm determination. He wondered if the man had any intention of letting the men leave here alive. He thought about messaging Tam, but he knew he'd get no signal so far below the earth's surface.

They were on their own.

CHAPTER 28

"We need to know what this thing does." Bones looked like a kid on Christmas morning as he looked over the Atlantean weapon. "Let me and Maddock take it out into the middle of the Gulf and give it a shot. Pun intended."

"I don't like it. What if it you set off some sort of natural disaster?" Tam gritted her teeth. She hated not knowing what this device could do, but was averse to the risks inherent in testing it.

"Why didn't you interrogate the old man and learn from him how it worked?"

"You didn't meet him," Maddock said. "I can read men, and this one was as stubborn as they come. We would have had to torture the information out of him, and he didn't deserve that."

"Tell that to the families of the men who lost their lives in those storms he cooked up," Tam snapped.

"It doesn't matter now. We didn't extract the information from him, and we need to know how this thing works." Maddock softened his voice. "Obviously, Daisuke experimented with the weapon before he used it against anyone, and he didn't set off any natural disasters—only small, localized events. I give you my word we'll exercise caution."

Tam sighed. What Maddock said made sense, and a good leader didn't ignore reason just because it came from an underling. Like her grandfather used to say, "Sooner or later, a stiff neck breaks."

"All right. I'm relying on you to keep the big dummy," she pointed at Bones, "under control."

"Great. We'll need Corey."

"I can't spare him. You can break in our two new team members. Don't argue with me!" she added sharply. "I've heard all I'm going to hear about Ihara and Professor. I have my damn good reasons for wanting them on board, and I didn't tell you before because I don't want to listen to your hissy fits. You're on the team; she's on the team. Deal with it."

"How long until my debt to you is paid in full?" Maddock's tone was perfectly polite and nothing more.

"When the Dominion is finished. Now you two get this contraption out of here before I change my mind."

Maddock hefted the device and carried it out of the room, Bones following with the bag of crystals.

"Lord, don't let them sink Havana," she muttered. Behind her, Kasey leaned against the wall, gazing thoughtfully at Tam. "Do you have a question?"

"What's the story with Maddock and Ihara?"

"Why do you need to know?"

"Because we're a team, and if there's an issue between them that could affect the way we work together, I want to know about it." Kasey grimaced. "I'm not questioning your choice. I just want to know."

"They used to be an item, but Maddock dumped her in favor of Bones' sister."

"Awkward," Kasey said.

"Very. But Ihara is an asset. I've profiled her thoroughly, and she's smart, tough, and resourceful. She's got a lot of what Maddock has, and I know for a fact she's not hooked up with the Dominion. In fact, she wants to see them done in as much as I do."

Kasey frowned.

"Don't ask why. That's her story to tell."

"Fair enough. Any word from Avery?"

"They found their target and are proceeding as

planned." Tam's cell phone vibrated. "It's a text from Matt." She read the message twice. "Do you know anything about caves in Naica, Mexico?"

"No. Hold on." Kasey moved to a nearby computer and performed a quick search.

"It's a small city in Chihuahua, about a hundred and fifty miles south of the border. Not much there except for mining operations." Kasey paused as she scrolled down the page. "The only cave I see mentioned is one that houses the biggest crystals in the world."

"Crystals?" Tam's blood turned to ice. Her eyes snapped to the crystal skull resting on a table, and then to the machine they'd recovered from the Cuban temple. "Lord Jesus, if they've found a way to power their tsunami machine…"

"Every city on the coast is in danger." Kasey's eyes went wide.

"I need boots on the ground in Naica as soon as possible. Call Maddock back, and tell Greg to scare up weapons and transportation. I want you three there as soon as humanly possible."

"You realize what this means?" Kasey said as she headed for the door. "Bones is going to try out that weapon without adult supervision."

"One battle at a time, sweetie. One battle at a time."

CHAPTER 29

"We're going to go inside the caves without protective gear. We will only stay for fifteen minutes. The purpose is to impress upon you just how dangerous the heat and humidity are." The guide turned, unlocked the door, and opened it.

Matt didn't need any convincing. It seemed like common sense. But, he followed the others inside.

The heat assailed him immediately. His knees trembled the moment he hit the wall of hot, damp air. His discomfort, though, was immediately forgotten when his eyes took in his surroundings.

The cave was magnificent. The giant crystals, gleaming in the dim light, were so huge as to give the experience a dreamlike quality. They were everywhere, jutting up at angles like countless, miniature Washington Monuments. He glanced at Joel, who appeared immune to the magic of the caves. His eyes flitted from one member of the group to the next, his face set in a look of concentration.

"What's up?" Matt kept his voice low.

"Just keeping an eye on things. I don't trust any of these men."

His words reminded Matt that they weren't here for sightseeing. He searched out Robinson, who stood off to the side, his expression bored and detached.

There was nothing memorable about Robinson; nothing to make him stand out in a crowd. To an ex-military man like Matt, however, subtle clues named the newcomer a fellow veteran: his posture, the way he walked, his general bearing. Of course, a military background wasn't a crime, but knowing he was associated with the Kingdom Church made him someone upon whom Matt and Joel would want to keep a close eye. Matt and the rest of Maddock's crew had run afoul of the Dominion's paramilitary elements too many times not to be on his guard around someone like Robinson.

"This place gets to you, doesn't it?" Bill came staggering up to Matt. "I'm feeling a little…" His legs gave out and Matt grabbed him before he collapsed.

"I think he needs to get out of here." Matt, aware of how weak he, too, felt, looked at Robinson, whose face remained impassive.

"All right." Robinson motioned to Rivera, who ushered the group back out through the door.

The temperature in the tunnel outside the crystal cave was probably more than ninety degrees, but stepping through the doorway felt like being immersed in a cool bath. Rivera opened a cooler and passed around bottles of water.

Robinson moved to the center of the circle of men, his presence commanding their immediate attention. "We'll take a ten minute breather," he began, "after which, we'll suit up and get to work."

"We're starting right now?" Bill sat with his back against the wall, clutching his water bottle like a lifeline.

"We have work to do, and it needs to be done quickly."

No one in the group seemed surprised at this. Apparently, only Joel and Matt had been led to believe this was a recreational trip.

"Do the rest of us need to be armed?" Matt asked.

"What?" The question had caught Robinson off guard.

"I notice you're carrying, though I can't imagine

what we might encounter in there. Some kind of underground dwellers?" He forced a grin and the others chuckled.

Robinson's face turned to stone, but softened in an instant. The smile he directed at Matt didn't quite reach his eyes.

"Just a habit. I won't be carrying inside."

Matt doubted that very much, but he didn't say so.

"Are you trying to put him on the alert?" It was amazing how well Joel could enunciate without moving his lips. "We're already the new guys. Why call attention to us?"

"I don't know," Matt admitted. "I guess I don't want him thinking he can bully us. Besides, isn't it the new guy's job to ask stupid questions?"

"Only if the new guy is stupid. You might want to let me take the lead until things get physical."

Matt set his jaw. He knew he was clueless as a spy, but he always trusted his instincts, and right now, his gut told him that Robinson needed to know that not all the men in this group were sheep.

"Time to suit up!" Robinson announced.

The suits they donned had two layers—an outer layer fitted with refrigeration tubes connected to a backpack filled with a cooling agent, and an insulating interior layer to protect the skin from the icy tubes. Each man was also outfitted with a breathing apparatus and a futuristic-looking helmet with a light on the forehead.

"I feel like a space marine," one of the group, a man named Davis, said. The others chuckled, except for Robinson and Greer.

Robinson explained that these suits would keep their body temperatures in the normal range for over an hour, and were an improvement over older models that were good for no more than forty-five minutes. "You might milk an hour and a half out of it if you're lucky, but I don't recommend it. You'll be exerting yourselves, which will raise your body heat and exhaust the cooling agent faster than if you were at rest. Exercise caution and good sense."

"Gentlemen, let us take a moment to reflect on our work today." Brother Bill had recovered from his bout of fatigue, and seemed ready to launch into a sermon. A stern look from Robinson nipped that in the bud, and he settled for a reminder that they were about the work of the church, which meant they were doing God's work, and that they numbered twelve, which assured His blessing upon them. When he had finished, they headed back into the cave.

That neither Bill nor Robinson had told them what, exactly, their work would entail, was not lost on Matt. Nor was the lump inside Robinson's suit. Evidently, he'd lied about leaving his weapon behind.

The journey into the caves quickly turned from fascinating, to laborious and, finally, to perilous. Several men slipped on the slick surface and just missed impaling themselves. They navigated several passageways, the way tight due to the forest of giant crystals in their path.

At one point, they climbed a sheer face seventy five feet high and crawled through a tiny passageway into a new set of caverns, an effort that left Bill gasping for breath and whispering prayers to Jesus.

No telephone pole-sized crystals filled this next system of caves. Instead, the floor, walls, and ceilings bristled with tiny crystal daggers, with the occasional head-high pyramidal-shaped selenite blocks. They navigated the treacherous caves slowly, knowing what would happen if one were to fall on the carpet of sharp crystal.

"How long do you think we've been in here?" Joel finally asked as they exited a winding chamber of white and blue crystal and entered a narrow crevasse.

Matt consulted his mental clock and conservatively estimated they'd been moving for at least thirty minutes.

"Long enough that we'll have to turn back soon if we want to make it back alive. Which means, wherever we're going, we must be almost there."

He was half-right. In the next chamber, they found a large tent into which several air conditioners pumped a steady stream of cool air. Here, the tired men rested and replenished lost fluids while Robinson outlined the next stage of the excursion.

"This is what we are looking for." He held up a tiny spike of transparent crystal. "As you saw on the way here, the crystals so far have all been opaque and white in color. Somewhere beyond this point is a single, tiny cavern filled with crystals of different sort. I won't go into detail about what makes this special." he brandished the crystal, which, Matt noticed, flickered blue in the glow of the bare bulbs hanging over Robinson's head. "In fact, I don't understand it myself, but that isn't our concern."

He turned to a dry erase board where the cave system had been sketched out. "We've had time to explore and completely eliminate this passageway." He marked a red X over a tunnel that branched out like the limbs of a tree. "These others," he tapped two more lines, "remain unexplored. That's why the map is open-ended in these places. We will divide into two groups and scout them out."

Matt raised his hand. "What if the cave we're looking for is farther than we can go with our cooling suits?"

"Fair question. A caver using the old-style suits managed to reach the cavern, recover this crystal and another, larger one, and make it back safely. That means it should be well within our reach."

"He couldn't tell you where the cave was?" Bill asked.

"Obviously not." A shadow passed over Robinson's face, but he quickly donned another of his phony smiles. "His cooling suit, which relied on ice and chilled water, lost its cooling capacity long before he made it out. He was disoriented and suffering from heat exposure by the time he reached the surface. He remembers the way to this cavern, but gets foggy after that." Robinson paused. "Any more questions?" Robinson's tone indicated that questions would be tolerated, but nothing more than that.

A rangy, sandy-haired man named Perkins raised his hand. "Why does the church need crystals? Aren't they part of the new-age heresy?"

"Imagine the rarest, most valuable mineral in the world." Robinson smoothed his gruff voice. "Now imagine the church owned it all. How much would it be worth, and how much good could we do with the proceeds?"

"And imagine how far down the road toward our aims we would be," Greer added. The others nodded, their expressions ranging from solemn to beatific. Once again, Matt realized that he and Joel, as newcomers, were out of the loop on something important.

They donned fresh cooling suits and Robinson divided them into groups of six, putting himself in charge of one of them, and placing Greer at the head of the other. He also handed out small backpacks

containing rock hammers, in case they found the
cavern quickly and had time to get to work. Matt and
Joel found themselves in Robinson's group, along with
Perkins, Brother Bill, and a red-haired man named
Logan. Before they entered the tunnels, Robinson
pulled Matt aside.

His senses on high alert, Matt tensed to fight
should Robinson reach for his weapon. Instead,
Robinson laid a hand on Matt's shoulder and
whispered in a conspiratorial tone.

"Keep an eye on Bill. He's not in good shape, and I
can tell you know how to handle yourself."

Matt nodded once but remained silent.

"You served," Robinson said. "I can tell. Army?"

Matt nodded again.

"Rangers?"

"Kicked out," Matt lied. No need to reveal too
much.

"It happens." Robinson thanked him in advance
for keeping an eye on Bill, and led the way into the
passageways.

The final pieces were falling into place in Matt's
mind. The Dominion believed these crystals would
power the Atlantean machines. But what did they plan
to do with them when they got their hands on them?
And, more immediately, what would Robinson do once
they found the cavern?

He spied a dagger-sized spike of crystal. Slowing,
he let the others get ahead of him, hastily used his rock
hammer to break it free, and then tucked it into his
bag. It might serve as a weapon later.

He caught up with Bill, who was already flagging.

"Are you going to be okay?" Matt asked.

Bill nodded.

"I'm curious. What are these 'aims' Greer

mentioned? I realize I'm new to the group, but I'd like to know what I'm working toward."

"It's more than I can tell you right now," Bill huffed. "For the short term, let's just say I wouldn't be buying any real-estate in Savannah if I were you."

Matt's heart lurched. So the Dominion planned to continue destroying cities. The loss in human life and damage to infrastructure aside, should a Tsunami strike the Savannah River nuclear plant, it could be an unmitigated disaster.

"But that's small potatoes. Wait until we find the Revelation Machine."

Matt swallowed hard. "What's that?" He tried to keep his tone casual.

"Can't say, exactly. I'm not even supposed to know about it, but I heard talk. When we get ahold of it, we'll make sure the world is a whole lot better than it is today."

Matt forced a smile. Whatever this Revelation Machine was, it didn't sound like something the Dominion ought to get its hands on. Somehow, he had to get word to Tam.

CHAPTER 30

"**The Great Library** of Alexandria was like nothing in the world at its time. It held the world's largest collection of books—legend places the catalog at well over half a million scrolls." Krueger handed Avery a coffee table book with a painting of the fabled library on the cover.

He'd taken up residence in Rachel's only apartment complex. From the looks of it, he'd quickly made himself right at home. He'd set up a computer station along with four cheap shelf units stuffed with books and papers.

"How did they get all the books?" Avery thumbed through the pages as she spoke. Unlike Sofia, her own knowledge of the library was limited.

"Any way they could. They borrowed and copied manuscripts or traded them. When a ship came into port, any books on board had to be lent to the library for copying. Sometimes they were even returned." Krueger winked. "Travelers passing through had their books confiscated, though they were reimbursed for them. Basically, anything in the world that was written down, the library tried to make copies."

Krueger filled four cups of coffee and set them on the battered coffee table along with milk and sugar. Avery and Sofia had taken the only chairs, so he and Willis sat on the floor.

"It was burned down, right?" Avery asked.

"It's not that simple. The library gradually declined over several centuries. Fires played a part, but so did war, politics, and religion. There are legends of

Christian and Muslim leaders, at different times, ordering documents burned that did not agree with their respective holy books. There's no firm evidence that the more sensational stories are true, but there's no doubt that some of that occurred."

"What about war and politics?" Willis asked.

"If you know the history of Alexandria, it was a Greek city founded in Egypt, eventually taken over by Rome, and torn apart by Roman civil war. We don't know exactly how much of the library was destroyed, but we do know that much of the contents of the library was taken back to Rome."

"I understand that you've managed to trace much of the lost contents," Sofia said. "Can you tell us how?"

Krueger took a drink of coffee and sat in silence for a few seconds, as if weighing his answer.

"First of all, we need to remember that most of the books in the Great Library were copies of books that came from somewhere else. It's not like many of the books were actually written in Alexandria. Virtually all of them existed in other parts of the known world. Also, part of the library's mission was to disseminate information. Sharing knowledge through copying and distributing books was a major part of the daily work. So, it's not completely accurate to call the library "lost." The building was lost—we don't even know where it stood, but the knowledge is still out there."

"All of it?" Avery asked.

Krueger smiled. "Good question. Let me show you my work."

He moved to the computer desk, turned on his laptop, and called up a map of the world. Circles in varying sizes and colors were dotted all across it.

"I'll give you the short version of what I do. I created a master list of all the "hot" topics, if you will, of the first few centuries of the library's existence: science, philosophy, you name it. To that, I added the names of the great thinkers and teachers of the day, and any scholars who were known to have been associated with the library.

"Next, I searched out the places where knowledge from this period seems to have been preserved."

"You mean, like, in museum collections?" Willis asked.

"Sometimes," Krueger said. "But it goes deeper than that. I looked for cultures or regions where the ancient wisdom appeared to have the greatest impact. I looked for literature that referenced the great teachers and contained unique insights. As you can see, there's plenty." He tapped the touch pad, and only the smallest dots, all pale green, appeared.

"The greatest concentrations are in expected places, like Rome, but there are others." He tapped the pad again, and larger circles, all blue, appeared. "I also considered the historical events, like the Roman civil war, that could affect the dispersal of knowledge."

He fell silent for no apparent reason.

"Are you all right?" Avery asked.

"Sorry. I have a flair for the dramatic." Krueger winked at her. "Finally, I assessed all the legends and theories—even the wacky ones. I evaluated them for frequency, consistency, and whether or not they made sense. Adding them in, you see the end result here."

A final tap and now only a few circles appeared on the map.

"The bright green circles are your repositories of basic knowledge: science, philosophy, and history."

"Cairo, Rome, Paris, London, Washington, no surprises there." Sofia sounded disappointed.

"What about the blue circles?" Avery tapped a

fingernail on a blue dot in Washington D.C.

"Those represent arcane knowledge. The special documents that would have been hidden away, either from religious leaders, or by them. Or hidden by governments."

"You think our government is hiding secrets from the ancient world?" Avery asked.

"Come on," Willis chided. "Do you really think there's anything our government won't hide from us?"

"I'm not saying the knowledge is definitely there," Krueger explained. "I'm saying all the signs point to these places. If such knowledge exists, that's likely where it will be found."

"Do you know where, exactly, in Washington?" Sofia rested her hands on Krueger's chair and leaned forward eagerly.

"I have a theory, but that's all that it is."

"What about the other places?" Willis asked.

"Jerusalem. Possibly beneath the Temple Mount, though I suspect whatever was hidden there is long gone. Wewelsburg Castle in Germany—a Nazi stronghold."

"And the other?" Avery asked.

"The Vatican's secret archives."

"You've got to be kidding." Sofia stood and pressed her hands to her temples. "I've tried so many times to get in there. There's no way."

"Well, I do have some good news." Krueger spun about in his chair. "Based on what you've shown me, there's little doubt that Atlantis, or a society that inspired the legend, existed, which means there almost definitely would have been a record in the library. Our best bet, though, is not the library."

Avery wondered if the expression on her face was as dumbstruck as those of Sofia and Willis.

"What is it then?" Sofia asked.

"We want the Egyptian Hall of Records."

"The what?" Avery and Sofia said in unison.

"It's a mythical library supposedly buried under the Great Sphinx of Giza. It's said to have housed the history of the lost continent of Atlantis, plus ancient Egyptian history. Sort of an Egyptian counterpart to the Great Library."

"That don't make sense," Willis argued. "Why wouldn't that knowledge be part of the library at Alexandria?"

"Because Alexandria was, essentially, a Greek city that just happened to be located in Egypt. Alexander the Great founded it. Ptolemy ruled after his death, and was responsible for founding the library. The Egyptians wouldn't have handed their knowledge over to foreigners."

Avery didn't know what to make of this new information. She turned to Sofia, who frowned at Krueger.

"I've never heard of such a place. Like you said, it's mythical."

"So was Atlantis until you found it," Krueger retorted.

"I love how people keep throwing that in my face." Sofia brushed a stray lock of hair out of her face. "All right. Suppose this place is real. How do we go about looking for it?"

"I can help you with that." Krueger smiled. "I know where the doorway is."

CHAPTER 31

"What do we know about this crystal cave?" Dane scanned a map of the area where the cave was located. He, Greg and Kasey were winging their way across the Gulf of Mexico in an S-6, a modified version of the Saker S-1, a jet capable of cruising at more than 1,100 kilometers per hour. While unable to reach such speeds, the S-6 could exceed 800 kilometers an hour, and carried six passengers. It was also equipped with an ejection mechanism so passengers could parachute from the plane. He had to hand it to Tam—she had some useful connections.

"The main access is through a mining operation," Kasey said. "It was discovered by accident, and it's only the turbines that pump underground water from the mine that prevent it from flooding. If the mine ever shuts down, the Mexican government will either have to foot the bill for keeping the pumps going, or let the caverns flood." She consulted her notes. "The place is dangerously hot and humid. You have to wear a special suit or you won't last long. We'll have suits waiting for us."

"How do we find Matt once we're there?" Dane took out a second map, this of the caverns. "There are so many channels to choose from. He could be down any of them."

"Matt *and Joel*," Kasey frowned at Dane's omission of their team member, "will probably be down one of the passages that hasn't yet been completely mapped. If there's a source of Atlantean crystal, it stands to reason that's where it will be found."

"I just got something from Tam." Greg tapped his iPad and read the message aloud. "Kevin Bray, geologist, was found dead in his apartment in Los Angeles."

"I hope there's more." Kasey didn't look up from her notes.

"There is. His laptop, journal, and all his research were gone. Cash and other valuables were still there. And the kicker? He had recently returned from an excursion to the Cave of the Crystals. According to his colleagues, he got lost, and when he finally made it out, barely alive, he had with him a crystal that he claimed was unlike anything known to science."

"That's promising." Dane leaned over and read Tam's message for himself. "Friends thought the heat exhaustion had messed with his head."

"I can see how a scientist who, all of a sudden, begins talking about crystal power could seem hippy-dippy to his colleagues," Kasey said. "So, the Dominion got to him first."

"If not, it's one heck of a coincidence." Greg closed the message and consulted his watch. "We're almost there. Get ready to jump."

CHAPTER 32

"What do you mean, you found the door?" Avery searched Krueger's eyes for signs of deceit, or even humor, but his gaze held firm.

"You've heard of Herodotus?" he asked.

"The Greek historian," Sofia supplied.

"Also known as the Father of History." Avery felt pleased by the others' surprised faces. "I was a history professor. Give me a little credit."

"Herodotus traveled in Egypt sometime after 464 BC," Krueger continued, "and wrote extensively about the nation and its history. In the course of my research, I came across a single piece of his writing that I've never seen anywhere else. It was part of someone's private collection. I don't think the man even knew what he had. To him, it was just another piece in his collection."

"I assume we're talking about a black market collector?" Sofia asked.

"Is that really important right now?" Krueger replied. "Anyway, in this scroll, Herodotus wrote an account of a massive temple complex he called the labyrinth. He said it contained 1,500 rooms and many underground chambers he wasn't permitted to enter."

"I've heard of a labyrinth being uncovered at the Hawara pyramid near the Fayyum oasis," Sofia said.

"One and the same." Krueger drained his coffee and headed to the kitchen for a refill. "Anyone need a warm-up?" he asked, sticking his head through the doorway and holding up the coffee pot.

Avery suspected he was stalling for some reason.

Willis apparently had the same feeling, because he stood and began pacing back and forth in front of the windows overlooking the dusty street.

Krueger noticed their discomfort immediately.

"I know I'm dragging this out. The truth is, I'm not a people person, but I do enjoy company every once in a while, and this is the first chance I've had to talk shop with anyone since I went into hiding. I'm having fun."

"We understand," Sofia said. "Can you tell us how Hawara connects to Giza?"

"Funny you should ask. It connects in a literal sense." Kruger pulled a battered notebook down from a shelf and turned a few pages. "Here's what Herodotus writes:

"There I saw twelve palaces regularly disposed, which had communication with each other, interspersed with terraces and arranged around twelve halls. It is hard to believe they are the work of man. The walls are covered with carved figures, and each court is exquisitely built of white marble and surrounded by a colonnade. Near the corner where the labyrinth ends, there is a pyramid, two hundred and forty feet in height, with great carved figures of animals on it and an underground passage by which it can be entered. I was told very credibly that underground chambers and passages connected this pyramid with the pyramids at Memphis."

"Memphis?" Willis asked.

"The ancient capital of Lower Egypt," Sofia said. "As Alexandria rose, it declined. The Giza Plateau, where the Sphinx and Great Pyramids are situated, was a part of Memphis." A tone of skepticism colored her words. "That sounds pretty far-fetched. After all, Herodotus was also called the Father of Lies."

"That name wasn't entirely deserved," Krueger said. "Yes, he had a habit of occasionally presenting his findings through the accounts of fictional eyewitnesses, but he collected folk tales and legends as much as historical fact. Also, many of his claims, even the ones that seemed most doubtful, have proved true. Take Gelonus, for example. No one believed Herodotus when he spoke of a city a thousand times larger than Troy, until it was rediscovered in 1975."

"We can debate Herodotus later," Avery interrupted. "Tell us how this relates to the Hall of Records."

"At first, I was as skeptical as Doctor Perez, so I continued my research and found even more accounts. The historian Crantor spoke of underground pillars that contained a written record of pre-history, and said they 'lined access ways connecting the pyramids.'" Krueger turned a page in his notebook and went on. "I found account after account: Pliny, Marcellinus, Altelemsani, and more. But these are the most powerful." He turned another page. "It's by a Syrian scholar named Iamblichus.

"This entrance, obstructed in our day by sands and rubbish, may still be found beneath the forelegs of the crouched colossus. It was formerly closed by a bronze gate whose secret spring could be operated only by the Magi. It was guarded by public respect, and a sort of religious fear maintained its inviolability better than armed protection would have done. Beneath the belly of the Sphinx were cut out galleries leading to the subterranean part of the Great Pyramid. These galleries were so art-fully crisscrossed along their course to the Pyramid that, in setting forth into the passage without a guide throughout this network, one ceaselessly and inevitably returned to the starting point."

He paused, glancing up from his reading, as if to see if they were impressed.

"And this I found on an ancient Sumerian cylinder seal:

"The knowledge of the Annunaki is hidden in an

underground place, entered through a tunnel, its entrance called Hawara, hidden by sand and guarded by a beast called Huwana, his teeth as the teeth of a dragon, his face the face of a lion, is unable to move forward, nor is he able to move back."

He closed his notebook with the solemnity of a liturgist.

"What's the Annunaki?" Engrossed by Krueger's tale, Willis had left his post by the window and now stood behind Avery. "I never heard of them."

"Mesopotamian deities," Sofia said. "Their name means, 'royal blood,' or 'princely offspring.' In the Epic of Gilgamesh, they are the seven judges who punish the world before the storm."

"Wait a minute." Avery sat up straighter. The connections were rapidly coming together. "The Epic of Gilgamesh is a flood story. And your translation of the codes indicates that the Atlanteans, for some reason, decided to flood their subordinate cities."

"Precisely!" Kruger said. "It all connects. And when I saw the inscription on Herodotus' tomb, I was convinced he'd had a life-changing experience at, or perhaps somewhere far below, the Sphinx."

"What was the inscription?" Willis asked.

"Herodotus, the son of Sphinx."

They lapsed into silence, with only the low hum of an engine somewhere in the distance to disturb the quiet.

"So, you think there's a door at Hawara that leads to the Hall of Records?"

"I know there is," Krueger said. "In fact, I found the entrance to the hall." His smile vanished in a blink, alarm spreading across his face. "Oh my God," he rasped. "They found us."

CHAPTER 33

"We'll have to turn back soon." Matt took a gulp of fresh air from his supplementary supply. "Maybe the cavern's not here."

"Is that a bad thing?" Joel asked. "We'd prefer the Dominion not find it."

"If our group discovers it, maybe there's something we can do to stop them in their tracks. If the other group finds it…" He left the rest unspoken.

"I think I've found something!" Up ahead, Logan stood at the edge of a five meter wide fissure. A single, meter-wide crystal spanned the yawing chasm, ending at the entrance to a cavern.

The others moved to join him, all training their lights on the cave.

"But the crystals in there are white, like the others." Bill gestured with his flashlight.

"Not the ones on top. See how that one cluster in the ceiling is transparent with a touch of blue?" Logan pointed. "They look like the crystals Robinson showed us."

"I think you're right. Truly, the Lord blessed you this day. You have found what He needs in order to continue His work." Robinson looked at the gathered group. "Who wants the honor of being the first to enter the chamber?"

"I found it," Logan said, and Matt could see zeal gleaming in his eyes. Or was it a touch of madness brought on by the heat? "I'm going in. It's God's will."

"We need a safety rope. The surface of that crystal has got to be…" Matt's words were cut off by a scream as Logan took two steps, lost his footing, and tumbled into the gorge."

"…slick."

They shone their lights down into the fissure. Logan lay impaled on a crystal spike, the blood pouring from his mouth redder than his hair. Perkins turned away at the sight, and Bill retched.

"A sacrifice for the Lord is the noblest sacrifice of all. We must soldier on." Robinson dug into his pack and pulled out a rope. "I wish Brother Logan hadn't been so hasty. Your idea," he leveled his gaze at Matt, "was a good one." He secured the rope to a stout crystal and handed the other end to Matt. "Lead on."

Matt's first instinct was to attack. Perhaps take Robinson by surprise and drop him into the cavern alongside Logan. But then he realized the man had already drawn his weapon.

"What's that for?"

"Times like these are when men tend to lose faith. Our task is too important for fear to take hold. Now, show us the way."

Grimacing, Matt secured the rope around his waist and moved out onto the crystal. The surface was slick as ice, and he had to choose each step with care. Once, his foot slipped and he teetered above the ten meter drop, arms flapping like a bird in flight, before recovering his balance. Finally, he made it to the cave and climbed inside.

The cave was about five meters deep, and the same across. The floor and walls bristled with tiny, white spikes. A few lay broken, presumably by the man who had originally discovered this place. Choosing his steps carefully, he moved to the center of the cavern where the transparent crystals hung from the ceiling. Somehow, perhaps through minerals leaching down through the bedrock, a distinctive type of crystal had formed here. It was a small cluster, enough to fill his backpack and no more.

"I've got this," he called. "It shouldn't take me long." He heard a rustling noise, and turned to see Bill, his face pale despite the heat, entering the cave, with Perkins right behind him.

"What's going on?" Matt asked.

"It's Robinson," Perkins whispered. "He's got your brother."

Matt peered through the cave opening to see Joel on his knees, hands behind his head. Robinson held his pistol at the base of Joel's neck.

"Insurance!" Robinson shouted. "Bag up the crystals and toss them to me and I'll let him go."

"I won't do it until you let him go." Matt knew the threat was empty, and Robinson did too.

"Fine. If you prefer, I'll shoot all of you and retrieve the crystals myself."

Matt glowered at him, vowing to kill Robinson the first chance he got. Why had he come without a weapon of his own? Foolishness. Rage burning inside him, he set about chipping away at the crystals. In a matter of minutes, he had filled his backpack.

"Walk out onto the bridge," Robinson said when Matt poked his head out of the cave. "Just a few paces."

Matt did as instructed.

"Toss the bag over there." He indicated a place off to the side. "If you attempt to distract me by tossing the bag directly at me, or if you do anything other than follow my instructions to the letter, your brother dies. And you'll be next."

Matt could see no way around the situation. Robinson was armed, and Matt had only a rock hammer and a crystal spike. Reluctantly, he tossed the bag of crystals onto the ledge near where Robinson stood.

"See how easy that was? Now, back into the cave with you."

"Let him go."

"When you're in the cave." As Matt backed into the cave, Robinson sidled away from Joel, keeping his pistol trained on the kneeling man. It was clear from the way his eyes kept flitting about that Joel was looking for an opening to attack, but saw nothing more than Matt did. Robinson was being careful, and he held his pistol like he knew how to use it.

True to his word, Robinson did not shoot Joel, but sent him across the crystal bridge and into the cave. He had just clambered inside when Robinson snatched something from his backpack, hurled it toward the cave, and ran. Matt saw the object over Joel's shoulder as it flew toward them.

"Grenade!" Matt shouted.

It seemed to happen in slow motion. Joel leapt out of the cave, catching the grenade in midair. His eyes met Matt's as he fell into open space. Matt hit the floor as the world turned to fire and ice.

Bill and Perkins barely had time to scream before razor-sharp shards of crystal shredded them like tissue. Pain like a thousand needles stung Matt's back, but, shielded by the low wall beneath the cave's opening, the worst of the blast passed over him.

Ears ringing, pain lancing through him, and heat creeping up his back through his damaged cooling suit, he pulled himself to his feet and looked out.

Joel was gone.

And so was the bridge.

CHAPTER 34

"Everybody get down!" Willis shouted.

Avery felt him shove her hard in the back and she hit the floor, her breath leaving her in a rush. The windows exploded in a shower of glass and the sound of gunshots boomed all around. She struggled to her feet, brushing glass from her hair. Willis had shoved the sofa against the front door and now peered out of one of the shattered windows.

"There's at least four of them. They'll probably come at us from both sides, and have another man guarding the door."

Krueger shoved a stack of notebooks into Avery's arms.

"As soon as I moved in, I cut a bolt hole in the floor of the bedroom closet. Move the shoes aside and pull up the carpet. It'll take you down into the basement, which runs the length of the building. You should be able to get out that way."

"We'll all get out that way." Willis flinched as the kitchen window shattered. "Come on."

"Somebody has to stay here, or else they'll know we've gotten away." He reached behind a bookshelf and drew out an assault rifle. Avery was no expert, but she knew an AK-47 when she saw it. "Those notes can't fall into the Dominion's hands, and you're more capable of getting the ladies out of here than I am."

A burst of gunfire shredded the front door, and Krueger fired back.

"Go!" he shouted. "Or else this is all for nothing!"

Willis hesitated for a split-second before ushering

Avery and Sofia toward the back room.

Avery found the bolt hole, yanked it open, and dropped down into the cool, dark basement. Above her, the gunfire continued. She heard another window shatter, Willis return fire, and a man cry out in pain. Good!

Sofia dropped down next to her and Willis followed a moment later.

"I'll get you away from here, and then I'm going back for Krueger." They dashed down the length of the basement, passing storage cubes made from two-by-fours and cheap chicken wire, each labeled with an apartment number, and ending in a laundry room.

Willis held up a finger for silence and then slipped out the door. He returned moments later.

"We can't get to the car. There are too many of them."

"I saw a couple of motorcycles in one of the storage cubes," Sofia said. "Too bad we don't have the keys."

A wicked smile split Willis' dark face. "I don't need keys."

"Can you not squeeze so tight?" Avery grunted. They were roaring south along the Extraterrestrial Highway atop a freshly-hotwired Honda Shadow. Willis had wanted them to take both bikes, but not only had Sofia never ridden one, she was deathly afraid of them.

"I'm not letting go." Sofia's voice quaked. "We don't even have helmets. What if we crash?"

"We'll definitely crash if you suffocate me." Avery felt Sofia's python clutch ease a little. "I don't get it. You're an outdoorsy girl. You SCUBA, you climb, what's so bad about a motorcycle?"

"What's bad is flying down the street with nothing between me and death but the clothes on my back."

"Fair enough. Just hang in there. Willis should catch up with us soon."

Ten minutes later, a man on a motorcycle appeared in her rear-view mirror. She recognized him immediately and pulled to the side of the road. Willis stopped alongside them and cut the engine.

"I called Tam. She says it's too dangerous to try to make it all the way to Vegas. She's hooking us up with a flight out of a little airfield about a half an hour from here." He grimaced.

"We wouldn't have had time to hit the casinos," Avery chided.

"Naw, it's not that. It's Krueger."

"What happened?" Avery had noticed Willis was alone, but didn't want to broach the subject.

Willis shook his head. "Right after you left, Krueger's gun went silent. Must have run out of ammo. They were hauling his stuff out of the apartment. I would have gone in, but there were more of them than I thought, and they were better armed than me. Besides, I needed to get the two of you out of here."

"Going in there would have been a suicide mission. You're not Bones; you're smarter than that."

"If you say so," Willis sighed. "Anyway, Krueger's either dead or their prisoner."

"Which means," Avery said, "the Dominion might soon know about the Hall of Records."

CHAPTER 35

"Two guards," Dane whispered into his mic.

"I see them." Kasey's voice didn't lose the serene quality it always held.

"Which one do you want me to take out?" Dane held his Walther ready to fire.

"We've got this one," Greg said. "Cover us in case we get into trouble."

Dane watched as two dark figures appeared seemingly out of nowhere. Greg took one out with a sharp strike to the temple and a knee to the forehead. Kasey eliminated her target with a strike to the chin and a roundhouse kick to the head as he fell. They dragged the men away from the entrance, bound them with zip ties, and motioned for Maddock to join them.

Keeping to the shadows, they passed through the gate and headed toward the mining company's main building.

They dispatched two more guards at the entrance. No need, Greg noted, to kill the men if they could help it. As far as they knew, these were locals and had no affiliation with the Dominion.

It wasn't until they located the security office that they ran into trouble. Two men burst forth, spraying the hallway with automatic pistol fire. Greg and Kasey hit the floor and, before they could return fire, Dane took both men down with head shots.

"Wow!" Kasey said as he helped her to her feet. "I guess the SEALs' reputations are deserved."

"Sometimes."

"Can Bones shoot like that?"

"Yep. Almost as good as me." Dane winked. "At least, that's what he claims."

"I figured he was full of crap." Kasey fell in alongside Dane as they followed Greg into the office.

"Oh, he's definitely full of crap, but he's also very good at what he does. The two aren't mutually exclusive."

"Do you think you two could manage to guard the door while you gossip?" Greg was already working on hacking into the computer system.

Dane and Kasey took up positions just inside the door where they could watch the hall in both directions.

"I have to admit, he handled himself pretty well in Paris."

Dane looked at Kasey. "Don't tell me you've got a thing for him. His ego doesn't need the boost."

"No. He's just… interesting." Kasey looked away, but Dane didn't miss the way her cheeks turned a delicate shade of pink. Bones was going to eat this up.

"I've accessed the security cameras," Greg called. "The good news is I don't see anyone between us and the entrance to the crystal caverns."

"Going by the tone of your voice, it sounds like you've got some bad news to deliver," Kasey said. "Spill it."

"Interesting choice of words. Come see for yourselves."

The heat assailed Robinson the moment he stripped off his useless cooling suit. The sudden wave of heat staggered him, but he smiled despite his weariness. Twenty minutes from now, he would be free of this hell and on his way back to Utah with the crystals that the Bishop so fervently desired. His triumph was certain to earn him a spot in the inner circle, one which he believed he richly deserved.

A harness hung at the end of a stout cable and he strapped himself in before pressing the button on the wall. Ten seconds later, a mechanical hum filled the shaft and he began to rise.

Two thousand feet deep, the Robin Hole was a ventilation shaft originally drilled by miners to ventilate lower chambers. When they broke through into this remote section, they widened the hole just enough to lower, or lift, a man through the hole.

The ascent seemed to go on forever as he scraped and banged against the stone walls. Sweat dripped from every pore of his body, and his breath came in gasps. It shouldn't be taking this long, should it?

Finally, he felt cool air on his face and he rose from the shaft to see Rivera's smiling face.

"You did as instructed?" Robinson asked as he removed the harness.

"I called the number you gave me and said what you told me to say. I also set off the charges I placed on the turbines." Rivera frowned. "What about the rest of your men?"

"They won't be joining us. Now, where's the way out?"

"That tunnel over there." Rivera pointed off to his left. "May I ask when I can expect the rest of my money?"

"Your money." Robinson smacked himself in the side of the head. "I almost forgot. Thank you for reminding me." He reached into his bag and took out his 9 millimeter.

The expression on Rivera's face turned from pleased to confused to panicked in the instant it took

Robinson to pull the trigger.

"Pleasure doing business with you. Sorry to run, but I have a ride to catch."

"What is it?" Dane's eyes went to the bank of monitors on the wall and his throat clenched.

Water was pouring into the caves.

"The pumps are no longer working. The caverns will be flooded in no time." Greg kept his voice calm, but strain was evident in his eyes as he pounded the keyboard.

"Can you turn them back on?" Kasey asked.

"I thought I might be able to, but check this out." He pointed to a screen showing what looked like a cavern filled with scrap metal.

"What is that?" Dane asked.

"Those are the turbines. Somebody didn't just shut them down; they blew them up."

"Joel and Matt?" Kasey's voice trembled.

Greg turned away from her, his posture rigid. He gazed at the bank of monitors for a second before finally giving his head a single shake.

"There's no hope."

The jagged outcropping sliced into Matt's hand as he hauled his weight ever upward. He didn't know if this crevasse would lead him out of the cavern, but it was his last hope. When Robinson blew the crystal bridge, damaging Matt's cooling suit in the process, the way back had been eliminated as a possibility. The gap was too wide and the sides too sheer to climb. Any thoughts of playing Superman were dashed with a single glance down at Logan's remains, now shredded by the grenade blast, still impaled on the crystal spike.

For a moment, he'd considered giving up, but then he thought about the man who'd found this cavern. Somehow, he'd made it to this cavern and out again. It was possible he could have made it to the cavern before his cooling suit gave out entirely, but there was no way he could have survived the return trip.

Unless he'd found another way out.

Matt had searched the cavern and found this narrow crevasse which, promisingly, climbed upward at a steep angle. His damaged suit would hinder his progress, so he'd removed it, chipped away a few remnants of what he now thought of as Atlantean crystal, and pocketed it, before beginning the climb.

Twenty minutes later, his strength flagging, he found himself flat on his stomach, feet pressed against the sides of the shaft, inching his way upward. His body, slick with sweat and blood, burned with the effort, and the heat, though intense, had abated somewhat. He felt like he was back in the midst of a firefight in some unknown patch of jungle, which was an improvement over crawling through the Fifth Circle of Hell.

He pressed his fingers into a crack in the rock and tried to pull himself up, but the stone crumbled in his grasp and he slid back. He tried again, and again his handhold crumbled. He lay there, gasping for breath, feeling the last of his strength melt away. He couldn't go on any more. He'd just lie here and gaze at the stars.

The stars! Up ahead, in the midst of unrelenting darkness, Orion's belt shone in a sliver of gray light. The way out!

Calling upon reserves he hadn't realized he possessed, he resumed climbing. Inch by painful inch, he moved toward the twinkling lights. They seemed to inch ever closer until he thought he could almost reach out and take hold of them. As if in a dream, he extended his hand.

A cool breeze raised goose bumps on his exposed flesh. He dragged himself out into the night air and rolled over on his back, relishing the shivers that racked his body. He was free.

He lay there, eyes closed, listening to the wind... and the roar of an approaching engine. He opened his eyes and spotted the approaching craft: a Russian Kamov Ka-52 Alligator attack helicopter. He staggered to his feet and watched as the chopper landed atop a nearby hill. A man carrying a backpack came running out of the darkness. Robinson!

Matt's hand went to his hip, reaching for a weapon that wasn't there. Cursing in impotent rage, he started running toward the chopper. There was nothing he could do, but he couldn't bear just standing there and watching the murderous Dominion operative escape.

It seemed someone else had the same idea. As the Ka-52 rose into the air, gunfire erupted from the direction of the mine. Who could be firing on the chopper? He strained his eyes, but could not make out the figures, only the muzzle flashes, always in different places, as the shooters remained on the move.

Undeterred, the chopper rose into the air, fired off a single burst in the direction of the shooters, turned, and zoomed off into the night.

Matt's knees went weak and he crumpled to the ground. Joel was dead, Robinson escaped, and the Dominion now possessed the crystals it needed to unleash their weapon.

Over the sound of his own ragged breathing, he heard shouts and the cries of someone in pain. At least one of the attackers was down. He could just make out some of the words.

"Hang on, Kasey! Help's on the way."

He knew that voice.

It was Maddock. And that meant they were another man down. Forcing himself to move, he headed toward his friends. How, he wondered, had this mission gone so wrong?

CHAPTER 36

"Kasey's out of commission for the foreseeable future." Tam looked around the table at her "Myrmidons," as they had taken to calling themselves. Everyone appeared shell-shocked. With Joel dead, and Kasey seriously injured, spirits were low. It was up to her to keep them going.

"I won't pretend to know exactly what each of you is feeling, but I can tell you I'm hurting. I knew Joel longer and better than most of you, and I've known Kasey almost as long. I also feel bad about Krueger. Just remember this. We are the last line of defense against the Dominion. Hell, we're the only line of defense."

"I take it our tip about an attack on Savannah wasn't taken very seriously." Greg sat rigid as a statue. He was taking the failure harder than anyone.

Tam laughed. The only response she'd gotten was, *"We'll give it due consideration and take all precautions we deem necessary."* Translation, *"We'll put it in the file with all the other crackpot tips."* She'd also shared the information with a few trusted contacts, but none of them had the power or the inclination to do anything about it.

"Not a chance. So it's all on us." She paused, and began pacing to and fro. Her uncle was a preacher, and he'd taught her a few oratorical tricks to captivate an audience, and the judicious use of silence was one of them. Too little, and you got no effect. Too much and you lost their attention. She watched for the little signs: narrowed eyes, a slight cock of the head, subtle demonstrations of interest. When the time was perfect, she continued. "We've got to find this Revelation Machine before the Dominion gets its hands on it. I think it's pretty clear that they believe it, whatever it might be, will bring about the end of days." She let that sink in for a long moment.

"I don't care how much pain we've suffered. I don't care if you don't approve of the people I've brought onto our team. And I really don't care about your relationships or family issues or your histories together. This is bigger than any of that."

Out of the corner of her eye, she saw Avery cast an embarrassed glance at Bones, who grinned and winked at her. Jade lowered her head a notch. Only Maddock didn't react to her words. The man could be hard when he wanted to be, but that wasn't all bad.

"I need to know right now. Is everyone here still committed to the cause? Because if you're not, I swear to Jesus I'll find somebody else who is, and you can put on a skirt and work as my secretary until this is over."

"Hell yes!" Bones pounded his fist on the table. "I mean, yes we're committed, not yes to the skirt thing."

The tension broke. Each person reiterated her or his commitment to bringing down the Dominion and paying them back for Joel and Kasey.

"So, what's the plan?" Greg asked.

"First of all, I don't know if there's anything we can do about Savannah, but we need to try."

"I think the biggest problem we face is the fact that the Dominion won't come in a destroyer or any other sort of military vessel," Maddock said. "They'll have attached the weapon to an ordinary ship so as not to draw attention."

"I agree, and that's both good and bad. Bad because it's difficult to spot; good because it's easier to sink." She looked Maddock in the eye. "Can we use your boat?"

"I won't be with it?" he asked.

"I need you somewhere else. Besides, it's Matt and Corey who make her go, right?" When Maddock didn't argue, Tam turned to Greg. "Take Matt and Corey and Willis. And take *Remora*. That way, you can patrol above and below the waterline. Maybe we'll get lucky."

She dismissed the four men with a jerk of her head.

"I want my archaeologists in Egypt. Maddock, Bones, Jade, and Sofia—I want you to take the information Krueger provided and find this Hall of Records, if it exists."

"I'm going too," Avery protested. "Sofia and I are the ones who've been working on…"

"You're not an archaeologist. I want you here. He gave you more information than just the Hall of Records research. Follow up on it. Besides, I need at least a couple of people to watch my back in case something comes up. If I send all of you across the Atlantic, I've got no one."

A touch of the Maddock obstinance flashed in her eyes, but she didn't argue.

Relieved, Tam dismissed the rest of the team, but grabbed Maddock by the arm as he walked by. He stopped and waited until the others left.

"I want to tell you," Tam began, "that no matter how much the things I do piss you off, I need you and I'm glad you're on my team."

"Same here." Maddock's eyes softened. "Like you said, I don't always love the way you operate, but you're on the right side."

Tam gave his shoulders a squeeze.

"Good luck," she whispered. "And try to bring them all back alive."

CHAPTER 37

Standing at the entrance to the Fayyum Oasis, the pyramid of Amenemhet III looked more like an Indian mound than an Egyptian monument. Constructed of mudbrick over a series of chambers and corridors, the pyramid once boasted a limestone facade. Over the years, the exterior stone had been stripped away for use in construction, leaving the mudbrick core exposed to the elements. Now, its original pyramidal shape was barely evident. The last rays of the setting sun lent a reddish-brown cast to the once-magnificent monument. All in all, it made for an unimpressive sight.

"It looks like a pile of dirt," Bones observed.

"That's a good thing," Jade replied. "It's not an impressive sight, which means it doesn't draw tourists like the Giza complex does."

"Where's this awesome temple and labyrinth?" Bones sounded affronted.

"All that's left are stones from the original foundation." Sofia gazed at the scattered remnants of Egypt's past glory, a sad smile on her face.

"We don't care about that. We need the entrance to the underground chambers, which, according to Krueger's notes, can be accessed through the main pyramid entrance." Dane had spent the entirety of the flight studying the notes. Sofia was already familiar with the details, but Jade and Bones hadn't had the chance to study them. Or, more accurately, Bones chose to sleep his way across the Atlantic, while Jade was either too proud, or felt too guilty about the way she'd treated Dane in Japan to ask for a turn. That, of course, did not prevent her from stealing glances over his shoulder whenever she got the chance.

Sand crunched beneath Dane's feet and a dry breeze ruffled his hair as he approached the pyramid. A hand-lettered sign identified the pyramid as Middle Kingdom, gave its height as fifty-two meters, its base width one hundred, and directed them toward the entrance which lay at the pyramid's south face.

A narrow walkway led to the spot where three monolithic slabs of limestone formed the entryway. Here, portions of the interior corridors peeked out from the eroded mound of bricks. Taking one last look around for unwelcome visitors, be they local authorities or Dominion agents, Dane led the way into the darkness.

They descended a stone staircase that ended in a small, rectangular chamber. Dane shone his Maglite on the ceiling, revealing an opening.

"Bones, will you do the honors?"

"Sure. I love being your personal stepladder." One by one, Bones boosted his three companions up to the chamber above them, and then, with a helping hand from Dane, climbed up himself.

This chamber ran at a ninety degree angle to the one below, ending in an alcove, where Anubis, the Egyptian protector of the dead, stood watch. The paint was faded, but the god was easily recognizable. Moving as if in sync, Jade and Sofia took out digital cameras.

"No time for that," Dane said. "Besides, I'm sure you can find pictures of this chamber online. It's not exactly a secret."

"But there is a secret passageway somewhere?" Bones asked.

"There is. This chamber was a decoy. Once upon a time, stout doors guarded that alcove. Grave robbers would waste time breaking them down, only to find themselves cursed by Anubis." He shone his light on hieroglyphs carved above the god's jackal head. "The true path lies above." He pointed to another trapdoor in the ceiling. "You have to pass through three of these dead-end chambers in order to get to the burial chamber. But we don't need to go quite that far."

"What do you mean?" Bones asked.

"You'll see in a minute."

Like the chamber they'd just exited, this one was also rotated at a ninety degree angle to the one below and ended in an alcove guarded by Horus.

"Do we go up again?" Bones glanced up at the ceiling.

"We would if the burial chamber was our goal. But what Krueger discovered is that this particular chamber isn't quite the dead end it appears to be." He made his way to the alcove, stepped up onto the ledge, and ran his fingers across the hieroglyphs, the ancient stone cool and smooth to the touch. A shiver passed through him as he reflected on the fact that someone had stood in this very spot, nearly four thousand years ago, and carved these symbols. For a moment, he felt a brief kinship with that workman. What was life like for him? Could he have imagined how long his work would endure?

"Are you awake?" Sofia asked.

"Don't mind him," Jade said. "He's a history buff and he sometimes gets weird around very old things."

"You should have seen him scamming on my grandmother last Christmas." Bones chuckled.

Dane ignored them. His fingers stopped on a flat hieroglyph that resembled a rowboat.

"This is the symbol for a door or gateway." He pressed his fingers against the glyph and felt it give way.

It slid back, creating a handhold which he gripped and rotated a quarter-turn, then released as the entire wall slid to the side.

"Awesome," Jade marveled, while Bones hummed the theme to Indiana Jones.

The passageway behind the trapdoor was so steep that they were forced to descend with the aid of handholds on the wall. By the time they reached the bottom, Sofia dripped with sweat and gasped for breath. Jade was in better condition, though she leaned against the wall to catch her breath.

"It's good thing we've got Krueger's notes, or else we'd be screwed." Bones shone his light down the corridor. It ran straight ahead, well beyond the Maglite's glow, and intersected a cross-hall every ten meters. An engraved column stood at each intersection. "There's something we need to decide right now."

"What's that?" Dane consulted Kruger's notes.

"Which one of us has to fight the Minotaur?"

"Wrong culture." Sofia laughed and squeezed Bones' arm.

Jade and Dane exchanged knowing glances.

"Straight ahead, seventh passageway on the left." Dane headed off down the corridor at a brisk walk, forcing the others to hurry to keep up.

"How did Krueger find his way through here?" Jade tried to walk and take in the scene all at once. She stumbled, and Dane caught her around the waist.

They froze for an instant, gazing into one another's eyes, the sudden closeness foreign, yet so familiar.

"Get a room," Bones jibed.

Jade pulled away from Dane and brushed invisible dirt from her knees. "Such tact." She shot a dirty look Bones' way. "It's truly a wonder some woman hasn't snapped you up."

"I'm a roller coaster," Bones replied. "I'm a short ride, but it's always fun while it lasts."

"You should try thinking about baseball," Dane suggested.

"I didn't mean…" Bones sputtered while the ladies laughed. "Forget it."

"Krueger found the chamber by looking for places where Anubis and the gateway hieroglyph appeared together. Like this." They had reached the seventh cross-hall. Here, Anubis faced left, the gateway symbol hovering between the tips of his long ears.

Aided by Krueger's notes, they followed where the jackal god led, winding through the labyrinth in a dizzying set of twists and turns, until Dane was certain the whole thing was an elaborate ruse and they would spend the rest of their short lives wandering through this dark maze of sand and stone.

"Does Krueger say how long it should take to get there?" Jade's tone held a hint of nervousness.

"It probably took him quite a while since he didn't have directions to follow. He would have been forced to inspect every column and make notes along the way." Dane flipped to the next page in Krueger's notebook. "If we haven't made a wrong turn somewhere along the way, it should be around the next corner."

"Don't jinx us, Maddock," Jade said. "I don't have the energy to go back and start over."

There was no need to start over. The next turn led them to a dead end, just as Krueger said it would. And to what he claimed was the doorway to the Hall of Records.

"It looks just like the photographs." Sofia beamed. Krueger's journal included several snapshots of this wall, where, beneath the now-familiar gateway hieroglyph, an Egyptian carver had rendered the constellation Orion.

"Orion? Here?" Bones gave Maddock a knowing look. This wasn't the first time Orion had figured into one of their mysteries.

"This definitely seems out of place." Jade reached out and ran her fingers along the curved line of stars that formed the hunter's shield. "But if this is a door, where's the handle?"

"And what makes you think we can get in when Krueger couldn't?" Bones added.

"Take a close look at his belt." Dane winked at Sofia while Bones and Jade shone their lights on the carving.

Bones saw it first. "The stars are shaped like the indentations on top of the Atlantean weapon we took from Daisuke."

"Avery and I both recognized the shapes the moment we saw the photographs." Sofia's voice trembled with excitement.

"Did anyone bring the crystals?" Jade asked.

Dane drew a small pouch from his pocket. "What? Did you think we were going to scout it out and then fly back for the crystals?"

"Don't be an ass," Jade snapped. "I was just asking."

"Quiet, you two." Bones hissed.

"He has no call to talk to me like that."

"I hear it too," Dane said. "Listen."

The corridor went dead quiet as they all strained to listen. Dane heard it again—whispered voices somewhere in the labyrinth.

They looked at one another. Jade and Sofia appeared stunned, Bones determined. There was only one logical conclusion.

The Dominion had taken Krueger alive, and they were about to catch up.

CHAPTER 38

It was a dark day on the Atlantic. A gray blanket of storm clouds cloaked the sky, and a chill wind stirred up waves that battered *Sea Foam*, sending icy salt spray over her gunwales. Soaked to the bone, Matt stood on the foredeck holding a pair of binoculars. He knew he should get out of the weather, but he felt as though he were doing a penance for his failure in Naica. He wanted his revenge on the Dominion for what they had done to Joel, and right now, this was all he could do to help. He felt impervious to the cold, maybe because he found it a pleasant change from the deadly heat of the crystal caves, or perhaps his anger kept him warm. Either way, he stood fast.

The foul weather kept all but the largest ships ashore, and Willis and Professor took *Remora* in for a closer look at every craft that plied the waters off the coast of Savannah, but they'd met with no success. He wiped the lenses for what felt like the thousandth time and traced the dark line of the horizon—an inky divide between dark sky and darker water. Nothing.

And then he spotted a white dot. He wiped the lenses again and tightened the focus on the binoculars. Something was there! Feeling a touch of hope for the first time in hours, he turned and waved to get Corey's attention. A moment later, Corey's voice sounded in his ear.

"Did you forget we can talk to each other?"

"I did. Still not accustomed to this high tech gear. Take us north-northwest. I think I see a boat."

"Must be a small one. Radar doesn't show… wait. There it

is!"

Sea Foam rolled in the choppy sea as Corey turned her about. A moment later, Greg joined Matt on deck.

"Can I take a look?" The tall, lanky agent, always so unflappable, still seethed with scarcely-contained rage. Matt knew no one blamed him for what happened to Joel, but he couldn't help but feel a pang of guilt around one of Joel's longtime colleagues. He handed the binoculars to Greg, who took a long look before handing them back. "Keep looking. Let us know when you have a visual." He turned and stalked back into the cabin.

Matt locked his gaze on the target and watched it grow larger in his field of vision. As they drew closer, the boat came into clear view. His heart leapt when he got his first good look at the boat.

"I think this is it!" he called into his mic.

"Dude, no need to shout," Corey said.

"What makes you think so?" Greg asked in clipped tones.

"That boat is identical to the one Bill took us out on for the so-called fishing expedition. Who, in their right mind, would be out fishing on a day like today?"

He felt the vibration beneath his feet as Corey opened up the engine and *Sea Foam* crashed through the waves, making a beeline for the fishing boat.

"Willis, Professor, did you hear that?" Greg asked.

"Roger," Professor replied.

"We're on the mother!" Willis cried.

Nervous energy boiling up inside him, Matt hurried into the cabin and grabbed an M-16. *Please let me get a chance to use it.* For a moment, he wished he had the Atlantean gun Maddock had found in Japan, but Bones had only managed to generate a few waves with it. For now, its secrets remained hidden.

Returning to the deck, he watched as they bore down on the fishing boat. He could make out two figures in rain gear looking in his direction. He dropped to one knee, rested his M-16 on the gunwale, and waited.

One of the men in the boat spotted Matt. He shouted something to his comrade, who sprang to the wheel and gunned the engine.

"They're running!" Matt called.

"Not for long," Willis said.

Ten meters in front of the fleeing fishing boat, mechanical arms extended like a creature from the depths, *Remora* surfaced. The pilot yanked the wheel to the right just as a wave crashed into the boat, nearly capsizing it. As he struggled to recover, Corey cut *Sea Foam* across their bow.

Matt stood and trained his rifle on the pilot.

"Hands in the air! Now!"

Both men raised their hands and stared up at Matt in horror. Up close, he saw that both had the weathered features of men who spent most of their time on the water. He had a sinking feeling they'd chased down the wrong craft. Willis seemed to confirm that a moment later when he reported no weapon attached to the craft's underside.

"Whatever you want, just take it." The pilot's voice trembled. "But we don't have much."

Greg appeared at Matt's side and flashed his identification.

"We're with the D.E.A. We need to inspect your boat." It was a lie they'd agreed on at the outset of the mission.

The men's frozen faces melted with relief.

"You two move to the stern and put your hands behind your heads," Matt ordered. No harm in maintaining the ruse.

Greg inspected the boat, proclaimed it "clean," and apologized for the inconvenience. The relieved men assured him there was nothing to apologize for, and headed back to port without complaint.

"Sorry," Matt said. "I really wanted it to be them."

"Me too." Greg gazed out at the sea. "But we're searching for a needle in a haystack here." His phone rang. "It's Tam." He answered, listened for a few seconds, grimaced, and then hung up. "We're aborting the mission."

"Why?" Matt protested. "There's no way those guys could have already complained about us. Besides, they think we're D.E.A."

"It's not that." Greg pocketed his phone and pounded his fist on the gunwale. "Bill gave you a bad tip. The Dominion just hit Norfolk."

CHAPTER 39

The sound of voices drew closer. Bones drew his Glock and took up a position at the corner where he could see the Dominion operatives' approach.

"Give me some light," Dane whispered. Jade and Sofia trained their Maglites on Orion's belt. Quickly, Dane placed the crystals in their proper spots. As he pressed each into its slot, some invisible force, almost like magnetism, snatched the crystal from his fingers and held it fast.

"I can see their lights," Bones whispered. "We're almost out of time."

"Got it." Dane set the last crystal into place and the door swung inward. He shone his beam inside, making a cursory inspection for booby traps, and then ushered the others inside. After they all entered the chamber, he pried the crystals free and pushed the door closed. With a hollow click, it locked into place. "Now, let's see if Krueger was right."

Turning around, he swept his light around the room.

"Oh my God," Jade whispered. Her free hand found his and squeezed. "This is it!"

Statues of Egyptian gods lined the Hall of Records. Between each statue, the walls were honeycombed with alcoves for storing scrolls. A band of hieroglyphs ringed the chamber just above the alcoves. It was laid out like the Atlantean temples, but with a large stone table at the center where the altar to Poseidon would have been.

Jade and Sofia immediately began snapping

pictures.

"We don't have much time," Dane said.

"Why not?" Sofia asked, still clicking away. "We're in here, they're out there, and they don't have the crystals."

"I don't think that will slow them down for long. The best we can hope for is they try the door for a few minutes. Once they realize they can't get in, I believe we can count on them to resort to other means."

"Like what?" Sofia asked.

"Like blowing the door," Jade said. "Maddock's right. We need to hurry. I just hope we can find the information we need in time."

"What happens when they do blow the door?" Sofia's voice dropped to a scant whisper.

"You two will hide while Bones and I deal with them." Dane wished he felt half as much confidence as he feigned. He had a feeling the Dominion would have sent enough trained men to make sure a job this important came off without a hitch.

"Guys, there's something weird in here." Bones pointed to the nearest statue—Osiris. "Notice how every statue has been defaced?"

"Every one?" Jade asked, moving deeper into the hall. "That can't be right."

"He's right," Sofia said. "Every face is smashed. That can't be an accident. Someone's been in here."

"That's not the worst part. Check out the alcoves." Bones shone his light along the wall.

Every alcove was empty.

"No!" Sofia wailed. She balled her fists and pressed them to her forehead. "All this work, and grave robbers beat us to it."

"Not grave robbers," Dane said.

"How do you know?" Jade cocked her head to the

side and fixed him with a questioning look.

"The thieves left a calling card." He shone his light on the wall above the door, where someone had carved a few squiggly lines and a familiar symbol.

"The Templars? No freaking way." Bones looked like he was about to say something else, but just then, they heard voices on the other side of the door.

Dane couldn't make out the words, but it was clear by their excited tone that they knew they'd found the entrance to the Hall of Records. He looked at Bones.

"There are a bunch of guys out there, Maddock." He said it with the clinical detachment of an engineer sizing up a challenging task.

"We'll have surprise on our side, and they'll have to come in two at a time." Dane thought fast. "We'll lay our Maglites in alcoves, with the beams directed at the door. They'll aim for the lights at first. That will buy us a little more time."

"Maybe we won't have to fight." Sofia grabbed him by the arm and pulled him deeper into the hall.

"We can't hide from them," Dane said. "When they find the chamber empty, they'll give it a thorough search."

"That's not what I mean." Sofia continued to pull him through the hall. Bones and Jade followed behind them, bemused expressions on their faces. "This place is laid out exactly like the Atlantean temples."

"So?"

"So, that means there should be an air shaft leading out. That's how I got away in Spain." She released Dane's arm and hurried ahead.

Dane glanced at Bones. "It's worth a try."

"It's here!" Sofia called. "Come on!"

"Okay, everybody into the shaft," Dane ordered. "Bones take the lead; I'll bring up the rear."

"No way. Why do you get the good view?" Bones winked. "Besides, I'm the biggest. If I get stuck along the way, everyone behind me is stuck too."

"Fine." Dane stuck his Maglite in his teeth and began to climb. He'd made it about ten meters when an explosion rocked the passageway. "I guess they blew the door." He wondered if the others could even hear him. If their ears were ringing half as loudly as his, he doubted it. He looked back to make sure everyone still followed, and continued the climb.

The climb through the shaft went on with agonizing slowness. The stones were fitted together with such precision that he found it difficult to find handholds. Every muscle ached from crawling in a hunched position. It felt like boot camp all over again.

As the ringing in his ears abated, the voices of the Dominion's men rose. Angry shouts and arguing reverberated through the shaft. *I know how you feel,* he thought. *You came all this way for nothing.* Listening to the men in the hall below, a sudden thought struck him.

"Everybody turn out your lights," he said around his own Maglite, which he still held between his teeth.

"Why?" Sofia asked.

"In case they look into the shaft." He paused enough to douse his light. "I don't think Bones' butt is big enough to block the light."

"Hey, my butt is perfect. Just ask your old lady."

"Your sister is my old lady," Dane retorted.

"Oh, yeah."

Even Jade laughed at this, though they quickly fell silent.

"Do you see anything yet?" Jade whispered. "Any light at the end of the tunnel?"

"Not yet, but we entered the labyrinth just before sunset. It will be dark outside."

He couldn't deny he was worried that the shaft wasn't a true air shaft that would lead outside. If a shaft this size were open at the other end, wouldn't it have been discovered by now? Nothing to be done about it, he supposed. At worst, they'd hide in the shaft until they were certain the hall was empty, then try to sneak out the way they'd come in.

His fears were confirmed minutes later when his skull met a stone wall. He halted, and Jade crashed into him a moment later. He heard twin grunts as Sofia and Bones joined the pileup.

"Why have we stopped?" Jade whispered.

"End of the line."

"There's got to be a way out," Sofia protested.

"I don't know." Dane ran his hand across the wall in front of him. It was smooth, just like the sides of the shaft. He felt for a seam, but the stone was seated tightly in the end of the shaft. "I think we're out of luck."

"Let me see." Light blossomed in the darkness and Jade squeezed in beside him.

"Warn me when you're going to do that." Dane tried to blink away the spots in his eyes.

"Somebody had to find the doorknob. Look."

He squinted against the too-bright light, and looked at the spot where she'd trained her beam.

"It's a slot for a crystal. I must have missed it in the dark."

"Duh. Now hurry up. I want a bath and a beer, and not in that order."

"Can I join you?" Bones asked.

"Only for the beer."

"Just like old times." Dane pulled out the bag of crystals, found the one that fit, and set it in place. Silently, the shaft swung open. Cool breeze and the glow of artificial light bathed his face. He looked around at his surroundings and laughed.

"What's funny?" Jade asked.

"You'll see. Just be very careful climbing out. Bones, be sure to take the crystal and close the door behind you." Carefully, he climbed out of the hole. When they all reached the ground, they stood, looking up, and laughing.

"I can't believe that we just climbed out of the eye of the Sphinx." Bones couldn't tear his eyes away from the battered stone face of the ancient monument.

"Believe it," Dane said. "Let's get out of here. If we hurry, we should be able to get back to the car long before the Dominion gets out of the labyrinth."

They took off at a slow trot. Dane and Bones could have stood a faster pace, and probably Jade, who always kept fit, but he didn't know if Sofia would be able to handle it.

As he ran, he punched up Tam's number. She wasn't going to like his report.

CHAPTER 40

"With us live *from his church in Utah is Bishop Hadel of the Kingdom Church."* Patricia Blount, the news anchor, was an attractive blonde of middle years, but her pleasant smile belied her reputation as a hard-nosed interviewer. She didn't quite manage to disguise her frown as she introduced Hadel. Though the Dominion was an organization unknown to most, Hadel was well-known, both for his altruism and his controversial opinions. *"Bishop, it is my understanding that representatives from your church are already on the scene in Norfolk, providing aid to displaced families."*

"We call them missionaries," Hadel corrected. *"And, yes, they are on the scene. When tragedy strikes, we reach out in loving compassion to our brothers and sisters in need."*

Hadel's easy smile turned Tam's stomach. She knew what a monster the man was, even if the world didn't, and the fact that she couldn't yet prove it made it all the worse.

"With thousands already confirmed dead, tens of thousands more having lost everything to the second freak tsunami to hit the United States in less than two weeks, how do you comfort people who might think to give up hope in your God?" Blount winced at her own brief lapse in professionalism.

"He's everyone's God, Patricia, whether they know it or not." Hadel smiled like an indulgent grandfather. *"And we provide reassurance through acts of mercy like those we are performing in Norfolk."*

"How did your missionaries happen to be on the scene so quickly?"

"We have sister and satellite churches throughout the nation

who assist us in our work." Hadel said with a touch of pride.

"What do you say to those who claim a merciful, loving God would not allow a tragedy like this to strike innocents?"

"I would say there are few innocents in this world. Norfolk, I am sad to say, is not immune to the infection that is rotting our nation from the inside out. Norfolk is rated as one of the hundred most dangerous cities in the United States, with crime rates well above the national average."

"May I ask why, in the face of this tragedy, you took the time to study up on Norfolk's crime statistics?" Blount bore down. *"It seems like you'd have other priorities."*

Hadel remained unflappable. *"I sought to understand the reason for this seemingly-senseless tragedy, and came to the inescapable conclusion that God's judgment and righteous wrath are at play here. This is a city peopled with some of the lowest of the low…"*

"Who do you consider the lowest of the low?" Blount snapped, but Hadel rode over her.

"Not to mention the strong presence of the United States military, which aids and abets our corrupt government."

Blount redirected the conversation. *"Bishop, we're going to play a cell phone video captured by one of the victims of the tsunami and we'd like your comments on it."*

"Of course."

"The video shows your missionaries rescuing a white family from the flood waters, and then, almost immediately, fighting off a drowning African-American man…"

Tam's phone vibrated just as an indignant Hadel shouted something about 'ambush journalism' and the tendencies of overcrowded boats to capsize. It was a text from Maddock. She fired off a reply and sagged against the wall, eyes closed. Why had she ever wanted to be in charge? What she wouldn't give right now to be out in the field, matching wits with her quarry.

Maybe she'd even get to shoot somebody. That would relieve her stress.

"What's wrong?" Avery looked up from Krueger's notebook. She was still upset with Tam for keeping her at headquarters, but she'd been working diligently since the others left on their respective missions.

"First the Dominion attacks the wrong city, making me look like a fool, and now Maddock finds the Hall of Records."

"Really?" Avery sprang to her feet, upending her chair. "Where was it? What did he find?"

"It was under the Sphinx, just like Krueger said. And it was empty."

The gleam in Avery's eyes flickered and died. "What?"

"The Templars got there first. He's sending me a picture of…" Her phone vibrated again. "Here it is. The Templars left a calling card." She handed the phone to Avery.

"The cross looks authentic. Lord knows we've seen enough of these lately." The Templars had been at the heart of a mystery Tam aided Maddock and his crew in solving. "But these squiggly lines are odd." Avery's gaze went cloudy and she bit her lip.

"What?" Tam could tell the young woman was deep in thought, but she dared not get her hopes up.

"I think I know where this is!" She snatched up the notebook and flipped through to a hand-drawn map. "See how the lines on this carving match up?"

Tam looked at the map. It showed a stretch of river and an island. "It's not an exact match. The Templar carving doesn't show this island." She tapped a chili-pepper shaped stretch of land that ran parallel to the shore, joined to the mainland by bridges at its north and northwest tips.

"That's because this island wasn't built until the 1800s but, according to Krueger, it's one of the Templars' most notorious 'hide in plain sight' constructions. He believes it's the place where the Freemasons, the modern descendants of the Templars hid their most sacred knowledge." She paused. "And it has Atlantean connections."

"Where is this place?" Tam held her breath. Hope stirred inside her again, though she was reluctant to believe it.

"It's in Washington D.C. I know it must seem like a stretch, but Krueger was right about the Hall of Records. Isn't it at least worth having Maddock and the others check it out?"

For the first time in she couldn't remember how long, Tam permitted herself a genuine smile. Now she recognized the location.

"Girl, forget Maddock. There's no time to waste. Besides, I'm the one who can get us inside. Grab your toothbrush. You and I are going on a trip."

CHAPTER 41

"You realize I know what you're up to?" Bones lay stretched out on the hotel bed, tossing his Recon knife in the air and snatching the falling, spinning blade just before it hit him in the face. He'd been at it for the past ten minutes, complaining all the while about boredom and insomnia.

"What are you talking about?" Dane groaned. Sleep eluded him as well, but he'd at least tried harder than Bones to catch some shut eye.

"Only getting two rooms. You're hoping I'll keep you from hooking up with Jade."

"I'm not going to hook up with her. You're the hookup guy in this partnership."

"You're not planning to hook up with her, but I know how things go when you meet up with an ex. It starts out friendly, and then it gets nostalgic. Next thing you know, you're wondering why you ever dumped her in the first place. It's psychology and hormones." Bones caught the knife again and flung it across the room where it stuck in back of the desk chair.

"You're paying for that." Dane sat up and rubbed his eyes. "You've been through this before?"

"Are you kidding? I hook up with my exes whenever I get a chance. It's a lot like makeup sex. The difference is, I don't get into long, committed relationships, like you do. I've tried a few times, but it doesn't last." He got up, retrieved his knife, and sheathed it. "It's bad enough you want me to run interference for you, but you're messing up my game. Sofia looks like a mountain I'd like to climb."

Dane ignored the labored metaphor. "Wait a minute. You think it's bad I want you to keep Jade away from me? I'm being faithful to your sister."

"It's not faithfulness if somebody has to make you do it. If you're going to go back to Jade sooner or later, I'd rather Angel find out now, instead of down the road. It'll hurt her less."

"It gives me a headache when you say something that makes sense."

"Screw you, Maddock." Bones smiled to show he had not taken offense. "I'm going to get some fresh air before I go stir crazy."

There came a soft knock at their door. Bones gave him a look that said, *What did I tell you?* He opened the door to find Jade standing there, looking abashed.

"I... needed to talk to Maddock about something."

"Go ahead. I'm going out for a few minutes." Bones left without looking back.

Jade sat down on the bed, facing him, and gazed at him, her brown eyes shining with deep emotion.

"What did you want to talk about?"

"I'm not sure." She looked down at her hands. "It was fun today. You know, solving the puzzle, proving a legend was true, almost getting killed." She laughed. "God, I've missed it. I know that sounds crazy, but I never feel more alive than when I'm with you."

"Nostalgia's a funny thing. It makes you forget the bad times."

Now, Jade met his eye. Her gaze was hard, but her words soft. "You're trying to sound callous, but I know you better than that. Tell me you don't feel it too."

"Of course I do. And yes, our highs are pretty high, but you can't deny that our lows were sometimes about as low as you can get." He poured all his effort into ignoring her eyes, which always mesmerized him, and her other features that he found just as enticing, and concentrated on the bad times: the fights, the jealousy, the months apart.

"It's called a roller coaster, and people love them. How boring is life if there aren't any ups and downs?"

Dane had no reply.

"You don't have to give me an answer. Just promise me you'll think about it. About us." Jade's smile faltered and faded into a tiny frown. She stood and headed for the door.

"Leaving already?" Dane didn't know why he'd said that. From the time they'd checked into the hotel, he'd wanted nothing more than for the two of them to keep their distance from one another.

"I want to get back to the room before Bones tries something with Sofia."

"He won't be happy."

"He will when I remind him about the punishment for adultery in a Muslim country." She looked back over her shoulder, a wicked gleam in her eye. "I don't actually know what the law is in Egypt, but I'll make up something suitably horrible."

"Nice one." Dane winked at her. "Sleep well."

Jade looked at him for another long moment before opening the door. "Goodnight, Maddock." She stepped outside and closed the door.

Dane stared at the door, fighting an irrational urge to go after her. What was his problem? He was in a good relationship with a girl he'd known forever. Why would he even consider throwing that away?

He turned out the light, yanked the covers over his head, and, when Bones returned a few minutes later, pretended to be asleep. It was going to be a long night.

CHAPTER 42

"According to Krueger, Pierre-Charles L'Enfant, who designed the master site plan for Washington, D.C., also known as the 'L'Enfant Plan,' was a French architect and Freemason handpicked for the job by George Washington, who was also a Freemason. L'Enfant's original design incorporated Freemason, Egyptian, and even Atlantean symbolism." Avery had spent the flight from Miami to Washington devouring all of Krueger's research on the Templars' connection to the capital city, and supplementing it with her own research. The more she learned the more fascinated she became. A scholar could devote her entire career to studying the connections between the ancient world, secret societies, and Washington D.C. Now, as their driver, a government agent driving a boring, gray sedan, drove them to their destination, she shared her findings with Tam.

"Skip to the part we care about." Tam was checking email on her phone, but seemed to be listening intently.

"Just like the labyrinth Maddock and the others found at Giza, a network of passageways runs beneath the national mall and all the major structures in the vicinity. Somewhere amid this warren lies a vault containing the accumulated treasures of the Templars in America. Beginning in the late 1930s, the Freemasons constructed a new passageway to the vault, and hid the entryway beneath a memorial that incorporated both Templar and Atlantean symbology; the symbols to serve as a sign to the initiated."

"Tell me about the symbology." Tam pocketed her phone and gave Avery her undivided attention.

"Look at this aerial photograph." Avery laid Krueger's notebook between them. "See how the entablature is a perfect circle?"

"I've been there before, and I can see how it's reminiscent of a Templar church. But I don't see Atlantis here anywhere."

"Look outward from the memorial. What do you see?"

Tam stared for a moment, and then her eyes lit up. "Rings of concentric circles on a piece of land surrounded by water."

"Is that Atlantean enough for you?" Avery could have gone on, but she could tell Tam was convinced.

"We're here, Ma'am." The driver stopped the car and opened the door for them. "Shall I come with you?"

"Remain here with the car. I'll call if I need you."

Bathed in moonlight, its interior lights glowing, the Jefferson Memorial stood enshrouded in the ethereal curtain of fog that rolled in off the Potomac. In the silence of the midnight hour, the place had a ghostly quality to it.

Tam made a beeline for the monument, and Avery hurried to keep up. As they drew closer, she noticed yellow tape encircling the monument and signs reading, *Temporarily Closed*.

"Uh oh. I wonder why it's closed."

"Are you kidding?" Tam gave her a quizzical look. "I closed it. Rather, a friend closed it for me. And there he is. Hey, Tyson!"

Daniel Tyson was a tall, dark skinned man who appeared to be about the same age as Tam. Light from the memorial reflected off his shaved head, and he greeted Tam and Avery with an easy smile and bone crushing hugs. His tailored suit was cut to accentuate his athletic figure.

"Tyson is a friend and former colleague," Tam explained. "He used to be FBI, now he's with the NPS and calls it a 'step up.' He's also a Lakers fan, which tells you he knows nothing about basketball."

"Please." Tyson's speech was flavored with a light touch of the Caribbean, adding to his aura of congeniality. "You've never balled in your life, Broderick."

"Not on the court, anyway." Tam gave him a wink.

"My court is always open if you ever feel so inclined to brush up on your...skills!"

Tam gave his arm a squeeze. "Thank you for doing this for us. We'll try to make it quick."

"Not a problem. Do you need anything else from me?"

"Just keep prying eyes away." Tam thanked him again, gave him another hug, and led them into the memorial.

"I found pairs of numbers, get this, written in the margins in invisible ink. I think they correspond to words in the various inscriptions on the walls."

"Invisible ink? How'd you know to check for that?"

"My father was obsessed with pirate treasure, legends, and secrets. I picked up a few things here and there."

"Good job. Let's get to checking the panels."

"No need. I looked up the various inscriptions online and worked on it during our flight. I think I've come up with something that makes sense." She opened the notebook and read aloud.

"Progress of the human mind. Enlightened discoveries. Truths remain ever in the hand of the master."

"The master? You mean Jefferson over there?" Tam assessed the bronze statue. "He's big, but I don't think there's a tunnel in his hand."

"I've got an idea about that." Moving to the statue, Avery climbed up onto the pedestal. There was little room to stand and the surface was slick, but she clung to the president's cloak for balance.

Ever in the hand of the master.

In Jefferson's left hand, he clutched a scroll. Avery wasn't tall enough to get a good look, but, if she stretched, she could just reach it. She ran her fingers across the top and found what she was looking for. A pyramid-shaped indentation.

"It's here! Give me the crystals."

Tam, looking bemused, handed her an envelope in which she'd put one each of the crystals Maddock and Bones had recovered in Japan. The first crystal was not a fit, nor was the second, but the moment the third crystal slid into place, the empty rotunda echoed with the thrum of cogs turning somewhere below ground. The statue lurched and Avery leapt off the pedestal, not quite pulling off a clean landing. She sprang to her feet, but Tam hadn't noticed. She watched as the statue slid to the side, revealing a stone staircase.

Tam looked at Avery and smiled.

"Who needs them boys? You did it!"

Avery couldn't help but blush a little at Tam's praise. She had to admit she was more than a little proud to have done all of it: tracking down Krueger, finding the connection to the memorial, and deciphering the clues, without her brother's help. Okay, a lot of the credit went to Krueger, but she was still going to enjoy the moment.

"You coming?" Tam was already ten steps down

the staircase, flashlight in one hand, Makarov in the other.

"Yeah, sorry." Avery took out her Maglite but left her 9 millimeter in her coat pocket. She couldn't imagine encountering anything down here that would require a weapon. Head buzzing with the thrill of discovery, she followed Tam down into the darkness.

The air grew damp and musty as they made their way deeper. After a long descent, they reached a level passageway. At first, Avery was taken aback at the relative modernity, but reminded herself that this tunnel had not been built by the Templars, but was a twentieth century link to the Templar vault. Cobwebs hung from the ceiling and a thin sheen of dust coated everything. No one had passed this way in years, maybe decades.

Minutes later, they found themselves facing a dead end.

"Okay. What now?" Tam shone her Maglite all around. "Did we miss a door somewhere along the way?"

"I don't think so." Avery moved closer and ran her hand down the wall. Her fingers passed over a soft spot and she paused. "I think I might have something." Pulling the neckline of her shirt up to cover her nose and mouth, she brushed away the accumulated dust and mold, revealing another indentation like the one on the statue. She quickly found the proper crystal and fitted it into the slot. Some unseen force tugged it into place and the door swung back.

They shone their lights through the doorway and Avery sucked in her breath. "This is really it!"

CHAPTER 43

The Templar vault looked like an oversize version of the interior of the Jefferson Memorial—round with a low, vaulted ceiling and columns interspersed around the sides. Shelves were carved into the walls between each set of columns, with piles of scrolls, books, and artifacts heaped onto them. The room itself was filled with statuary from all over the world and various historical epochs. She recognized Greek, Egyptian, and Chinese sculpture, as well as Roman busts on pedestals.

"This is…" Tam couldn't finish her sentence. "To think this has been down here all this time and no one knew."

"Someone knew," Avery said. "I can't imagine the Freemasons let the knowledge die."

"I wonder," Tam mused, "if they kept the knowledge within an inner circle, and something happened to those in the know before they could pass the information along. It would explain why nobody's been down here in forever." She shook her head. "That's a question for another day. We need to get to searching. Where should we start?"

"Um." Avery bit her lip. She hadn't considered how they would go about sorting through the accumulated treasures of the Templars. "This could take a while."

"Time we might not have. Unless the men they sent to Egypt were idiots, the Dominion knows the Templars cleared out the Hall of Records. They'll try to extract the information from Krueger. He's unlikely to hold out any longer than he did before he revealed the secret of the labyrinth."

"In that case, we'd better hurry. You go left, I'll go right?" Avery skirted the perimeter of the vault, examining the contents of the various shelves. She saw that there was at least some organizational system here. The first section contained Hebrew texts, a golden menorah, and a few artifacts she didn't immediately recognize. In addition to the ancient texts, the section also contained more recent copies of various writings, some in Latin, others in Greek, and still more in English. So the material was organized by topic as well as origin. Perhaps they should search out, not the Egyptian collection, but one devoted to Atlantis.

The next section contained Christian writings and a few small chests that likely contained relics. She took a few steps back to get a different perspective on the layout. As she ran her light up and down the wall, she noticed the symbols carved above each set of shelves— a menorah above the Hebrew section and a cross over the Christian section.

As her eyes followed the beam of her light as it swept in a circle around the vault, she saw more symbols: the eagle of Rome, the Eye of Horus, and…

"The trident! It's over here." She hurried over to where a statue of Poseidon guarded the shelves. Tam joined her a few seconds later.

"Some of this is really old. It might crumble if we touch it." Tam passed her fingers over a scroll, as if she could capture its contents through proximity. She hesitated. "How do we know which of these contains the information we need?" She swept her light up and down the shelves. "There's too much to carry."

"We need Sofia," Avery agreed. "I've picked up on the meanings of a few of the symbols but not enough of them to translate." Her eyes roved over the collection and fell upon an object so different from the others she almost wondered if it were mislaid.

Laying her Maglite on the shelf, she picked up a leatherbound journal and opened it to the first page.

"That's anachronistic," Tam said.

"It's more than that." Avery's hands trembled. "This journal is an eighteenth century scholar's attempt to tell the true story of Atlantis based on a lifelong study of this archive." She turned the page and almost dropped the book.

"Are you all right?"

"Look." Avery could scarcely manage to believe her eyes. A hand-drawn map of the world showed the locations of Atlantean cities: in Spain, Cuba, Japan, and the middle of the Atlantic. Dotted lines connected them all to one mother city. With trembling hands, she passed the book to Tam, whose jaw dropped.

"That can't be right," she whispered.

"Yes it can. You see, it wasn't always..." She paused as a beam of light coming from the direction of the doorway, sliced through the darkness.

"Oh, my God. What have you two found?" It was Tyson.

"What are you doing down here? I asked you to keep people away." Tam's eyes narrowed at the sight of her friend.

"I'm sorry. I looked in to make sure you were all right and I saw the Jefferson statue moved to the side. Then I noticed the staircase and I just couldn't believe it. I called down to you and, when you didn't answer, I thought you might be in trouble." He shone his light around the vault, taking in the treasures of human history. "What is this place?"

"Sort of an old library," Tam said.

"Right." He glanced at the book in Tam's hand,

and the map. Avery didn't miss the way his eyes widened. Without warning, he drew a Glock and leveled it at Tam's face. "Give me the book."

Tam didn't flinch. "How can you possibly be one of them?" She bit off each word, fire blazing in her eyes.

"Who? The Dominion?" Tyson laughed. "Not a chance. I'm too, shall we say, tainted by the blood of Cain for their liking."

"Then why are you helping them?"

"Let's just say that, on occasion, we have mutual interests."

"Who is we?"

"The Trident." As if by reflex, Tyson's free hand moved to a spot below his throat.

"You're a traitor to the country you devoted your life to serving."

"America." Tyson laughed again. "I never served this infant nation. I serve the oldest people of them all. Any job I took in this foul government served to put me into a position to help prepare for the return."

Tam held Tyson's full attention, and Avery took advantage of that fact, sidling away. What could she do to help? The man was too big to fight and, even if she could take him on, she couldn't do anything before he pulled the trigger.

"You're crazy," Tam whispered.

"And you're dead."

Before Tyson could pull the trigger, Tam struck, smashing the journal book into his gun hand.

As Tyson's shot went wild, Avery threw all her weight against the Poseidon statue. It toppled over with agonizing slowness, striking Tyson in the shoulder and knocking him to the side.

Tam lashed out with a roundhouse kick, knocking

Tyson's Glock free. He reached for his weapon, and Avery remembered her own pistol.

She drew it, took aim, and shouted out with more confidence than she actually felt. "Hands up or I'll shoot!"

At the sound of her voice, Tyson flung his flashlight at her head and rolled to the side. Avery's shot went wild as the big man fled. She spun around, following the sound of crashing statues as he fled the vault, and fired a desperate shot.

"Let's go!" Tam had regained her feet, her Makarov, and the book. Avery snatched her Maglite off the shelf and followed. At the door, she paused to retrieve the crystal, then sprinted to try and keep up with Tam, whose light bobbed up and down ten meters ahead. Tyson stood well over six feet tall and looked like an athlete. It was unlikely they'd catch him, but Tam appeared determined to try.

They took the steps two at a time, their footfalls reverberating through the stairwell. And then, all sounds were drowned out by a low rumble. Avery felt the vibration in the soles of her feet.

"He must have taken the crystal! He's trying to lock us in down here!"

Up above, the statue slowly moved back into place. The square of bright light inexorably shrinking. Tam hurtled through the opening, which seemed to be shrinking even faster. Did Avery dare try it? But what if Tyson had taken the crystal? She might be stuck here?

She had an instant to make up her mind. What would Maddock do? With a cry something like terror, she flung herself upward.

She stumbled.

And fell, her legs half in and half out of the stairwell. She scrambled to crawl, but she slipped on the slick, stone surface. Almost there. She felt the statue's massive pedestal close on her foot.

Suddenly, Tam grabbed her wrists and yanked. For an interminable instant, she felt frozen in place, and then she slid forward. Something grabbed her toe and she jerked her leg. Her foot slid free, leaving her shoe behind.

"Could be worse," she mumbled as she scrambled to her feet. When Avery reached the portico, she saw Tam standing on the bottom step, Makarov at her side. The thickening fog rendered visibility almost nil.

"We lost him."

"It's my fault. If I hadn't fallen, you might have caught him."

Tam shook her head. "He had too big a lead, and the dude is fast. You saw them long legs. Besides, he'd have killed me if it weren't for you."

Avery doubted that, but appreciated the words of reassurance.

Through the fog, they heard the sound of running feet. They both aimed their weapons at the sound, but lowered them again when they recognized their driver.

"I've been trying to reach you," he said, skidding to a halt in front of Tam. "A terrorist group just claimed responsibility for the tsunamis. They've got a list of demands, and if they aren't met, they say a major city will be the next to fall."

"Does this group have a name?" Tam's tone of voice was razor sharp.

"The Dominion."

CHAPTER 44

Bishop Frederick Hadel read through a report from his agent inside the CIA. The contact was a low-level operative, and seldom had much of use to report but, on occasion, he delivered valuable information. Today, he'd picked up a useful tidbit. Someone within the agency had tried to warn the government about an attack on Savannah. Specifically, a man-made disaster.

"Our first leak," he said aloud. His mind ran through the list of false trails he'd laid. The Savannah rumor had been planted with the leader of the church in Key West. He'd have to address that situation immediately. A shame, really. Some of his most ardent supporters were members of that particular congregation, and they'd served him well during the tsunami and in Mexico.

Now, he opened a browser window on his desktop computer and navigated to the major news sites. As he expected, the internet was abuzz over the proclamation the Dominion had just released, in which they claimed responsibility for the Tsunamis and demanded the President's resignation, along with that of the Vice President, a few select Supreme Court justices, and most of congress.

His demands would not be met, of course, but the implicit message would not be missed. One look at the list of representatives and justices whom the Dominion considered acceptable would deliver the message. The nation needed to change, and he would make it over by any means necessary. The next attack would prove the Dominion's power, and when they obtained the

Revelation Machine…

His phone buzzed, interrupting his musings. He tapped the speakerphone button.

"Yes?"

"Mister Robinson to see you, Bishop. He says it's urgent."

"Send him in."

As always, Robinson knocked exactly two times before pushing the door open. It was an idiosyncrasy, or perhaps a compulsive behavior, that Hadel was happy to ignore, given Robinson's reliability.

"I just received a report from a contact within a friendly organization. A CIA agent named Tamara Broderick sought his help in accessing a vault beneath the Jefferson Memorial—one that, she claimed, contained a Templar archive."

Hadel sat up straight. "And?"

"It was there. Inside, she found information that pinpoints the location of the capital, if you will, of Atlantis. He failed to obtain the document in question, which he said appeared to be a journal of some sort, but he saw the map and knew exactly where it pointed."

Hadel laid his hands on his lap to prevent Robinson from seeing them tremble. He couldn't remember ever being so excited. But, when Robinson told him the location, he found himself puzzled.

"I've never heard of such a place. Just a moment." He returned to his computer and called up the location. When the first images appeared on his screen, he relaxed. "Atlantis," he whispered, "has been hiding in plain sight all this time."

"I'm assembling a team as we speak," Robinson said. "We await your instructions."

"Activate the failsafe plan."

"Bishop?" A furrow creased Robinson's brow. "But the failsafe is…"

"I know what it is, and now is the perfect time to activate it, because I'm going with you."

CHAPTER 45

The Range Rover bounced across the barren landscape, jostling its passengers. Dane slowed the vehicle to a halt atop a rise. The sun beat down on the dry, rocky landscape below. It was hard to believe this was their destination.

They all climbed out, stretching tired limbs and knuckling sore backs.

"The Eye of the Sahara," Sofia whispered. "I never would have thought it possible."

Located in Mauritania, the Richat Structure, or the Eye of the Sahara, was a thirty kilometer-wide, collapsed volcanic dome. Visible from space, when seen from far overhead, its circular shape and symmetrical rings bore an eerie similarity to elements of Plato's description of Atlantis. Indeed, when Sofia had shown him satellite photos of the location, he'd been shocked no one had considered it before.

"It looks different from here," Bones said. "Not like Atlantis at all."

"That's because we aren't looking at it from overhead." Jade rolled her eyes.

"But how could Atlantis have been here? We're so far away from the ocean. I don't see how it could ever have flooded."

"Researchers have found evidence of salt water fishing in the area ten to twelve thousand years ago," Jade said. "So it's possible that the ocean extended farther inland than it does now."

"Another possibility is that Plato's flood story referred to the site in Spain, which flooded and was buried beneath mud, just like the story says," Sofia said. "If the mother city stood here, it might have been so isolated that it could have been lost to memory."

"Seems like an awfully big place to just get lost," Bones said.

"Up until a little over ten thousand years ago, settlements in northern Africa were largely restricted to the Nile Valley. By the time the Sahara went through its monsoon period, the Atlanteans were gone. At least, that's our best guess." Sofia looked out across the landscape and smiled in disbelief. "I've worked at this for so long, and now we're right on the verge of finding it. I just can't believe it."

"Where do we start?" Dane asked.

"There are no explicit directions, but it seems there's a system of caves somewhere near the center."

"According to my research, there's a small hotel there," Jade said. "That could make for a good base of operations while we search."

"As long as we can see the Dominion coming." Dane hopped back into the Range Rover and cranked it up while the others piled in. Deep inside him, the thrill at the prospect of finding Atlantis battled with apprehension over the Revelation Machine. What if the Dominion got there first? Or, and he hated to entertain the thought, what happened if he found it first? Did any government deserve the power to destroy the world? But that was a problem for later. First, they had to find it.

"Were we supposed to make a reservation?" Bones asked as they pulled up in front of the tiny hotel that rested right in the center of the Eye. "Looks like they didn't leave the light on for us."

The small hotel appeared deserted. Dane cut the engine. All was quiet. "I imagine this place doesn't get much business, but I have a bad feeling about this." Drawing his Walther, he climbed out of the Range Rover. Bones was at his side a moment later.

"Do you want us to stay here?" Sofia asked.

"I don't want you two to be alone, just in case."

"Maddock, you see these tracks?" Bones swept his hand in a half-circle. "At least two different vehicles were all over this place, and not too long ago or else the wind would have blown the tracks away." He narrowed his eyes. "Looks like Hummers to me."

Dane didn't reply. He hoped that, if two Hummers had come this way, they weren't packed with Dominion agents. He led the way to the hotel.

The coppery scent of blood filled his nostrils as soon as he opened the door. He didn't need to look far to find the source.

A man lay bound to an upended chair. His eyes gazed blankly up at the ceiling. Congealed blood pooled on the floor around his head. Dane grimaced at the ragged cut in the man's throat.

"Cause of death is pretty obvious." Bones pursed his lips as he looked at the grisly scene. "Looks like he was tortured."

The man's hands were smashed, his fingertips sliced and his fingernails torn out.

"I guess the Dominion got here first." Dane hoped he caught up with the men who did this. He was eager to repay the favor.

"I can't imagine they got any useful information from a desk clerk," Bones said.

"We can hope," Jade said. "Say, what if it's not the Dominion? What if it's this Trident group Tam told us about?"

"All we can do is be prepared. Let's check the building and get out of here."

It didn't take long to determine no one else was about. Thankfully, they found no other bodies. When they'd completed the search, they gathered outside the door.

"What's our next move?" Bones asked. "This place is too big to just go wandering."

"I don't see that we have a choice." Jade turned to Sofia. "Unless you think there's something you missed in what Tam sent you."

Sofia shook her head. "I'll look again, but I don't think so."

"I have an idea," Dane said. "I think it's safe to say the man inside didn't know the way to Atlantis. But, if he was local, he probably would have been familiar with any caves in the area."

"Which would mean the Dominion now knows the way," Bones grumbled.

"How would they know about the caves without the book?" Sofia asked. "Tam said her so-called friend only saw the map."

"It stands to reason that Atlantis, if it's here, is beneath the volcanic dome," Jade said. "They'd have wanted to know about any tunnels or caverns that might lead underground."

"So we do what?" Bones asked. "Drive around until we find some locals?"

"We could do that," Dane said. "Or we could follow their tire tracks."

CHAPTER 46

The moment he spotted the Hummers parked at the base of a steep rise, Dane pulled the Range Rover behind a rise, blocking it from view. Urging Jade and Avery to wait with the vehicle, and failing spectacularly to convince them, he and the others moved closer to scout the area.

"I'll bet it's somewhere on that ridge up there." Dane pointed to a steeply-sloped wall of volcanic rock. "It stands to reason the entrance would be somewhere difficult to get to, and that doesn't look like an easy climb."

"Not for some people." Bones winked. He and Dane had always been competitive when it came to climbing. "So, do we wait until Tam gets here with backup?"

"I don't think we can. If the Dominion, or anyone, for that matter, is ahead of us, we'd better catch up to them before they find the machine."

"Ladies, you should wait with the Range Rover." Bones held up a hand.

"Not a chance." Jade glared at the two men. "We've got as much right as you to see this through. Heck, Sofia has more right than any of us. This all started with the Dominion killing her team. Besides, you're probably outgunned, so you'll need all the help you can get."

"Someone needs to be here in case Tam tries to make contact."

"Have you checked your phone lately?" Sofia held up her phone. "We haven't had a signal for hours.

Might as well be a tin can and string."

Dane had had this same argument too many times to count, and not only with Jade, and he'd never won.

"No point in arguing. Let's move."

They found precious little cover as they moved toward the spot where the Hummers were parked, but they arrived without incident. Whoever had gotten here first here hadn't left a lookout. Dane made a cursory inspection of the vehicles. Both were empty, save a Bible lying on the passenger seat of the second vehicle. It wasn't confirmation that it was the Dominion they tracked, but it increased the likelihood. Meanwhile, Bones began tracking their quarry, complaining all the while about stereotypes and racial insensitivity. He identified eight sets of bootprints, probably belonging to men based on their size. As they expected, the tracks led up the rocky slope, part of one of the raised rings that gave the Eye its distinctive appearance.

The way up was easier than Dane had anticipated, with plenty of natural hand and footholds. Jade was a skilled climber in her own right, and Sofia held her own. They experienced a bit of good fortune when, approximately two-thirds of the way up, they came upon a climbing rope affixed to pitons hammered into the rocky face.

"Nice of them to help us up the steepest part." Bones grunted as he heaved his bulk up the rock.

"Putting these in would have slowed them down, at least a few minutes," Dane added. "We'll take any break we can get at this point, no matter how small."

Reaching the top, they fanned out and began searching for the caves that would, they hoped, lead down into the earth and to the fabled lost city. Minutes later, Dane spotted a ledge a few meters below the place where he stood. From this vantage point, only a fraction of it was visible, but his sharp eyes espied it, as well as a scuff mark that might have been made by a boot. He waved the others over and then climbed down for a better look.

Rubble lay scattered across the ledge where someone appeared to have cleared away a rockfall, exposing a dark passageway.

"I think this is it," Dane said.

"How will Tam and the others find us?" Jade looked doubtfully into the dark cave.

Dane considered the question, then took his cell phone out of his pocket and stuck it in a crack in the rock.

"Maybe they can trace it." He made a noncommittal shrug before entering the cave.

A few meters in, the cave floor dropped down at a steep angle before leveling off in a small chamber where three round tunnels converged. Seeing no signs left by the Dominion's agents, they decided to take them one at a time, beginning with the one on the left.

"This is a lava tube." Jade shone her light around the rock-encrusted tube. "And maybe not the most stable one. There are cracks everywhere."

Dane looked up at the fragmented crust coating the tunnel and winced.

"Maybe Bones should walk a little more softly," Sofia said.

"The day a white person teaches me how to walk softly…" Bones began.

"Hello? Latina here."

"Oh. You shut it too."

"I've got an idea," Dane said. "How about we hold it down in case there's a Dominion agent or two waiting around the corner?"

"He's such a killjoy, but I suppose he's right."

Bones checked the safety on his Glock.

The lava tube ended in a wall of rubble, and they were forced to retrace their steps. The second passageway was similarly collapsed a short way in.

"That leaves door number three," Bones said.

They entered the third passageway moving cautiously, not knowing when they might happen upon the Dominion. This lava tube was in a condition similar to the others, with cracks running through the rocks and shattered stones all over the floor, remnants of minor ceiling collapses. More than once, Dane froze when he thought he heard the sound of cracking rock.

"It's held for more than ten thousand years," Jade whispered. "Surely it can last a little longer." She snaked her arm around Dane's waist and gave him a quick squeeze.

"It'll be all right. Just keep moving."

Several anxious minutes later they came to a spot where two tunnels crossed.

"Holy crap." Bones glared at the tunnels as if they'd given offense. "This is going to take forever."

"Now I see how Atlantis could have gone undiscovered for all this time," Sofia said. "It's in an unlikely location, the cave was hard to find, and even if a local were to stumble upon it, they could wander around down here forever without ever finding anything of interest."

"And I'll bet you need a crystal to get inside." Dane thought of the door to the Hall of Records and what Tam had told him about the entrance to the vault beneath the Jefferson Memorial.

"You figure the Dominion will blast their way in?" Bones asked.

Before anyone could reply, a deafening explosion rocked the ground beneath their feet. Dane covered his head as chunks of ceiling began to fall.

"Which tunnel did it come from?" Bones cried, dodging a chunk of rock.

Dane looked around and saw dust drifting out of the nearest tunnel. "That one. Come on!" He grabbed Jade by the arm and ran, Bones and Sofia hot on their heels.

As they ducked into the lava tube, the ceiling continued to crash down. They kept running along the curving passageway, the sound of falling rock loud in their ears. Finally, when they heard no sound except that of their own feet pounding the floor, they stopped to catch their breath.

"What's your plan, Maddock?" Bones shone his light back the way they had come. The tunnel behind them had completely collapsed. They were trapped.

"We do the only thing we can. Keep going."

CHAPTER 47

"I don't understand." Robinson nudged a silver box with his foot. "In most ways this place is primitive, but some of the things we're finding seem advanced— alien, even."

"Do not make assumptions. I am sure all will be made clear in time." Hadel kept his voice calm, though his mind was in turmoil.

In searching for Atlantis, he'd expected to find the remains of an ancient, human civilization, one that had perhaps stumbled across a previously unknown, yet terrestrial, power, and the discovery of the crystal-powered weapon seemed to confirm that, but now, he was not so certain.

It was true that there was an ancient world feeling about this place—every passageway or chamber they passed through thus far had been a natural formation or a room carved from stone. No one else seemed to notice that those rooms were carved with more precision than even the most advanced of the ancient stone masons. And their shapes were... off—the angles not quite square, the ceilings undulating, rather than flat. The deeper they'd penetrated into Atlantis, the more uneasy he felt. This place felt... wrong.

They entered another of these disorientingly-skewed rooms and Hadel felt his insides twist into knots as his mind sought to resolve what he saw into a normal picture. Here, the walls were hive-like, with oval pockets carved everywhere. It appeared to be a storage room of some kind, with clay pots and jars in some, and more alien-looking objects of various size and shape in others.

"I don't like this place," Robinson muttered under his breath.

Hadel turned an angry glare on Robinson, who did not wither under the Bishop's stare as so many of his underlings might have. It wasn't that he disagreed with the statement. It was the way Robinson gave voice to Hadel's own fears that annoyed him.

The artifacts, the crystals on the wall that absorb light and pass it along. What if they're dangerous?" Robinson asked.

"Some of them are likely to be dangerous," Hadel said. "That is why we are here, is it not? To find the Revelation Machine so that we may complete our work."

"Yes, but with so many things down here we don't understand, maybe we should take you somewhere safe, and then the men and I can come back here and complete the search."

"Is this a coup? Do you want to control the Revelation Machine?" Hadel snapped. He'd never have believed Robinson capable of such machinations.

The blood drained from Robinson's face. "Of course not. I only meant that we're expendable. You're essential."

"Very well." Hadel forced a smile and struggled to calm his nerves. Where had that flash of paranoia come from? Robinson had always been one of his most loyal lieutenants.

Somewhere in the distance, a shot rang out. Robinson froze, listening. After a few seconds, he turned to Hadel. "That must be Thomas. He wouldn't fire unless he had reason."

"Whatever is happening at the door, these men can see to it." Hadel inclined his head toward the five operatives who trailed behind them. "You and I will find the Revelation Machine."

It took one shot to eliminate the guard posted in front of the door to Atlantis. Dane kept his Walther at the ready as he crept forward, keeping his eyes peeled for more enemies.

"Nice shot," Bones whispered. "Next one is mine."

Dane relieved the guard of his AK-47 and paused to examine the remains of the door to Atlantis. The Dominion had blasted a hole in it large enough for a person to crawl through, but most of it still remained— a stone block half a meter thick, twice his height and nearly as wide. Like the door to the Hall of Records, someone had carved Orion into the stone.

"I could be wrong, but I'm beginning to think Orion is important," Bones said.

Dane ignored him. He climbed through the hole, and waited for the others to join him. They were still in a lava tube, but here, the floor was perfectly level. Up ahead, the passageway shone with opalescent light.

"That looks familiar." Dane shone his light on an opaque, diamond-shaped crystal. As soon as the beam struck the crystal, the surface swirled, and the light became brighter and more iridescent, gaining in strength until the passageway shone as bright as day. It set off a chain reaction as crystals further down the hall absorbed and amplified the light.

"I've never seen anything like this," Sofia marveled.

"We have," Dane and Bones said in unison.

Dane thought back on all places he and Bones had been and the things they had seen in the past few years: so many devices, and even weapons, powered by crystals, the powers of some of which were nothing short of miraculous. Was Atlantis the source of it all?

"Looks like there's a room up ahead." Bones raised the AK-47 to his shoulder and took the lead as they moved along the silent corridor.

A low wall barred entry to the first chamber, which was empty.

"Maybe it's a guard room?" Jade offered.

"Makes sense. All I know is, it's weird." The room was almost square, the walls almost perpendicular, but off just enough to give Dane a feeling of discomfort. The arched, ribbed ceiling bulged in places, and the center line not quite straight.

"It's like we were swallowed by a snake," Bones said.

"All I know is, looking at it makes me dizzy." Jade rubbed her eyes. "Let's get out of here."

Up ahead, the lava tube ended, with a passageway running off to either side. They chose the one on the right, and found it to be cut at the same, not quite square, angles.

"Don't look at the walls," Dane said. "Keep your focus straight ahead and you won't feel so dizzy." Taking his own advice, he locked his gaze on the way ahead, and they soon found themselves in a much larger, if no less disorienting, room than the previous one. What they found stopped them all in their tracks.

The walls were covered in maps and star charts, cut with such precision that they could not have been made with primitive tools. Running all around the base of the walls, like a giant honeycomb, a waist-high band of meter-wide, hexagonal cubes held stacks of stone tablets. Stone benches ringed a table in the center, where more tablets lay, as well as a few crystals and an object that looked like a titanium pencil.

"This is their archive!" Sofia picked up one of the stone tablets at random and examined it. "The writing is the same as in the codex I found in Spain. I'll bet," she looked around, eyes as big as saucers, "the whole story of Atlantis is here. What might we learn about human history once we translate them?"

"I think we'll find that the Atlanteans, at least the original ones, came from somewhere out there." Bones pointed to a star chart. "Probably from a planet orbiting one of the stars in Orion."

"Five years ago, I would have laughed at you," Dane said. "But it makes sense. Remember Goliath's sword?"

"How could I forget?"

"If you guys are going to reminisce about things we weren't there for, you really ought to give us a bit more information." Sofia sounded affronted.

"It's a long story. Actually, it's several long stories." Dane wondered how long it would take to recount their exploits of the past few years.

"I've heard bits and pieces of them from Avery. Just hit the highlights."

Dane paused, considering how to sum it all up. "We've found things made of metal that didn't come from earth. We've found things powered by crystals that could do things that were so advanced that they seemed like magic… or very advanced technology."

"Like the tsunami machine and the gun," Sofia said.

Bones nodded. "That and more. An almost perfect cloaking device, a blade that could cut through stone, spears that fired bolts of energy, and all of them were powered by ambient light. And that's not even all of the things we've seen."

"And we found them in different places: Jordan, Germany, England, Ireland, even America." Dane looked around as he spoke. "Looking at these maps, and taking into account the book Tam and Avery found, I think it's a reasonable assumption that this is where it all started."

"They had knowledge of the entire world," Jade said. "Every continent is mapped accurately."

"Some people believe that the great accomplishments of the ancient world were made possible by contact with aliens," Bones said. "But that's definitely a story for another day."

"I know you'd like to stay here and begin your studies," Dane said, "but we should keep moving. I want to catch up with the Dominion before they get their hands on the Revelation Machine."

They left the library and entered a crypt. Skeletal remains filled alcoves in the walls. They were tall and slim, their arms too long for their bodies and their fingers too long for their hands. Their heads were overlarge, the skulls elongated, and their eye sockets large and round.

"These look like... aliens," Sofia breathed.

"Another thing we've seen before," Dane said. "We..."

A thunder of gunfire cut him off in mid-sentence. Sofia's body jerked as a torrent of bullets ripped through her. Dane knew in an instant there was no hope.

Jade dove behind one of the stone benches while Dane and Bones took shelter behind the table and returned fire. Dane saw a Dominion operative fall, clutching his throat, and felt a wave of satisfaction.

"You two duck out the back!" Bones shouted. "I'll cover you." Not waiting for a reply, he opened up with the AK-47.

Dane grabbed Jade by the back of her belt, hauled her to her feet, and shoved her toward the exit beneath the world map. Bullets spattered the ground at their feet as they fled.

"Keep going!" Dane shouted. "We'll catch up."

Jade looked up at him, tears streaming down her face and grabbed his collar. "You kill them, Maddock. she rasped, her voice husky. "Kill them all."

"I'll try."

Jade yanked down on his collar and kissed him, hard and fast, and then turned and ran.

Dane heard Bones' AK-47 fall silent and hurried back to the doorway.

"Your turn, Bones!" Dane emptied his Walther while Bones, ducking down as low as his frame would allow, ran for it.

More shots rang out as Bones dove for the tunnel, hit the ground and rolled, and came up in a kneeling position. He squeezed off two shots with his Glock.

"I've got one reload left. How about you?"

"Same here." Dane ejected the magazine and reached into his pocket for a reload.

"Don't bother," said a cold voice. "Now, turn around slowly or the girl dies."

(HAPTER 48

Jade stood, hands on her head, her lips pressed tightly together. She trembled slightly, but the fire in her eyes told Dane she wasn't frightened, but enraged. A tall, weedy blond man stood behind her with his rifle pressed against the back of her neck. A second man, dark-haired and broad shouldered, trained his weapon on Dane and Bones.

"You two drop your weapons, put your hands on your heads, and stand up slowly." The dark-haired man gestured with his rifle.

Dane assessed the situation in an instant and knew there was nothing he or Bones could do without Jade paying the price. Charging the men or throwing their knives was out of the question—the distance between them was too great and retreating to the archive room wouldn't work. The men would kill Jade and probably get to Dane and Bones before they could reload their weapons. And then there were the men coming up behind them. He dropped his Walther and stood, Bones following suit an instant later.

"Don't hurt her. We'll cooperate." His only hope was to stay alive long enough to rescue Jade and, hopefully, sabotage the Revelation Machine.

"I'm sorry, Maddock. I didn't see them until I ran right up to them," Jade said through gritted teeth.

"It's all right."

He heard footsteps behind him, and felt the cold metal of a gun barrel pressed against his neck.

"Wilson, they got Douglas," a voice behind him said to the dark-haired man. "I think we should waste them right here."

"I don't know. I think the Bishop should make the call. Frisk them. And if you two," Wilson's eyes moved back and forth between Dane and Bones, "do anything stupid, I'll kill you in a second. The girl, I'll kill slowly."

The agent patted them down one at a time, relieving them of their recon knives and spare magazines. When he got to Dane's front pocket, he paused.

"I'm not your type," Dane said.

Ignoring him, the agent reached into Dane's pocket and drew out the pouch that held the Atlantean crystals. He tossed the bag to Wilson, who upended the contents into his hand. He held the crystals out, letting the light dance off their surface.

"What do these do?"

"I found them on the floor and thought I'd add them to my rock collection." Pain blossomed through Dane's skull as the man behind him struck him at the base of his skull with the butt of his rifle. Dane grimaced but didn't fall or even cry out.

Smiling, Wilson pocketed the crystals.

"We'll take you to the Bishop. If, by the time we get there, you haven't decided to come clean, we'll cut pieces off of your girl until you tell us what we want to know."

Dane and Bones exchanged glances. Bishop Hadel was here? Dane made up his mind then. If he decided escape was impossible, he'd find a way to kill Hadel.

The Dominion's operatives escorted them, at gunpoint, through the Atlantean complex. They passed through empty rooms and others where alien-looking artifacts lay on shelves or in the strange, hexagonal alcoves. This place would be a treasure trove of information if they could ever get away, but Dane scarcely considered the thought. Rage burned hot inside him. His failure to protect Jade and Sofia was almost more than he could bear.

Bishop Hadel stood in the midst of a massive chamber—the largest they'd seen since entering the underground city. Dane took in his surroundings. This room was clearly the model for the Atlantean temples they'd discovered. It had the same exact layout as the others, down to the pyramid-shaped facade at the back. But it was what stood at the center that separated it from the other sites they'd uncovered.

A circle of crystal spikes, each twice a man's height and breadth and tilted inward so that their points almost touched, stood behind a ring of gleaming silver metal reminiscent of the Stonehenge-like altars in the temples. A silver hand, its palm open, rose from the altar.

The bishop paced back and forth, staring at the crystals.

Another man, large and powerfully-built, stood nearby. He turned his gaze on Dane and Bones as they entered the room. His green eyes bored into Dane.

"Who are these people?" he snapped.

Before anyone could reply, Bishop Hadel turned on his heel and stalked toward the captives. His hands trembled and there was a gleam in his eyes that bordered on manic. Dane had seen Hadel on television and in pictures, but the man always seemed so calm and self-assured. What he'd seen down here had unhinged him.

"I know who they are." Hadel's voice shook. "The Indian is Uriah Bonebrake, which makes this one," he pointed a trembling finger at Dane, "Dane Maddock."

He lowered his voice. "You two have a knack for stepping on my toes. I ordered you killed months ago, but we couldn't locate you. And now, here you are." He laughed, a cold cackle that echoed in the stone chamber. "Did you imagine you would stop us from setting off the Revelation Machine?"

Dane glowered at him, but remained silent. If Hadel planned to set off the machine, the situation was worse than he had feared. Of course, now that he saw the device, if that's what this crystal circle was, he realized it wasn't something that could be carried away. If Hadel wanted to use it, he'd have to do it here.

"Bishop," Wilson began, "he had these with him."

The bishop took the pouch containing the Atlantean stones, looked inside, and smiled. "I think we now have what we need." He leaned in close to Dane until their faces were inches apart. "Are you ready to die?"

Dane didn't speak, didn't think. Instead, he head-butted Hadel across the bridge of the nose.

Hadel cried out in pain and reeled away, his hands unable to hold back the crimson flow that streamed down his chin and dripped onto the stone floor.

Behind him, the Dominion operative clubbed Dane across the back of his head with the butt of his rifle. Dane dropped to one knee, his head swimming. Hadel was about to use the machine. What could he do?

The big, green-eyed man hurried to Hadel's side, but the bishop shook him off.

"I'm fine, Robinson. Just keep an eye on these three in case they try anything else." His broken nose still dripping blood, he turned and headed for the machine.

"Shall I kill them?" Robinson asked.

"No. Let them see it happen. I want them to feel

their failure deep in their bones before they die."

"With all due respect," Robinson said, "I don't think we should try the machine until we're certain of what it does."

Hadel turned a beatific smile in Robinson's direction. "I know what it does. It will bring about the end of times, as promised in the Book of Revelation."

Robinson swallowed hard. "I understand, but we should learn to control it before we use it."

"Control? You do not presume to control the power of God."

Dane's vision cleared and he noticed the guards behind Jade and Bones shift uncomfortably. The time was drawing near and the only possible action would be desperate and likely fatal. Of course, if Hadel discharged the machine, the result would be the same. As Dane planned his last, desperate attack, Hadel continued to rant.

"You saw what lies in this place. Abominations! The earth must be cleansed of this filth."

Robinson tried to argue but Hadel went on.

"This world has become an abomination. Our faith is persecuted daily as people bow to the altars of science and government. Imagine what the idolaters would make of what we've found here. They would use it as *evidence*," he spat the word, "against the truth of our Lord." His voice fell to a hoarse grunt. "Better they die in the Lord than live in confusion."

The bishop turned again and, as he approached the machine, the crystals in his hand began to flicker. He knelt before the machine and began to recite the Lord's Prayer.

"Robinson?" one of the guards said.

"Stand firm." Robinson ordered. "He is about the Lord's work."

Hadel laid a gleaming crystal in the silver hand rising from the altar. It snapped into place and began to glow. Behind the rail, the giant crystals that formed the machine also began to glow.

High above, unnoticed by anyone except Dane, crystals set in the stone began to glimmer as Hadel laid more crystals into place. With each one, the machine shone brighter and the crystals in the ceiling sparkled.

Soon, Dane recognized their shape. He took another glance in the direction of the machine, and then back up at the crystals in the ceiling. He now understood the machine's purpose.

As the bishop made to place the last stone, Dane stole a glance at Bones and Jade. Their eyes met and he mouthed instructions. He didn't know for certain if they understood, because, just then, the last crystal clicked into place and the world exploded in blue light.

CHAPTER 49

"Where the hell are you, Maddock?" Tam stood, hands on hips, staring at the small hotel that stood in the middle of the Richat Structure. They'd found plenty of footprints and tire tracks, but no sign of Maddock or the others. Until they'd arrived, she hadn't appreciated how vast this place was. "I shouldn't have sent him in ahead of us."

She looked up as Greg and Professor emerged from the hotel.

"There's a body inside," Greg said, "but no sign of our people."

"Do you think they were here?" Tam asked.

Greg shrugged. "No way to tell."

"Damn! If Willis and Matt don't find any sign of them, I guess we'll follow the tire tracks and hope it's them." Tam sighed. "And that's another dollar in the jar, too. Working with those two is going to break me."

Willis and Matt appeared a few minutes later, looking sweaty and frustrated.

"We didn't find nothing." Willis cast an angry glance in the direction from which they'd come. "I don't know where those boys got off too."

"We'll have to keep looking." Tam turned toward their vehicle, where Corey sat, pecking away at his laptop. "Any luck tracing their cellphones?"

"No signal out here," Corey said. "You should have issued satellite phones."

Tam bit off her reply as the ground began to tremble.

"What the hell is that?" Willis scanned the horizon.

"Somebody drop a bomb?"

A low rumble resounded from somewhere deep beneath the earth, and with it the ground shook even more violently. Tam staggered and grabbed hold of Willis' arm for support.

A column of brilliant, blue light shot up from the ground, consuming the hotel. Tam shielded her eyes from the blinding light. Oddly, it generated no heat, but she felt as if every hair on her body were standing on end. It went on for the span of ten heartbeats, and then stopped without warning.

"What in the name of Jesus?" she muttered, blinking the spots out of her eyes.

"It was like a beam of pure energy." Professor's face was ashen. "It went straight up into space, almost like a…"

"Like what?" Tam asked.

"Like a beacon." He turned his eyes up to the sky. "You know, like the way researchers send messages into space, hoping to make contact with alien life."

Tam's breath caught in her throat. She remembered Tyson's words. *"…prepare for the return."* Could this be what he meant? Was the so-called Revelation Machine designed to send a message into space? No, she couldn't even contemplate that right now. They still needed to find Maddock and the others.

"Tam, look at this," Greg called.

Where the hotel once stood, a shaft, perfectly round and smooth, plunged deep into the ground. She joined Greg at its edge.

"The stone seems to have melted away, but it's cool to the touch." He ran his fingers along the inside of the shaft to demonstrate.

"Dissolved is more like it," Professor added. "How is that possible?"

"We can figure that out later," Tam said. "Look at what's down there."

Down at the bottom of the shaft, a circle of crystals flickered in the darkness. Tam's sharp eyes could just make out a metallic ring around the crystals. It had to be the Revelation Machine, which meant there was a good chance that was where they'd find Maddock.

Or the Dominion.

CHAPTER 50

When Bishop Hadel placed the last crystal into place, Dane closed his eyes and shielded them with his hands. The surprised cries from the Dominion's agents told him he'd guessed correctly.

He spun about and struck at the Dominion agent, who had been rendered temporarily blind by the brilliant light from the Revelation Machine. His fist connected solidly with the man's chin. His legs turned to rubber and Dane kicked him in the temple on the way down. Beside him, Bones had eliminated his guard with ruthless efficiency, and now closed in on the agent who guarded Jade. She, too had understood Dane's plan, and now grappled with the man for control of his AK-47.

Dane turned and made a dash for Robinson, who squinted against the bright light and looked around for a target on which to bring his weapon to bear. He reached Robinson, drove his shoulder into Robinson's chest, and knocked his rifle barrel upward just as the man squeezed the trigger, sending bullets ricocheting through the chamber.

Like a football player hitting the blocking sled, Dane drove the larger man backward. Surprised, Robinson lost his grip on his rifle, stumbled backward, and hit the rail. For a moment, he struggled to regain his balance, but Dane drove a sidekick into Robinson's chest, sending him toppling backward.

Robinson's head struck the nearest crystal and a blue aura engulfed him. His body jerked, his mouth twisted in a silent scream of anguish. His hair blackened and crumbled to dust in an instant. Even after the burst of energy ceased, Robinson continued to thrash about like a fish on dry land.

Slowly, the crystals dimmed, flickered, and died. It felt like an eternity, but Dane knew the phenomenon couldn't have lasted much more than ten seconds. He looked around and saw Bones hauling a whimpering Bishop Hadel to his feet. Jade hurried to him and crushed him in a tight embrace.

"Are you all right?"

"I'm fine." He gently extracted himself from her arms. "You okay, Bones?"

"Hell yes. I almost fell asleep waiting for you to decide what to do."

Dane recovered their weapons from the fallen Dominion operatives and assessed the situation. The men who had guarded Bones and Jade lay dead, while the man Dane had taken out wobbled on hands and knees as he slowly regained consciousness. Dane gave him another kick to the head and then bound him with his own belt.

Still holding on to Hadel, Bones glanced up at the ceiling, where the blast had carved a perfect circle where the apex of the temple had been moments earlier. "I saw you looking up there. What did you see?"

"Orion." Dane pointed at the remaining crystals. "Most of it's gone, but you can still see his bow. His belt lay centered at the top of the ceiling and the crystals were pointed right at it. It just didn't seem like a weapon to me. With all we've seen, the connections to Orion, I just had a feeling."

"You think Hadel just sent a signal to the aliens?" Bones asked. "I should have thought of that myself."

"I don't know. If we assume the Atlanteans came from a planet orbiting a star in Orion, he picked the wrong time of day. Orion won't be overhead for several hours yet."

"But signals sent into space will diffuse over great distances," Jade said. "They might get the message someday."

Hadel, who stood stock-still next to Bones, his nose still dripping blood, slumped to the ground. "No," he whispered.

"Seriously, dude? You kill thousands of people and don't bat an eye, but make one little call to E.T. and you lose it?"

"You don't understand what will happen if the people find out..."

"Find out what? The truth?" Dane said. "People are resilient. How about putting a little faith in them instead of in your twisted version of God?"

"People are sheep. They must be shown the way, else they stray into peril."

"After all the people you've killed, you're going to talk about keeping them from peril?" Dane clenched his fists and, with a supreme effort of will, stopped himself from decking the man.

"Better a temporal death than an eternal one." The madness now receded from Hadel's eyes. Now a crafty grin spread across his face as he rose to his feet. "Besides, I have killed no one."

"Neither did Hitler," Dane retorted, "but you're responsible for every killing done by your minions. For Sofia Perez, for the people of Norfolk and Key West, and all the others."

"Key West?" Hadel forced a laugh. "A modern day Sodom. I was proud to give the order."

"I'd watch what I say about Sodom," Bones cautioned, "considering where you're headed. We work for the government now, and I can guarantee you our boss will find you an affectionate cellmate to comfort you in your declining years."

Hadel blanched. "You'll never get a conviction. The government can't hope to match the attorneys I have at my disposal."

"Who says you'll be going to trial?"

Dane turned to see Tam, in rappelling gear, lowering herself to the floor. A few seconds later, Willis and Greg followed.

"Where's Matt?" Dane asked.

"Watching our backs with Professor. They weren't happy about it but I couldn't trust nerd boy to do it by himself."

"What do you mean I won't be going to trial?" Hadel demanded.

"Shush!" Tam held up a finger, silencing him. She turned in a slow circle, taking in the chamber. "Lord Jesus. So this is it."

"This is just a tiny bit of it," Jade said. "There's a library, a crypt, and all sorts of chambers. Lots of Atlantean instruments and devices, too."

"It would take years, maybe even decades, to glean all the knowledge from this place," Dane said. "But I don't think that's a good idea."

"We've had this conversation before, Maddock, and my opinion hasn't changed any more than yours has. Technology can be dangerous, but I'd rather have it in our hands than in those of an enemy." Tam paused. "Where's Sofia?"

Dane tried to answer, but his mouth was sandpaper and emotion held his throat in a chokehold. He felt Jade's hand on his shoulder.

"The Dominion got her." Bones voice was as tight as his fists, which he clenched so hard that his arms trembled.

"Damn." Tam put her hands on her hips, took a deep breath, and composed herself.

And then she whirled and drove her fist into Hadel's gut. His breath left him in a rush and he slumped over. Tam grabbed a handful of his unkempt hair, kicked his feet out from under him, leaned down, and whispered in his ear. "I'll tell you why you won't be getting a trial any time soon, if ever. First of all, I don't plan on letting anyone know we've got you. We'll let them think you're dead while you rot away in Guantanamo Bay. And then we'll label you an enemy combatant."

"It won't stick." Hadel grunted. "I'm a citizen. I have rights."

"That's okay, sweetie. By then, I'll have taken my pound of flesh and squeezed every last secret out of you. The Dominion will be dead. Broken. Have fun using a public defender to fight charges of high treason, murder, and whatever else we can think of throwing at you."

"You have to let me go. You have no choice."

"I don't think so." Tam yanked Hadel to his feet. "Greg, bind this fool. And don't be gentle."

Greg pulled out a pair of cable ties and grabbed Hadel by the wrist.

"Do you think I would let my plan, my purpose, die without me? If, at any point, twenty four hours pass without my people hearing from me, or if they learn I have been captured, the failsafe is activated. One city every forty-eight hours. Can you let that happen?" Hadel winced as Greg yanked his arms behind his back and bound his wrists.

"We'll stop you." Only a slight twitch in her cheek belied Tam's resolve.

"How? You don't know where the next attack will

be, and the Atlantean weapon can be hidden on any boat. You can't guard every inch of the American coastline. Then again, perhaps your hubris is so great that you believe exactly that."

Dane thought Tam might punch Hadel again, but she smiled instead. "You're going to tell me where the next attack will take place."

"You *are* an arrogant little girl." Hadel had regained some of his bluster, if not his self-assurance.

"Or you will tell Bonebrake." Tam turned to Bones. "You and Willis take our guest somewhere out of sight of us witnesses and teach him some of your traditional interrogation techniques."

"What?" Hadel gasped.

"Can I just scalp him?" Bones drew his Recon knife and licked the blade.

"If that don't work, I got some tricks I can show you." Willis bared his teeth and mimicked biting Hadel's face.

"I don't care," Tam said. "Just make it slow and make it hurt. For Sofia."

Bones and Greg hauled Hadel, who struggled and hurled racial epithets at them, into one of the passageways leading out of the chamber.

Dane watched them go, wishing he could feel good about this turn of events, but unable to put Sofia's death out of his mind. "You do realize Bones doesn't know any kind of Indian torture methods, unless you want him to wear Hadel down with juvenile banter."

"I know that and you know that, but Hadel doesn't know that." Tam gave him a wink and then turned to Greg.

"As long as we're waiting, I'd like to check out the alcove back there." Jade pointed to the small room on the far side of the chamber.

In the other Atlantean temples, the small room was the adyton, a place exclusive to priests. Here, it served a very different purpose.

A tall, impossibly thin man with an elongated head lay perfectly preserved in a coffin of blue-tinted crystal. Jade gasped and Greg took a step back, but not Dane and Tam, who had seen something like this only months before.

"There's another connection," Dane said.

"I wonder who he was." Jade moved in for a closer look.

Dane took in the sight. The man had long greenish-brown hair and beard, wore sea green robes and a silver crown inset with mother of pearl and topped by the largest shark's teeth Dane had ever seen. His long, slender hands gripped a crystal tipped…

…trident.

"Poseidon."

The name hung in the air while the others struggled to reconcile this alien being with the god out of Greek mythology. Tam finally broke the silence.

"You're saying the Greek gods were real? Or, at least, this one was?"

"I'm saying I think this guy was the source of the Poseidon myth. He was important enough that his was the only body they preserved. I'll bet he was the Atlantean ruler, which is why he's represented in their temples, though in a form to which humans could relate. Think about it. The Atlanteans' alien appearance and their advanced technology would have made them seem godlike to primitive humans. I wouldn't be surprised if other Atlantean leaders provided the inspiration for other ancient world myths, legends, and gods."

Tam turned and hurried away. She stopped,

dropped to one knee, and rested her hands on the rail that encircled the Revelation Machine. Her shoulders heaved and her head drooped.

"I'd better check on her." Jade took a few steps toward her before Dane laid a hand on her shoulder.

"No, let me. I've spent more time than you coming to grips with this stuff." He hurried to Tam's side and knelt down beside her. When she didn't tell him to leave, he took her hand and gave it a squeeze. "It's okay."

"How is it okay? Everything I've believed all my life isn't true. Adam and Eve were aliens? All the miracle stories are just advanced technology from another world? What does that mean for the world if there's no more power of God to believe in? If it's all a lie?"

"Never underestimate the power of denial." At Tam's angry frown, he hurried on. "Seriously, though. Some might lose faith, and many didn't believe in the first place, but others will hold on. Heck, in some cases, it might even make their faith stronger. These crystals, they're miracles. The Atlanteans harnessed their power, but where did that power come from? And maybe the Atlanteans did intervene in human history, but that doesn't explain where humans come from or where Atlanteans come from, for that matter."

"It's not enough. An awful lot of people need to believe in the power of God, and in spite of all that we've seen, I need to believe it."

Dane hesitated. He'd lost his religion when his wife died, but honesty compelled him to go on. "You know Bones and I did some serious damage in Utah a few years back, but do you know what we found down there?"

Tam shook her head.

"It's too long a story to tell you right now, but I

promise you, it will restore your faith. Not only did we find treasures from out of the Old Testament, we experienced something that couldn't be explained by crystals or advanced technology. It was miraculous."

"I want to believe you," Tam said.

"Ask Jade and Bones. We all saw it."

"Ask me what?" Bones emerged from the hallway holding a pencil.

"Never you mind." Tam composed herself in an instant and sprang to her feet. "What did you find out?"

"New York City. It's hidden inside an Ellis Island tour boat."

"How can you be sure he's not lying?" Tam asked.

"Because, once he confessed, I cut the tips of his thumbs off just to make sure he kept his story straight."

"You didn't!" Jade gasped.

"Of course not, but he believed I would, so it amounted to the same thing. Besides, I don't think he could have given so many specific details under duress. Willis hung back with him to do some fact checking, but I think we've got what we need to know." He recounted the specifics of the Dominion's plan, and Tam sent Greg back to the surface to report this new information.

"You think they'll believe you this time?" Dane asked.

"Oh yes. Issuing that public ultimatum had to be the stupidest thing the Dominion has ever done. Hadel must have thought he had the Revelation Machine in the bag. When that announcement came out, a lot of people started taking me seriously. They'll come down on those operatives in New York like a hard rain."

They took a minute to fill Bones in on their final

discovery and on Dane's theory. Having long supported the theory that aliens intervened in the ancient world, Bones agreed with all of Dane's conclusions and proclaimed himself vindicated.

"From now on, Maddock, no more calling my theories 'crackpot,' okay?"

"No promises, Bones."

"What I want to know," Jade piped up, "is how you got Hadel to confess in the first place."

"Easy. I gave him time to get nervous and then I asked Willis for a pencil, a light, and some flammable liquid. I was just messing with Hadel's head, figuring I'd let his imagination run wild before I tried something less exotic, but Willis actually had a pencil on him. He said he's taken up Sudoku."

"And?" Jade asked.

"I showed Hadel how a pencil can be used to stretch open any orifice." He illustrated by placing the pencil between the corners of his mouth. "And then," he said around the pencil before spitting it out onto the floor, "I pulled out my Zippo, bent Hadel over, and pulled down his..."

"Okay, I get the picture." Jade covered her ears and turned away, but not fast enough to hide her smile.

"What happens now?" Dane asked Tam.

"We take the Bishop and any of the operatives you left alive into custody for enhanced interrogation."

"They can have my pencil if they need it," Bones offered.

Tam rolled her eyes. "Our embassy is already negotiating for us to have unfettered access to this area for research purposes. As soon as Greg reports in, we'll have men on the way to secure the site, just to be safe. That blast will have drawn attention. Right now, I imagine scientists all over the world are trying to figure out what in the hell happened. We need to clean this place out before there's an international incident."

"So there's no way we could keep it a secret even if we wanted to," Dane said.

Tam shook her head.

"Like it or not, you've changed the world, boys. Let's just hope it's for the better."

CHAPTER 51

"We're going to need another keg!" Bones proclaimed as he handed Corey a cup of beer. "That's the last of this one."

Corey frowned at the mound of foam in his blue cup. "That's all I get?"

"I'll check the kitchen. Maddock hasn't re-stocked his frig, but I think Professor brought a cooler. It's probably Bud Light or something else crappy." Bones wobbled back inside and reappeared with a cheap Styrofoam cooler. "Perfect. A cheap cooler for cheap beer."

"I happen to like Bud Light." Professor sat with his feet propped up on the rail, gazing out at the Gulf. "Besides, I'm not a highly-paid government employee like you."

"You will be if you take Tam's offer." Dane turned a questioning look at Jade, who shrugged.

"I'm thinking about it, but it's been a long time since I've had bullets flying in my direction. I'm not sure I want to go back."

"Hey, if I can handle it, so can you." Kasey had been out of the hospital for one day, and had foregone the beer due to the painkillers she was taking while she recovered from her wounds, but she'd managed to put away more ribs than Dane would have thought possible for a woman of her size.

Dane leaned against the rail and bathed in the warmth of the sun and the sounds of revelry. They'd spent the early part of the afternoon filling in Kasey and Avery on all that had transpired since they'd left for Mauritania. Kasey had bemoaned the injuries that put her out of action, while Avery took some consolation in finally having an adventure of her own to share with the others. Tam had already told them about the discovery of the Templar library, but Dane and the others listened in rapt attention as if the story were brand new to them. By the time Tam arrived with a box of polo-style shirts embroidered with a Spartan helmet and the words "Myrmidon Squad" over the breast, they'd finished swapping stories. They shared a drink in Sofia's memory, and then let the Dos Equis do its work.

Inside, Greg pounded out an Irish drinking song on his portable keyboard, while Willis, Tam, and Avery sang along. Where a kid from inner-city Detroit had learned an Irish song, Dane had no idea, but the sound washed over him in a pleasant way and he allowed his mind to drift.

It had been a week since they'd uncovered the Atlantean mother city. Tam had shut down the Dominion's plot to attack New York City before it got off the ground, and even managed to get Krueger back in one piece, if a bit worse for the wear. Meanwhile, the U.S. Government had pulled enough strings, or greased enough palms, to buy time for its researchers to go over the complex with a fine-tooth comb. Working around the clock, they'd removed everything they could—even the remains of the Atlanteans. Soon, they'd reveal their discovery to the rest of the world.

For what felt like the thousandth time, Dane wondered how people would respond. Although most of the trappings of alien technology, and all of the alien remains were gone, the star charts and engravings on the walls remained, as did the Revelation Machine. As expected, the world had taken notice of the massive blast of energy shooting up into the heavens, and the absurd claim by the American and Mauritanian governments that it was part of a joint experiment in solar energy, would soon be put to lie.

He supposed it didn't matter. It was out of his hands now.

"I swear, you think longer and harder than any man I've ever known."

Dane was surprised to discover that he and Tam were now alone on the deck.

"Long and hard. That's me."

"That's unworthy of you, Maddock."

"You spend enough time around Bones, he starts rubbing off on you." Dane offered her a seat and then sat down next to her.

"I like your place. If we keep our headquarters here, I guess I'll need to invest in some real-estate myself." She smiled as a pair of seagulls drifted past them, floating on an updraft.

"I'm surprised the squad's staying together now that we've shut down the Dominion."

"We've shut down the Kingdom church, but there's plenty still to do. And that's only here in the States. Or have you forgotten your Heilig Herrschaft friends?"

Dane frowned. He, in fact, hadn't spared a thought for the German branch of the Dominion.

"On top of that," Tam continued, "there are definitely elements in Italy, and we've got hints of them in a dozen other places. I'll be chasing them down until I'm old and gray. Plus, there's the Trident to investigate. Lord only knows what they're about."

"I'm never going to be free of my obligation to you, am I?"

"Baby, you can leave any time your conscience

allows it." Tam paused and ran a finger through the condensation on her cup of beer. "That's not fair of me. You've more than repaid me for the help I gave you. If you want to be free, I won't stand in your way." She stood and moved to the rail, where she perched on the corner and turned her gaze on Dane. "But I wish you'd stay, and that goes for the rest of your crew. Even Bones. We've got a good team here, and I want you to remain part of it. Not just for what you can do, but because you keep me honest. You challenge me without being insubordinate, and you make me think."

"I thought I just pissed you off."

Tam smiled and raised her beer. "Cheers."

Dane returned the salute. "I'll think about it."

"That's all I ask." Tam slid down off the rail and gave him a quick hug. "I think somebody else wants to talk to you." She glanced to the doorway where Jade waited. "Tag. You're it."

Jade took up the spot Tam had occupied moments before. She sat there, chewing her lip and not quite meeting Dane's eye, while Dane finished his beer and tossed the cup in a half-filled garbage bag at his feet.

"I don't know the right way to say this," Jade began, "so I'm going to dive in. Just don't interrupt me, okay?"

Dane nodded. He knew how Jade felt about being interrupted and it was never pretty.

"You don't want to spend your life fighting the Dominion. You're more than capable, but that's not your passion. You're a treasure hunter at heart. There's nothing in the world you love more than finding a mystery from the past and solving it. And that's what drives me, too. We're perfect for each other. I love to dive and climb and I love Archaeology, maybe more than you do. Yes, we drive each other crazy sometimes, and we even fight, but so what? That's because we're passionate. I'll bet you never fight with Angel."

Dane was about to correct that misconception when he remembered he'd agreed not to interrupt.

"Let's do it, Maddock. Let's spend the rest of our lives solving mysteries and making discoveries. Someone else can dodge bullets. You've done your time." She lapsed into silence, her eyes boring into his. After a suitable pause, he decided it was safe to talk.

"I can't imagine how Bones would react if I broke up with Angel and brought you on to the crew."

"That's not a reason to stay with someone, and you know it. Besides, didn't Bones just dump your sister? It would be awkward, but we'd get through it. It wouldn't be the first time he and I were at loggerheads."

Dane didn't have an answer. He couldn't remember ever being so confused.

Jade came and knelt before him. She took his head in her hands and drew his face close to hers. The familiar scent of jasmine was strong in his nostrils and her eyes, deep dark pools, filled his vision.

"I know I've said it before," she whispered, "but it's time you started doing what you want instead of what you should."

She kissed him softly and left him alone with his thoughts.

EPILOGUE

Angel drove her fist into the heavy bag, relishing the solid feel of a blow well struck. She bobbed, doubling her jabs, digging in hooks, and delivering crushing roundhouses and vicious spin kicks. She poured her anger into her workout, attacking as if it, and not Maddock, had wronged her.

Two days! It had been two days since Maddock, Bones, and the others returned from wherever the hell they'd been off to on their latest mission to save the world. Since then, all she'd gotten from Maddock were a couple of lame text messages. She wondered if Jade had been a part of the mission, but when she'd asked, Bones had pushed her off the phone, and Avery wasn't picking up her phone. She'd taken that as a *yes*.

"Argh!" She slammed her elbow into the bag again and again, imagining Jade's face and then Maddock's. Tears welled in her eyes, and she knew she should take a break, but she was out of control. She continued to slam the bag until rough hands pulled her away.

"What the hell are you doing?" Javier, her striking coach, shouted. "What happened to your composure? Your discipline?" Though now in his sixties, Javier retained the strength and fire that fueled a successful boxing career in his younger days. "You are better than this."

"I know." Angel jerked away and headed for the locker room. "I've got a lot on my mind."

"You've got a fight in one week!" Javier shouted. "Do you think you can clear your head by then, or are we wasting our time?"

Angel stripped her gloves off and gave him the finger with both hands. She didn't bother with the doorknob, but kicked the door in instead. It wasn't until she reached the shower that she let the tears flow. How had she messed things up so badly? She'd carried a torch for Maddock for years, and when she finally got him, she let jealousy get in the way. She deserved to lose him.

She turned the hot water all the way up and waited for it to get warm. One at a time, she removed her ankle braces, trunks, and tank top and flung them all against the wall as hard as she could. None was a satisfactory substitute for a heavy bag or someone's face.

"Need somebody to wash your back?"

"Crap!" Though she still wore compression shorts and a sports bra, she snatched a towel and wrapped herself in it before turning back around. "Maddock! What the hell?"

His eyes, so like the sea on a stormy day, captivated her. She took an involuntary step toward him and then froze. There was something about the way he looked at her that didn't seem quite right. His jaw was set, his posture rigid, and she saw a hint of uncertainty in his eyes that was so unlike him. He smiled, but it was a small, sad thing.

She wanted to run to him, to wrap her arms around him and cheer him up like she'd done so many times before, but she held back. "Why are you here?"

"Because I can't get you to talk to me. Texts don't count, especially the ones you've been sending."

"I suppose that's fair. So what do you want to talk about?" She wasn't sure she wanted to know, but she supposed it was better this way. She steeled herself for the worst.

"I couldn't do this over the phone." Maddock took a deep breath. "I've made some big decisions."

ABOUT THE AUTHOR

David Wood is the author of the Dane Maddock Adventures series and several stand-alone works, as well as The Absent Gods fantasy series under his David Debord pseudonym. He enjoys history, Archaeology, mythology, and cryptozoology, and works all of these elements into his adventure fiction.

David co-hosts ThrillerCast, a podcast about reading, writing and publishing in thriller and genre fiction. When not writing, he can be found coaching fast-pitch softball or rooting on the Atlanta Braves. He lives in Santa Fe, New Mexico with his wife and children. Visit him online at www.davidwoodweb.com.

Made in the USA
San Bernardino, CA
14 March 2014